Broken Eye Books is an independent press, here to bring you the odd, strange, and offbeat side of speculative fiction. Our stories tend to blend genres, highlighting the weird and blurring its boundaries with horror, sci-fi, and fantasy.

Support weird. Support indie.

brokeneyebooks.com
facebook.com/brokeneyebooks
instagram.com/brokeneyebooks
bsky.app/profile/slgable.bsky.social

"*Song of Spores* is a rare find: a truly innovative science fiction novel with psychological depths as nuanced and complex as our own world. Takács reveals emself to be a true heavy hitter, marrying the sharp, cinematic coolness of Peter Watts with Le Guin's lyrical, unbounded imagination. The characters are fascinating, the plot both riveting and batshit unpredictable, the writing beautiful. An absolute gem." (**Maria Dong**, author of *Liar, Dreamer, Thief* and *Psychopomp*)

"A rollicking adventure full of fungi, shapeshifters, and groupmind shenanigans. *Song of Spores* bursts with inventive exuberance. As always with Bogi Takács, it's also a thoughtful book with light to shed on gender, collective identity, neurodiversity, religion, and what happens when an organization is more concerned with cleaning messes up quickly than with protecting its own." (**Ada Hoffmann**, author of *The Outside* and *Resurrections*)

"Is it enough that *Song of Spores* revives the zesty weirdness of the classic space opera without the self-important bloat and anthropocentric pulp baggage? No! Because Bogi Takács effortlessly models the kindness and curiosity we'll need to find our way among the stars, not by fetishizing what it means to be human but by celebrating how all sentient beings grow by being humane." (**Cody Goodfellow**, Wonderland Award-winning author of *Radiant Dawn* and *New Tomorrow*)

"What does it mean to be alien among humans as well as extraterrestrials? These characters connect and intersect in a kaleidoscopic gamut of identity and experience: insect and mammal, hive mind and individual, investigator and criminal. That's not even mentioning the tensions of strict religious Judaism versus queer genders boosted by practical alien shapeshifter tech. Yes, please. I need more science fiction as original as *Song of Spores*." (**Evan J. Peterson**, author of *Better Living Through Alchemy*)

"*Song of Spores* is a fast-paced interstellar adventure with a diverse cast and sentient fungi! I loved the premise and the characters, and I hope to see more set in this world." (**Catherine Lundoff**, publisher at Queen of Swords Press)

"Takács's first full-length novel is a SF procedural set in a far-flung part of space with a shapeshifting protagonist and an alien crew [...] They deftly weave intersex, trans, and other identities into this fine book that thrillingly crosses genre lines." (*Booklist*)

SONG OF SPORES

SONG OF SPORES by BOGI TAKÁCS

Published by
Broken Eye Books
www.brokeneyebooks.com

978-1-940372-75-4 (trade paperback)
978-1-940372-76-1 (hardcover)

SONG OF SPORES

BOGI TAKÁCS

CHAPTER ONE: EMPATHIC MIRRORING

DOVBER WAS STANDING IN UTTER DARKNESS, LISTENING TO THE SOFT gurgling and clicking noises of the spaceship. He had been praying, but he stopped. Even after many years, his mind would sometimes roll along its well-worn tracks, inertia making his lips trace the words he was taught as a child. *Blessed are you, G-d, our Lord, King of the universe, so that you have not made me a woman.*

He coughed nervously and corrected himself. *Blessed are you, G-d, our Lord, King of the universe, so that you have made me in accordance with your will.*

The ship declined to comment.

Mawu, the jump pilot, was peeling out of the ship's connection berth, nerve-tentacles detaching from their back and their own tentacles folding back in an intricate, overlapping pattern. They sighed and ran their hands along their loose turquoise robe, which obediently closed its slits. They turned around and smiled at Dovber, nodding their head, dark-brown curls bouncing.

"Good morning," they said, perky as ever.

"Good morning to you too." Dovber fought the urge to groan in response. He leaned back in one of the shapeforming chairs. He didn't feel like he knew anyone on the ship well enough to be informal, even the operations team who he'd been working with for years—let alone Mawu, a newcomer. He knew all too well that he appeared out of place. People looked at him, and they saw a short, round, pale Jewish man with long sidecurls, a reddish-brown beard, and the traditional attire of the Olimpianer Chasidim from Mars.

That was, of course, unless they saw someone else entirely.

He ran his fingers along the sides of his black overcoat, belatedly noticing that he was mimicking Mawu's gesture. He looked up at them and grinned. "So what's the situation?" he asked. It came out more formal in the Alliance trade language than it would have in Hebrew. He hadn't spoken Yiddish in a long while.

"Anayāun talked to Counterintelligence Command, and she said there was some kind of, er, difficulty on Hidi-Niruy that they wanted us to investigate."

Dovber grimaced. "That's what, five jump points away?"

"I don't mind! I've totally recovered from the last round!" Mawu shook their head. Indeed, their skin had regained their healthy light-brown shade from the previous ashen pallor, and their motions were firm, their hands no longer twitching.

"If you say so," Dovber shrugged.

"I can jump to Hidi-Niruy any time!" Mawu frequently spoke in exclamations. "What, directly?"

"Sure! Would I need any effort to go through the *jump points*?"

Operative Hlaz-mlan Mm strolled into the ship's control room, her six legs rhythmically clacking on the hard flooring and her carapace glittering with age. Click-click-CLACK-click-CLACK-click, and again; her two artificial limbs making a different, louder sound. She was the only sentient on the operations team with a non-humanlike body template. "I don't think we need to rush," she said, her speech resonant with soft buzzing. "The Alliance hired you for transportation, not for heroics, young one." She shook her torso for emphasis. Dovber was wondering when would Hlaz-mlan start calling him "young one" too. If you're three hundred years old, everybody looks young to you.

"But I—"

Dovber chuckled. "You heard the lady."

Hlaz-mlan belted herself into her chair-frame, though there was no need for it as long as the ship and Mawu kept some attention on gravity control. Operative Anayāun arrived last, wearing her uniform of Ereni Security as usual, black with silver trim. She was delegated to Alliance Counterintelligence by the Free State of Eren, and Dovber thought she never missed a chance to indicate that she did not entirely belong to Counterintelligence. She took off her cap and rubbed her scalp, bald in Ereni custom. She was tall, muscular, and dark-skinned. She moved with confidence, glancing around while checking some display only visible to her.

Mawu turned to the three Alliance operatives once they'd all settled. "Open flag?"

Dovber, Hlaz-mlan, and Anayāun nodded in unison.

Mawu scratched their head but went ahead—expecting some kind of ambitious false-flag operation, no doubt: the ship masquerading as traders, tourists, or even pirates. But none of the operatives felt they had any reason to hide their presence from the local authorities, who'd requested their visit.

"Mawu of Dahond, jump pilot of the sentient ship Kheinu of Downstream Clutch, requesting permission to board the station. We are an Alliance Treaty Enforcement vessel with three operatives on board."

"Permission granted. We've been expecting you. Our police liaison will be waiting for you in the docks."

They're not wasting any time, Dovber messaged the rest of the crew on the backchannel. *Is this really such a backwater as Command made it sound?*

On the outskirts of the Alliance, you never know what you might find, Hlaz-mlan replied.

Dovber stopped himself mid-sigh—realizing he'd never heard anything about Jews living on this planet.

Dovber and Mawu were sitting in one of the small, badly aged dock lounges while Anayāun was trying to sort out their incorrectly transmitted credentials with the local police, and Hlaz-mlan vanished in the maze of the dockworks.

Dovber was vaguely annoyed at himself. This would be a great opportunity to change, go stationside as a woman, but he didn't feel woman today. He would soon need to go back to his home planet for the holidays, and there he would need to present all man, all the time. He wasn't looking forward to it. He felt that he was wasting an opportunity by not changing right there and then.

He wished he had someone to discuss his complicated feelings with, and

Mawu also came from a people who, like his own, were quite invested in their binary gender concepts. But the young jump pilot was content to ignore gender for the most part and was not genderfluid at all. Dovber remembered Anayāun telling him that Mawu was intersex, or maybe he misunderstood? It felt too personal to ask Mawu for clarifications.

Maybe he could have a good, lengthy heart-to-heart with the ship. His options: a brash teenager and a giant pufferfish.

"I'm hungry," Mawu said. "Let's go find something to eat?"

Dovber resisted the urge to explain Jewish dietary laws. "I can only eat what comes from the ship's fabricator," he said. "And probably so should you. Who knows who might want to poison us here, G-d forbid."

Mawu blinked at him, eyes shimmering with the promise of adventure.

"Don't get your hopes up," he added.

The police liaison, a tall white woman in a charcoal-gray uniform, was not in good spirits. She stared at Mawu and Dovber with open hostility. She glanced over the ship, now safely berthed. Kheinu's gray skin was tinted more purplish than navy blue; probably from anxiety or aggravation, Dovber thought. They'd also withdrawn their surface spikes almost completely.

"I said you will *all* need to present your credentials in *person*," the police liaison said. "I need to verify you are who you claim to be. Where is the third operative?"

"Hlaz-mlan Mm will also be back shortly." Anayāun replied and then added mildly, "From the *restroom*."

Dovber suspected this answer was untrue, but he also knew most humanlike, I-type sentients knew very little about insectoid anatomies and would be hesitant to betray their ignorance. He was happy to cover for Hlaz-mlan, who had a special talent for finding exactly what she needed while ostensibly looking for a restroom.

"You first," the woman barked at Mawu. "I have in my file—Mawu of Dahond, union jump pilot employed by Alliance Treaty Enforcement, body type I, subtype J/O. What does this even mean?"

Mawu blinked in confusion, opened their mouth and closed it.

She pressed on. "Is this your original subtype?"

"Sorry?" Mawu finally managed to say.

"Were you born with this, or were you modified?" She enunciated every word slowly with rising anger.

Dovber decided to intervene. "J/O is a jump pilot subtype, officer. No one is born with it."

The officer shot him an aggrieved glance. Dovber smiled. She snorted and looked in the distance, no doubt consulting some kind of visual interface. "Let's see the rest—cognotype Ereni. So you are Ereni, I take it?"

"Um, no, maybe, not yet, I don't know," Mawu said all with one breath and paused, perplexed. "I am on a temporary . . . immigration thing . . . I applied . . ."

"Why is this relevant, officer?" Dovber crossed his arms. The officer grimaced at him. He knew he did not look threatening—but rather, amusingly traditional, from one of the many religious splinter groups dotting Alliance space. Even if the officer had no idea which group, she likely got the impression correct.

Oh well. Almost.

"I'm just going through the file," the officer said. "You do your job, I do mine."

Hlaz-mlan strolled in, waving her antennae. "Is it my turn yet?" She chuckled deeply, warmly. "I can tell you *all* about my body type."

Finally, they were allowed to pass through. They walked along a seemingly neverending, narrow, and damp corridor in single file. The officer had not even told them about the case, just instructed them to head to Central Police Headquarters for more information.

"They could've sent a car or something," Dovber complained.

"I don't think this station is big enough for cars," Anayāun told him. "I wish! I miss racing. Maybe I can get some downtime out in space, among the asteroids . . . want to come with?"

Dovber made a noncommittal noise. He liked sports, just from a safe distance.

Mawu ran their hands along the scratched and dented panels of the corridor but was otherwise quiet. When they had to stop at another gate and wait for entry, Dovber decided to message Mawu.

Are you afraid of the police?

Well, I guess I shouldn't be. I mean, we're also the police now, aren't we? Mawu responded, their thoughts erratic with worry.

We're counterintelligence, technically, Dovber replied. *Local law enforcement is supposed to cooperate with us . . . in the best-case scenario.*

I'm not an operative, Mawu messaged back after a pause. *I'm just helping you jump around.* Another pause. *Do I even need to go to that meeting? With the police investigator?*

If you're interested.

Mawu fell silent again. Dovber would have liked to have them on his side, include them as much as he could. There was also a utilitarian aspect to this: Mawu could get the three operatives all out of harm's way if they needed to be transported instantaneously back to the spaceship. And as a high-level operative, Dovber had the right to make these decisions about need-to-know. But he felt like he couldn't trust anyone.

With a loud hiss, the door opened wide.

"My apologies," the tall Nesker man said. "My colleagues do not quite understand the urgency of this investigation. I came out here to meet you as soon as I could, so we can go back to the station together."

His golden fur shone even under the annoyingly cold, artificial light, and he seemed aware of the effect. He brushed his mane back with his left hand, his large claws still extended. Then he retracted them and offered his right. Anayāun shook hands with him firmly, Hlaz-mlan bowed—he returned the bow—and Mawu waved hi from the back. Dovber hesitated.

It was sometimes impossible to observe the Jewish rules of touch. How to avoid touching members of the opposite sex when it is no longer clear what is your sex—let alone what is its opposite? Dovber shrugged internally: right then, he was a man. By the time he made up his mind, the Nesker man already decided he wasn't about to shake hands—the moment gone.

"Well met," the police officer said, grinning in a massive show of teeth. "I am Bih Avhadessen, junior investigator, Central Police Department, Hidi-Niruy Station Orange."

Dovber smiled back, not showing his annoyance. A junior investigator? It was no doubt his pet project to drag an entire team of Alliance Treaty Enforcement operatives here to the back of beyond. Trying to prove something? He was probably one of the only Nesker on the station, so he stood out even more than Dovber himself in his kaftan. But he must have convinced the Alliance somehow—maybe his case had some merit or maybe someone in Dispatch was having a bad day and decided to foist the case upon them, let them sort it out.

The officer opened a secure channel. As the five of them walked along more narrow corridors and damp storage-caverns streaked with fluorescent mold, he explained the case.

"With our government's current Isolationist policies, you can probably imagine how strictly we control the flow of people in and out of the border stations."

A chill ran over Dovber. Was this an immigration case? *Hashem, let this not be an immigration case.*

"ATEF does not ordinarily handle immigration matters," Anayāun said. It was good to know their thoughts ran along parallel lines—for while strictly speaking the team had no leader, Anayāun did often take the lead, even though Hlaz-mlan was senior in age.

The officer shook his mane. "No, no, we are quite clear that there is a possible counterintelligence angle to this."

"So is it *clear* or is it *possible*?" Hlaz-mlan said mildly.

He said in a defensive tone, "We know there is one additional person on the station than we have records for—someone who entered but didn't exit. Also, we're not managing to locate anything out of the ordinary with our monitoring equipment. There is an additional person, but whenever we're running checks on any given group, everything appears in order."

Dovber held up a hand. "You're not able to run a check on every person at the same time?"

"When we do that, the additional person vanishes. The only explanation we've come up with is that someone is tinkering with our systems. Someone who's beyond our means to catch. Someone who's desperate enough to go to such huge effort."

"I still think this is an immigration case," Hlaz-mlan said. "Someone came, and you want to deport them."

"This is not the only tinkering we've noticed. There has been . . . infrastructural damage. Most worrisomely, to ventilation. I don't think I have to explain to you how, on a small station, this can endanger everyone." He paused and puffed up his chest in a very humanlike manner. "I was the investigator who managed to correlate the damage with the appearance and disappearance glitches."

"Do you think it's malicious or just someone poking their head into where they don't belong and accidentally breaking things?" Dovber asked.

"I would err on the side of malice," the officer said. "Checking to see what can be blocked, how to redirect flow—it looks like someone is planning on flooding the docks and the main public areas with something airborne. A pathogen perhaps? We do get the impression that the instances of smaller damage are leading up to something bigger." He looked embarrassed for a moment. "We know how stragglers hide in the ducts, and believe me, this is nothing like that."

"We can definitely look into this," Anayāun said quickly, glancing at the ceiling vents. "If you could share the details . . . ? And we will need a secure area as our living quarters."

The officer nodded vigorously. "That's where I'm taking you. If you can bear with me for just a bit more, we'll be there shortly."

More storage-caverns. The fluorescent moss was replaced by giant flatworms stuck to the plastic paneling and creeping slowly forward to their mysterious destination. Dovber idly wondered if they produced oxygen.

Wouldn't they need some kind of computer hacker for this? Mawu pinged Dovber.

He tried not to roll his eyes. *They think we are experts in everything.*

But . . . ?

We'll try to do our best not to prove them wrong.

Mawu sighed loudly behind him. *I only know about jumping a ship and other magic stuff. Um, māwal, sorry. I'm still not used to Alliance terms. All I know about electronics is how to avoid breaking them with my power. Er. Energy. Something. With my mind. Sorry, I'm babbling.*

Dovber replied, *Don't worry, we'll figure something out.*

The officer turned into a narrow side corridor, and Dovber wondered if the flatworms would follow them all the way into their rooms.

"I actually don't think it's an issue with the sensor systems," Hlaz-mlan said. She was sitting on a sizable ottoman and munching on one of the flatworms she had snatched from the living room wall. "It says here that they also physically checked people."

Dovber leaned back on the sofa. It made a cracking sound, and he winced. "I'm not the only rapid response shapeshifter in the universe."

Anayāun had been pacing around the entire living area, but she stopped behind Dovber and put her hands on the back of the sofa. "The Alliance has records on all of you. And on the transformation containers left over from the Old Empire."

Dovber craned his head. "That's not true," he said. "There are plenty of those barrels out in the universe still, just beyond Alliance territory. There might be any number of worlds not re-Contacted yet after the collapse of the Empire."

"So you think this is someone from beyond Alliance space?" Hlaz-mlan asked.

Dovber nodded. "That's possible. Wasn't there a case just a few months ago when ATEF sent two Ereni operatives . . . ? And they stumbled into a bunch of containers and people turning into trees and giant flying bats and whatnot?"

Hlaz-mlan rose from the ottoman with difficulty and bent her head toward Mawu. "Hmm?"

Mawu startled. "Uh, me? I don't know anything about that!"

"And you *shouldn't*," Hlaz-mlan said, the vague threat in her voice more directed at Dovber and Anayāun.

Dovber sat up, ready to defend Mawu. "They—"

Mawu paled. "I can't disclose anything—to third parties—I mean, like—the things you tell me! At all!" Dovber noticed they were trembling slightly. "I'm literally not able to! They made sure of that!"

"I was about to suggest we include Mawu of Dahond in our deliberations," Dovber said slowly.

Hlaz-mlan chirped. Dovber knew this was the sound of strong disapproval. "We shouldn't have brought them into the station," she said.

"We *had* to bring them into the station," Anayāun said. She was keeping calm. "I can't jump all three of us back to the ship by myself if there is an emergency."

Mawu nodded, their mouth tightly shut.

Dovber was becoming aggravated. "So do you want to just shut them out of our communications altogether, so when someone ambushes us, Mawu will have absolutely no idea what's going on and will not be able to react?"

Hlaz-mlan chirped again. "I don't like this. I see your point, but I don't like this. If we still had Syuf . . ."

"Syuf retired," Anayāun said wearily. "And retired for a reason."

"Yes, because the Alliance *loves* to go through young māwal-active operatives like disposable—"

"Hlaz-mlan!" Anayāun gripped the back of the sofa with such force that Dovber was afraid she would crush it altogether. "That was inappropriate."

Mawu sighed. "I know how it goes, okay? I'm from a backwater. But a warlike backwater. And I'm not an ATEF operative for a reason. I didn't *want* to sign up."

"Well, watch them force you into it," Hlaz-mlan said, but she was already lowering her nether segments back onto the ottoman. "Until you have no other choice because you know too much."

"That was not my intent," Dovber said with forced calm.

"What it comes down to is, do you trust Ereni psychotechnology?" Anayāun said. "If we say Mawu will not speak, Mawu will not speak."

Mawu shrugged. "I consented. It was a precondition."

"We still need to minimize risks." Hlaz-mlan shifted around on the ottoman.

"The question is, which risks do we want to minimize?" Anayāun pushed herself off the sofa and started pacing again. "I'm in favor."

"Well, well. Fair enough. Just don't say I didn't warn you. I've been around longer than the two of you combined," Hlaz-mlan chirped. "And young one, know that it's not about your person. It's about operation security." She paused. "Keep your eyes on these two. They are crafty. You might trust them for your own reasons, but . . ."

Dovber sighed heavily and leaned back again. He wished his biggest problem would be presenting as a man or a woman. That would be big enough.

Their bedrooms were little more than curtained-off sleeping berths. Dovber contemplated going back to the ship, but it was a lengthy walk.

He didn't even have enough space to say his evening prayers. He stood on top of his bed, but it wobbled. He tried to lean against the wall and bumped his head on a storage shelf that jutted out from the wall. He stopped himself from swearing and yanked the curtain open, strode out into the common living area.

"I'm going for a walk," he half-grunted, half-yelled. Mawu looked up at him. They were sitting on the floor with their back against a wall and looked likewise uncomfortable.

"Can I come along?" they asked.

"I'm trying to find a place to say my evening prayers," Dovber said.

"I don't mind it if you don't mind me."

"I—" Dovber paused. *Why not,* he thought. "Fine." He motioned the young pilot to come along.

They headed in the opposite direction from where they had come from, and the corridor widened into a quite busy public space. Dovber took a deep breath—the air smelled stale but otherwise ordinary. He looked around, trying not to think of the possible death toll. Tiny stalls stood on either side of the passageways, offering finger food and brightly colored drinks that looked like local fruit mixes. In a corner, people were queuing up in front of an industrial-sized fabricator. Dovber was surprised to see that, despite the wealth of hand-baked snacks on display, many people were using the fabber to produce meals.

"Can I get myself something? I'm hungry." Mawu steered them toward the queue. "I have to eat a lot, you know. Because I use a lot of energy."

The line seemed to move fast enough. Dovber nodded. He was wondering if he could imitate Hlaz-mlan, bump into the most important people and find the most crucial locations on the station simply by accident. He suspected he didn't have enough māwal for it, though neither did Hlaz-mlan; she was simply very savvy. Then he realized Mawu did—

"Hold on a moment," he said.

Mawu was leaning forward to see what kinds of foods people fabricated. "Mmhm?" they murmured without turning back to Dovber.

"Do you ever wander around and accidentally bump into something important? You know—"

"Sure, all the time." Mawu still didn't turn around. "It's because of my māwal." They shrugged.

"Do you think we could try doing that together?" It seemed more fruitful than spending dreary days tracing an elusive hacker across the networks and crawling through ducts.

Mawu finally looked at him and furrowed their brow, tilted their head sideways. "I don't think that's how it works," they said in a dismayed tone. "Now that you've said it, it's going to be harder because we're expecting it to happen. I could try to do something still, but . . ." They sighed. "Can I eat first? And then we can try to figure it out."

Dovber nodded. The line had ground to a complete standstill. Mawu turned back to stare. Dovber closed his eyes and rocked back and forward on his toes, even his body eager to get his prayers over with. He was wondering if he could say the entire ma'ariv while standing in line, though it did not quite strike him as properly respectful.

Someone ahead of him was yelling. Dovber opened his eyes. The person was thumping the lid of the fabricator. Dovber frantically searched for a translator package. There! His interface worked surprisingly well with the local nets. Maybe this place hadn't always been so Isolationist—but he had no time to reflect.

"Your circumnavigable male genitals should wave in the wind!" the person shouted at the fabricator.

The translator package was clearly *trying.*

"YOU - ARE - A - GONAD!!!"

Dovber pulled up the stranger's public profile, almost by reflex. He was a local man in his fifties, a dockworker, played some kind of instrument that looked like a tin whistle in his spare time—

Someone was trying to pull the man off the fabricator. "Hey, you're ruining my *dinner!*"

"GONADS! Ovaries! Testicles! Ovarian duct!" The man shoved back.

Dovber pushed people aside and stepped closer. "Can I help, comrade?"

He really, really did not want to pull his newly assigned police privileges, but he thought everyone would be better off if he could stop the fight that was about to break out. At the same time, he was tired at the end of a long day.

The two men glared at him. He could feel their anger seeping into his skin.

"They were late with my compensation, the hermeneutic dockworks," the man grunted. Was *hermeneutic* also a swearword? "And now this accursed machinery doesn't allow me to log in to create my nourishment either."

Dovber nodded. He hoped the translation worked better in the other direction. "I can try to log in for you," he said, fervently hoping the system wouldn't display a blatant police override. He was just a stranger passing by.

He stepped to the fabber. It was an old-fashioned model with a handprint reader. He put his palm on the surface.

ACCOUNT UNRECOGNIZABLE, it said.

"Gonads," Dovber hissed at it.

The man looked confused. Clearly the word didn't make it across. "See what I'm explicating?" He nodded at the fabber and kicked abruptly from the hip.

"Stop!! My dinner! My nourishment!!" The other man jumped on top of him.

Dovber tried to grab them both and push them apart—so much for not having a fight—so much for not creating a spectacle—so much for not having to use force—

The fabber made a cheerful tinkling sound.

"I logged in for you," someone said. Dovber was twisting his neck to see the third stranger, but they had already vanished in the crowd by the time he managed to shake the two hungry brawlers loose.

"Who was that?" The swearing man asked.

"That fellow, he lives in our dormitory where he has recently moved, I gather. A repairman of wind processing?"

They both shrugged and turned to the fabricator.

"Did you see that?!" Mawu yelled in Alliance Common.

"See what?" Dovber was trying to downregulate his fight-or-flight response now that the trouble was past.

"It works backwards!" Mawu pulled up a scrambling ward to keep other people from overhearing their conversation. Dovber wasn't sure why they wouldn't just message him, but they seemed so agitated that maybe they didn't realize. "Backwards!"

"What works backwards?" Sometimes it was harder to understand people across cognotypes than across unwieldy translation algorithms. Dovber had no idea what Mawu was saying.

"You wanted to see something important but accidentally! And I said it was too late and you shouldn't have said! But we were already there where the something important was happening when you asked!" Mawu waved their arms in utter desperation.

"What was important?" The pieces weren't clicking into place.

"That person logged in!"

"Sure, they had an account . . . ?"

"No, they logged in with the angry person's account!" Mawu grimaced.

"The hacker . . . ?"

"They changed their handprint! They physically changed it!"

Dovber was perplexed. "How did they know the other man's handprint?"

"Maybe they saw? Just now? Snapped a pic while those two were fighting? Or in their dorm? Wait, that was the other guy. I don't know, okay?" Mawu's eyes were open wide. *They* clearly did not downregulate their fight-or-flight respo—

Dovber gasped. "Wait, you mean we should *pursue*?"

Mawu looked as if they were about to cry. "Yes? No? I don't know? I was trying to track them and lost them right away? There are too many people?"

Dovber shook his head. He suddenly felt exhausted.

"You can only track them with the māwal, but I can track them with my new police account," he explained.

The line was already moving, people planting their hands one by one—so he probably wouldn't get a good organic sample from the palm plate anymore.

He quickly reloaded the swearing man's public profile, put in his override, and looked at the man's list of interactions. The other brawler was listed twice, as he expected. Dovber wanted his address. The dormitory entrance was right behind him, half-covered by a curtain smeared with food grease.

"Well then," he said. "Let's grab some food, and then I can pray."

Mawu was confused. "We're not pursuing?"

"We will, but we need to work out our strategy. Hlaz-mlan might have been right. It's possible that this infiltrator isn't hacking systems but rather changing their body."

"How fast can one do that?" Mawu frowned. "I'm sorry, was that offensive? My planet doesn't have much Imperial leftover technology."

Mine doesn't either, Dovber thought, but he was concerned it wouldn't come out right. "I can show you after I'm done praying."

It was out of his mouth before he knew it. He never offered to demonstrate. He never offered. But he just did.

He didn't want to be comfortable with Mawu. He didn't want to trust people. It was always a risk. But if the infiltrator realized people were on to their plan, they might push into action. The air might be contaminated already.

Anayāun trusts Mawu, he reminded himself, and Anayāun was probably the safest person in the entire universe. But Hlaz-mlan remained skeptical . . .

He took another deep breath, smelling the damp—and maybe a faint undercurrent of mold. Spores?

He hoped it was just his overactive imagination at work.

He wanted to rush through his prayers, but the familiar words were such an unexpected comfort in an unfamiliar place that he held onto them, allowed them to linger.

He did his three steps at the end of the Amida and straightened up, closed his eyes. The thoughts that had been quieted down came to the fore again—his mind running through hypothetical sequences of Mawu, asking questions of varying intrusiveness. He began singing the final Aleinu prayer, loudly, firmly, his voice resonating in the deserted corridor. He felt there was no space for his voice though. The station constricted around him, the air maybe unsafe already.

Then it was done, and all he had to do was slog back to his room. That and . . .

"Thank you for letting me listen," Mawu said.

Dovber murmured something and waited for the moment he'd just imagined. Mawu remained silent.

"Let's go back," Dovber finally offered.

Mawu only spoke up when they were almost back at their lodgings, past the crushing crowds and into the deserted final stretch. "Um, I just want to let you know that I don't want to push you into doing anything? Like when I was still training for the Navy, back on my home planet, some people treated me like . . . you know. Do this, do that, work your magic . . . can you teleport to the top of the shrine . . ." Their voice trailed off.

Dovber sighed with a measure of relief. "I hear you. But I offered first. Can you hold on a moment?" he said to Mawu's back, the teen so intent on marching back to their rooms that they didn't realize Dovber had stopped.

They turned around, a lopsided, embarrassed grin on their face. "Sorry about that. I was just thinking . . ." They looked away. "This is so hard! I was just thinking, you also have a nonstandard body shape like me, you're also trans like me, and people constantly demand you to perform something rare. These are three separate things. One would be hard enough. But also for example, I'm intersex, and you're a shapeshifter, which is of course not the same thing, but—"

Dovber held up a hand, interrupting the rapid-fire words. "Ssh. It's fine. Watch."

He smiled broadly, let his face go slack, and then allowed the flesh to mold into Mawu's features—just the face. This was easy enough, his systems had a subroutine for this. He shivered as his beard retracted into his head.

Mawu gasped. "Wow, that's fascinating. Weird implications. But cool. Can you do"—they stopped themselves—"I shouldn't ask."

Dovber chuckled. "I'll guess."

He had a subroutine for this too—to assume the shape of someone the person in front of them would *like* to see. He didn't have to know.

"Wow, you look just like my niece!" Mawu frowned. "I miss her a lot . . . how did you do that?"

"My systems track your very subtle reactions in real time and adjust accordingly. Your eye muscles relaxing a fraction, your smile. It doesn't use any māwal, just pure physiological data." He had to admit he enjoyed talking about it. "It's called empathic mirroring. Sometimes, the end result is a composite of people, not a specific person."

"Can you do the reverse too?" Mawu's eyes shone with enthusiasm. "Like make yourself into someone really terrifying?"

Dovber laughed. "I certainly can, but do you *want* me to?"

Mawu laughed too, their voice pitching high. "You would turn into my Navy trainers!"

"Watch! This is going to be different." He was used to imitating Hlaz-mlan, and it was especially easy to do just the head. He rubbed his antennae together and chirped. "You shouldn't trust Dovber. He is very dangerous!"

Mawu slapped their knees. "Stop, stop, they're going to hear—" They dissolved into childlike giggles.

Dovber hesitated only for a moment. "I might as well." He'd designed the eldritch monster shape for a Purim party, but he never actually used it. His jaw cracked open wide, and tentacles spewed forth from his mouth, marched around his face, heavy like a beard but much more sinister. Crests split his scalp, and his skin hardened into scales. He enjoyed the tickly sensation. He waved his tentacles gleefully.

"By the Powers, that's amazing! I'm totally a fan! You should do this all the time!"

"Might help me with local law enforcement," Dovber said through a mass of tentacles and then retracted them and shifted back—slowly, gradually drawing out the change, fish scale by fish scale.

He felt less conflicted about Cthulhu than about the ordinary man-shape. Or the ordinary woman-shape, for that matter.

"I think it's time to return. The others are probably already asleep," he said.

He lay in his bed, pondering how Mawu still hadn't seen his woman-shape. But he didn't feel a woman now, he didn't feel like women's grammatical forms, he didn't feel like any of that. Sometimes, it seemed to him it always happened at the most inopportune moment. He would pray in the men's section and suddenly feel an unassailable certainty that he should be in the women's section. Once she tried, back on Alliance Central, to go to an entirely unfamiliar synagogue as a woman—Dvora Kalonymus instead of Dovber Meyerson—but people quizzed her on her relatives, and she could not possibly answer. And then once the prayers finally started, he was again sure that he should be on the other side.

He heard a series of soft pops from the air ducts and got up, stood on his wobbly bed. He couldn't see anything—so whatever it had been, it must have echoed through the station. The pops hadn't sounded purposeful; probably just his professional wariness at work. He lay back down, but his thoughts were still churning.

He had to admit to himself that he envied Mawu—entirely undecided about their gender or, if anything, entertaining the possibility of having none. He could leave Orthodoxy and go for some interesting third option.

He didn't want to leave Orthodoxy. But even his family didn't know about him being a shapeshifter . . . or being a senior operative of ATEF. They only knew he had a job that took him all over Alliance space.

Bigender, genderfluid, *and* a shapeshifter. He thought the shapeshifting would come in handy. He'd signed up for the transformation. He'd been enthusiastic. But he still remembered the gaze of the ATEF doctor who stuffed him into the giant silver barrel—a leftover of Imperial technology—and as the nanomaterials tore his body apart and reassembled him on the molecular level, the doctor held on to that complicated expression of sadness and concern.

Dovber could change himself into any shape now. But he would never be able to tell his family. He could not turn into Cthulhu to entertain kids on Purim.

As for his colleagues . . . they mostly came from planets and cultures where gender changes were commonplace even without shapeshifting. Except Mawu, but Mawu was still an unknown—and against his expectations, somehow a fan of his?

He turned to the wall, wrapped himself tight in his blanket, and said his bedtime prayers, but sleep wouldn't come. In the end, he had to manually override his askew biorhythms and force himself into unconsciousness.

In the morning when the operatives got together, Dovber knew exactly what he had to do. Sleep didn't bring rest, but it had brought a solution.

Anayāun was unconvinced. "So we go stake out this dormitory, but what makes you think our target is going to be there? They could've fled many times over."

Dovber adjusted his large black kippah on his head and put his wide-rimmed black hat on top. "They are staying for the same reason they intervened to break up the fight. They want to keep out of sight of the local police, and a fight would bring more attention from law enforcement—patrols, maybe even a raid on the dorms."

"I'm sure that person didn't realize who we were," Mawu said. "Even if they are māwal-active, we are shielded tight, and there was a big crowd."

Dovber chuckled. "We look like strangers, but we look entirely unlike *dangerous* strangers."

Mawu looked down on their jump pilot's robes. "I look like a jump pilot, but um, a small and slightly confused one?"

Anayāun tilted her head, surveying the two of them. "Fair enough. So you say you got . . . lucky."

"The kid has enough māwal to blink the station out of existence, including their own self if they're not careful. I don't think it's about being lucky," Hlazmlan added dryly.

"Well, it wasn't pre-planned . . . ?" Mawu looked apologetic, possibly even for their own existence. Dovber felt sorry for them.

"But you deliberately don't pre-plan," he said. "Let's just go."

The cafeteria was large and crowded with workers getting ready for their morning shift in the docks. People grumbled and yelled, chatted about any number of topics, elbowed each other out of the way as they made their way to the small, mushroom-like stools around the haphazardly arranged tables.

Anayāun shook her head. *I can't sense anything out of the ordinary,* she messaged them. *They must be warded well too.*

Mawu kept on frowning. *I thought I wasn't doing it right the first time around, but I guess it's not just me. They're really hard to spot.*

"I need to go to the restroom," Dovber said out loud and then messaged them: *Watch this.*

He had a plan, something that was clearly not regular procedure but still within the flexibility allowed him as part of the team. Anayāun nodded at him to proceed.

He didn't go to the restroom. He stepped outside into the swirling crowds and found himself a secluded space.

He fashioned himself into someone most people would find attractive—the latest Alliance looks, straight black hair, a muscular androgynous build. Sleek clothes like on a current drama serial set in the Emerald Spires. He made himself as gender-ambiguous as possible, knowing the crowd's attentions would pull his appearance in multiple directions.

This wasn't his shape, but it was the shape he would need.

He walked back to the dormitory and engaged the subroutine he'd shown Mawu, the one that adjusted his appearance to his conversation partners' delight. Dovber was glad there were very few non-humanlike sentients in the crowd, and he made a point to avoid them. From the corner of his eye, he noticed Hlaz-mlan slip out of the room, understanding his plan right away.

People stared at him as he passed by. Workers of all genders commented, sometimes loudly, sometimes rudely. There were whistles and catcalls. Some people flushed. The air was stuffy; too stuffy? He pushed the thought away from himself.

His skin tightened and loosened, its color paling and darkening from the medium-brown shade he started with. His chin wavered ever so slightly as the people near him preferred a more masculine or feminine bone structure. He walked around slowly, hoping the changes wouldn't be as noticeable to any given person if he just kept on moving. He grabbed a bowl full of hot soup, giving him the excuse to walk cautiously and a reason for others to get out of his way.

"You're gorgeous, sweetie," a woman told him in an eerily fetishizing tone. "Are you a boy or a girl? Oh I do hope you are a girl."

Dovber was growing frustrated. The moment he'd been waiting for hadn't arrived, and his soup would soon get cold. He murmured, "Check my profile.

That's what it's for," and passed by the worker. He had no attention to spare for a snappier comeback.

Get ready, he messaged the rest of the team. *A fight might break out.* He looked around to see if he could spot the plainclothes officers they'd requested from Investigator Avhadessen, but he couldn't—and that was probably good. He turned on his police overlays, which helpfully tagged the officers.

They were positioned well. Better and better. Now, if only . . .

Another circle around the cafeteria, and he might need to call this off.

He slowed even further and stopped by a crowded table. "Hey, I'm looking for my friend," he said. "I'm sorry. I'm not from around here." He hoped the translation would not enrage them, but they seemed to understand.

"The offbeat newcomer, correct?" a woman said, glancing up from fidgeting with a complicated-looking tool. "Those fellows at that table, they might be aware."

Another table and then another. Dovber felt like he was being sent on a wild goose chase, but at the same time, he was sure he must be closing in. His scalp tugged.

His scalp wasn't supposed to tug.

He took a deep breath and turned around. Took a few steps ahead. He closed one eye to see his own nose better—was it acquiring a subtle turquoise shade?

He felt his tongue split in three inside his mouth.

This was it.

Another step forward and then another gingerly to the right. He was feeling his way toward the unfamiliar change.

The infiltrator might have been in human shape, but their preferences still followed their original.

Dovber was sure he got the right person—an average-looking dockworker in grimy overalls, though clearly a professional at his trade. Though that trade was probably espionage rather than ship repair.

Then he realized he forgot about something. Where was Mawu? Mawu was supposed to help him remove the target from the crowd.

He could have slapped himself. With all his convoluted thoughts, he simply forgot to tell them.

He needed to gain a moment of time. Just a few seconds would be enough.

He pretended to trip and dropped his bowl, careful not to splatter anyone.

He didn't want to start a fight before the fight that would inevitably break out once he was out of here. "Gonads!" he yelled out. "This was fine nourishment!"

He hastily marked the target and sent it over to the team. *If Mawu can, jump them back to the ship now,* he messaged. He turned off empathic mirroring.

"Aw, too bad for you," someone said.

He slowly rose. Behind him, Mawu kicked out their stool and made a dash for them. The person in front of him made an odd, soft noise—suspicious? Scared? There wasn't enough time—

Suddenly, he saw the cafeteria from an entirely different vantage point, rushing forward, and then he fell, fell across expanses of swirling gray—

He was sprawled on the floor of the ship, lying on his belly. He struggled to all fours, still disoriented.

"Power," Anayāun said, the tone clearly an order. "More. Now."

What was *Anayāun* doing here? How?

Dovber looked up to see the dockworker utterly terrified, eyes bulging. "I said now!"

Mawu coughed and mumbled something like, "Sorry," behind him.

Then he felt Anayāun grab ahold of Mawu's power and direct it. Even with what little māwal he had, he could sense a vast surge slamming into the stranger's wards, annihilating them.

The dockworker slumped on the floor, unconscious, and as Dovber got up on his feet, he could see them melt into an iridescent silver puddle, losing their shape as long as their consciousness wasn't holding them together.

"We got the right one," Anayāun said. "Hlaz-mlan is on the way, and in the meanwhile, we can figure out what kind of containment we can use. We should've probably done that first, but jumping back inside the ship is much easier than . . ."

Dovber turned around, the world turning a bit too fast. He was still dizzy from the jump. He took a deep breath.

Mawu was lying on the floor of the spaceship. "I'm okay . . ." they croaked. "I just need to . . . rest a bit . . ." They closed their eyes and were out cold, though Dovber gladly noted they were still breathing.

He spun around again, coming close to losing his stomach contents, and glared at Anayāun. "Did you have them jump *four* people?!"

Anayāun shrugged. "I also joined in. They can do it. It got us out of harm's way, and it was easier than knocking the target out first and risking who knows what kind of reaction."

"Well, I clearly didn't expect a puddle." Dovber carefully bent forward. He could see a set of small fan blades and some screws and clips amid the goo, probably the contents of the infiltrator's pockets—something they'd just removed from a duct. He shivered and sent a quick message to Avhadessen to check if anything had been deposited in the ventilation system, even in the smaller ducts. The Nesker man was probably in for a major promotion. Dovber leaned even closer to the puddle.

"Don't poke at it," Anayāun said. "This might be a Contact situation. And we need biohazard containment."

Dovber knew that was correct. "Will Mawu be all right?"

"After some sleep, yes."

Dovber summoned a floater pallet. "I'll get them to their room to rest. You know, they gave me the idea."

He gently rolled Mawu onto the pallet. The back flap of their robe was open, their ship connection tentacles dangling out in disarray. He closed the shirt flap but was unsure about what to do with the tentacles. He queried the ship.

I can help, Kheinu said, their vast mental presence echoing in his mind. *Just get them back to their room.*

As he pulled the pallet along, he was wondering about transformations, differences, and trust.

CHAPTER TWO: DEFEND HEARTH POSITION

I'S NOT ABOUT HAVING AN EGG SAC, PER SE, HLAZ-MLAN THOUGHT TO herself. *With age, there's just more and more trouble with it.*

She shifted in her chair, her original legs aching. Her replacement legs were fine, and again she wondered if she should just swap the old ones all out. But that would be more trouble than what it was worth. She was a bit envious of humans, who only had to deal with two legs, not six, though they were so much less graceful—so there was that tradeoff.

"You just feel motherly toward Mawu. Admit it," Dovber told her.

Mammals. So much effort spent on raising their young, and they assume it applies to all sentient species equally. Hlaz-mlan sighed. "Not every impulse to care is related to parenting," she said.

This made the human uncomfortable. Dovber started to fidget with the long threads hanging out of his clothing—they were a religious object of some sort— and scratched his belly. He finally said, "I'm sorry. I didn't mean to imply that."

Hlaz-mlan wasn't sure whether Dovber could have children or if his shapeshifter transformation had made that infeasible. She knew it would be intrusive to ask. "Don't worry about it," she said mildly.

Mawu wandered in, looking sleepy and munching on a bar. Jump pilots were hungry all the time, but Mawu was also sleepy more often than not. Hlaz-mlan did want to take care of the small, young human. So much more vulnerable than her own young, and their young, and their young . . .

"We're almost there, just waiting for our turn to approach the station," Mawu mumbled, stifling a yawn. "They're preparing containment for the . . . the spy you've taken into custody?"

"Let's not jump to conclusions about whether the person in question is a *spy*," Hlaz-mlan said. "People have the most unexpected motivations."

"Well, we practically caught them in the act." Dovber pulled again at those threads. "Not just intelligence-gathering but also sabotage. Your interrogators can sort it out, and we can all get our well-deserved leave planetside."

"I'll go lie down a bit," Mawu said. They tossed the wrapping of the bar into the fabricator for recycling and then rubbed their face and ran their fingers along their dark brown curls. "You're Alliance Treaty Enforcement. I'm just the driver." They wandered off.

Dovber got to his feet. "Hlaz-mlan? Let's go prepare our captive for transfer, and then you can go home and see your grandkids."

"With how little leave we get, I might have great-grandkids by now," she said, only half jesting.

Dovber and Anayāun were fiddling with the controls of the floater pallet that was supposed to go under the sizable containment unit. Hlaz-mlan stood back and let them sort it out.

Hlaz-mlan had more of a desire to rest in her wonderful treetop lounge and eat the choicest confections than to see her unruly grandchildren. They had a certain charm, and she did have maternal feelings toward them, if not in the same ways mammals tended to have. But on such a short leave between missions, she felt she could not get her thoughts to revert to an off-duty mindset. She didn't want to snap at her offspring, to hurt them. But someone in Alliance Treaty Enforcement thought that it would be a good idea for the captive to be interrogated here on her home planet, no doubt assuming that the captive was also a mammal who would potentially be terrified by large, sentient insectoids.

Hlaz-mlan wondered how the Alliance bureaucrats could miss the crucial detail that the captive was a shapeshifter like Dovber, and no one knew their original shape.

The captive's shape. She had a quite good idea of Dovber. He kept his original shape most of the time, primarily not to unsettle his very religious family. They were so hung up on their egg sacs or whatever they had.

Dovber finally pushed the containment unit on the pallet, huffing.

All of them got the incoming message. *This is Alliance gunship* Treasury of Legends. *We will match course with you and board. Do not change course or attempt to board the station.*

Anayāun glared at nothing in particular. "I hope they don't want us to spend our leave on the gunship too."

If a human wearing an ATEF dress uniform did not want to spend time on a gunship, who would?

They didn't meet the soldiers at first. They met the hazmat team bumbling around in their bulky yellow suits, treating the operatives as if they'd witnessed the aftermath of a nuclear explosion. They looked like a backup team, using leftover gear while the real elite bio-squads must have been gallivanting in a distant corner of Alliance space.

The hazmat people yelled at each other over the comms about decontamination procedures. They wanted to dress Hlaz-mlan in some kind of bag. They wanted to undress Dovber altogether, though they did not get far. They glared at Mawu as if the young pilot was a piece of furniture, clashing with the decor. Anayāun made faces behind their backs, and this was so unexpected that Hlaz-mlan chirped in amusement—just a little.

They finally declared everyone clean and passed them on to the soldiers actually managing the ship.

The ATEF soldiers were also humans, and they looked like Anayāun, except their skin was a much lighter brown, comparable to Mawu's. They all wore identical gray uniforms instead of the bulky suits. There was no one from Hlaz-mlan's planet. *The ship must have come a long way just to pick up the captive,* she thought.

The soldiers all seemed distressed or, at the very least, trying to avoid the containment unit sitting in the middle of the empty loading deck. They clung to the walls like fertilized egg deposits.

One of the officers gingerly stepped closer and touched the containment unit with one finger. "This looks tightly warded. Did you do it?"

Anayāun answered, "I did it, and I also asked the jump pilot to help. We wanted to make sure. We don't know much about the infiltrator's capabilities beyond their being a rapid-response shapeshifter."

The officer grimaced. "That's bad enough."

Dovber imitated the officer's grimace but didn't say anything. Hlaz-mlan was relieved. They were just doing their job. There was no sense in picking a fight with them. The faster the captive could be handed over, the better.

Two other soldiers were dragging in a much larger containment unit. They plopped down the floater pallet next to the original one on the floor.

"The whole box goes in? Good," Hlaz-mlan said with relief. She was worried about the infiltrator simply leaking out at the seams.

"We're concerned about contamination," one of the soldiers said. "We'll check your ship quite thoroughly too, and then you can be on your way. I know you're eager for your leave planetside."

They are poking around in my guts, the ship—Kheinu—said, their vast inhuman voice resonating in the crew's minds.

Patience, young grasshopper, Hlaz-mlan messaged back. *They will be done soon.* She had not realized the ship could speak while Mawu was asleep. Was Mawu already awake? She knew little about either of them and their symbiotic nature.

Dovber paced around the small central chamber of the ship, fuming. "They wanted me to undress! It makes no sense. I'm also a rapid response shapeshifter. Most of my clothing is a part of my body!" He pulled at the loose strings. "Except for my tallis, the rest is just—"

"What did you tell them?" Hlaz-mlan asked cautiously.

Dovber turned to her and blinked, thirty-two eyes popping open on his forehead like so many tiny eggs, the skin slicing apart. "This."

Mawu was standing in the doorway. "Wow, do that again! That was awesome! Can you grow them this fast, or do you have them, like, stored under your skin?"

Dovber looked embarrassed. "I was preparing to scare somebody, yes." His additional eyes smoothed back into his face. "This is just a party trick."

"You have the coolest party tricks," Mawu stated firmly and strode into the chamber.

Hlaz-mlan chuckled. "Operative, you have a fan."

Dovber grinned uneasily. Uncomfortable being in the spotlight? "So I have noticed. Where is Anayāun? I want to be planetside for our break already."

The warm bubble of the planetside station already radiated the smell-taste of home. Hlaz-mlan waved her antennae to get more of it.

"It's time to say goodbye for now," Anayāun said. "Ping me if you need me. I'll be meeting with an old friend, and we're planning on going rock climbing in the Pinstripes. We won't wander far from the station in case I need to get back up into orbit fast."

Dovber nodded. "The two of us will go see the sights. Neither Mawu nor I have been here before." The young jump pilot was beaming.

Hlaz-mlan tilted her head. "Just don't forget, you're all invited to dinner tomorrow. And if you change your minds about staying, just let me know."

"We're coming, but we really would rather not impose on your family beyond that," Anayāun said. "We already reserved our hotel rooms."

Hlaz-mlan could tell that Mawu was curious. Then again, Mawu was curious about everything and had little sense of danger. It was good they were not an operative, and Hlaz-mlan had already been on guard for attempts at recruiting the young pilot into ATEF operations.

They all waved goodbye—Mawu peeking over their shoulder well after they'd turned away—and Hlaz-mlan walked to the waiting area to find her grandson Mlhlh-af.

Mlhlh-af was lounging by the snack trays, poking at the sugary goop. He only noticed Hlaz-mlan when she was already by his side.

"Grandma," he buzzed eagerly. "So glad to see you home! You look great. Did you manage to talk your friends into coming to the festive dinner tomorrow? A true brood-celebration!"

He buzzed and chirped all the way to their floater-pod.

On the landing, she stopped to stare, ordering Mlhlh-af behind her. She needed just a moment to take in the sight.

The house was the way she remembered: a central building with three globular wings to the sides, towering above the grassy meadow like a mushroom. Old-fashioned, so not only biomorphic but actually bio-framed, carefully grown, woven and bound by her grandparents and their parents. A nest of branches.

For a while, she had been responsible for its maintenance with two nieces assigned to assist her. She knew intimately how to reglaze floors and walls, how to make sure bird droppings would not stick to the roof, how to make sure all the ventilation and piping was in good working order.

Those had been her worst years by far.

But the house . . . the house still felt warm and welcoming, populated by four generations of her family by the last recount.

Four kids ran around in the grass, weaving in and out between the wings, chirping in delight. Her great-grandchildren? It could not be. None of her grandchildren had kids of their own yet—or had they in her absence? She had meant that as a joke, but maybe . . .

She chuckled as the kids ran up to her, and she reached into her bag for some sugary treats. They dashed off, leaving her to wonder. There would be ample time for introductions later. She would just have to make sure not to let Mlhlh-af out of her sight. He was such a gangly, awkward adolescent with one molting too many for his nervous system to catch up with his body size. Maybe that's why he was so eager to help her. Away from all the other youngsters.

"Let's go, Grandma," he prodded her gently. "Your old room on the top floor is waiting for you. Iyiii-nh put up some new decorations. I'm sure you'll enjoy them. We'll drop your stuff, and then we can go downstairs for the welcoming feast."

Hlaz-mlan nodded an antenna at her luggage. "It's mostly gifts. I figured, if I needed anything here, I could just use the fabricator." She chuckled. "Assuming Yn-dladlan hasn't broken it again."

Mlhlh-af seemed embarrassed. "No, Grandma, everything is in best working order." He lifted and spread his middle legs. "The house is all ready for its matriarch!"

Hlaz-mlan suppressed an annoyed buzzing. While she had been feeling her age, she was not ready to relax into the role of the matriarch yet, to retire to the warm embrace of her family. And besides, what would Counterintelligence do without her? All those young sentients!

Yet it was tempting to give in, to let go. To allow herself to be pampered, just for a week . . .

She followed Mlhlh-af inside, trying not to grumble. *I'm becoming a crotchety old lady,* she thought.

The giant entry hall reached all four floors high, and the climbing wall was directly across from her. Light filtered through the lower-floor membranes, tinted a charming yellow. Dessert bulbs were stacked on a small table by the entrance, and she snatched one, poked it open.

The warm smell-taste of home surrounded her entirely. She could feel the tension in her legs decrease, seep into the ridges of the freshly reglazed floor.

"Welcome home, Grandma," Mlhlh-af said, and from all directions, people rushed out to greet her.

But Grandma, you have to seeeeeeee—

Grandma, just this one more, it is really tasty, I gathered it myself—

Aunt, if you please—

But Mother, you don't need to be so reticent—

GRAMMMAAAAAAAAAAAA—

Hlaz-mlan shuddered and shifted in her sleeping-tendrils. Her head was full of all the shouting of the preceding hours. Everyone had been glad to see her and tried to make it as clear as possible as fast and as loud as possible.

She wanted to sleep and relax, but it was impossible. All the cheerful yelling was still echoing in her head, taking on a nightmarish quality. She was glad she was not particularly māwal-active, and she understood why Anayāun'd turned down the invitation. Such a crowd of eager but pushy minds; it must be very aggravating for anyone with even a semblance of telepathic awareness. Poor Mawu would be discomforted too, but they were so curious, they probably wouldn't mind. And Dovber? She couldn't even pin down the extent of Dovber's māwal capabilities. Not a huge amount but definitely something, yes? He had secrets.

But Grandmaaaa—

It felt like her family members had imprinted all their buzzing upon her brain. She pulled her aching legs close and reminded herself that all this was just an expression of their love. But it was also a good reason for her to spend most of her time off-planet.

Amidst all the noise, she did feel lonely. She wondered how Mawu was faring with Dovber. Dovber would be a good mentor, both an experienced operative and someone who knew the Alliance inside out—while Mawu was still a newcomer. Both of them were trans too and from unwelcoming cultures, which gave them something in common. And they also had atypical bodies beside being trans . . .

Hlaz-mlan had to admit to herself she was somewhat of a matchmaker—not necessarily in the romantic sense, just in the general social sense. These people would work well together, those people would be good friends, and *those* over there could have a passionate love life. She was good at it, across species too. *It probably just came with age,* she thought. Better this than the replacement legs. And did she need to go to the restroom *again*? She groaned and looked up from her hammock, tracing the movements of the two moons through the transparent window slits in the ceiling that imitated a tree canopy. The walls curled up around her, and everything was peaceful, belying her inner turmoil. There was a greenish tint to the moons tonight.

Greenish and oddly bright.

She shifted among the tendrils, turned around in place. Then she realized there were green patches on the walls, glowing softly. Some kind of fluorescent moss. She'd seen something like this before. A new trend in interior design? The decorations Mlhlh-af mentioned? She felt hopelessly out of date with local fashions. Was her home even her home any longer?

The glowing decorations bothered her. She wouldn't be able to sleep.

She tossed and turned, but it felt comforting to find another cause for her upset, something that was at least a little bit removed from family. She will blame the decorations, not the screaming little grasshoppers.

She reveled in her grumpiness a bit before she summoned Mlhlh-af to complain. And oh, how she would complain.

Mlhlh-af pulled a grass-curtain aside, chirped just once and stared.

"Grandmother, why are you glowing?"

Her mind ran through the possibilities. Contamination—it had to be. From the infiltrator? From the station where they caught the infiltrator? Hadn't she seen some kind of green glowing moss on the walls there too? But no one had seemed alarmed by it.

She resisted the impulse to poke at the glowing squiggles. She glared. She harrumphed, leaning close.

The pattern seemed to be spreading. Slowly but perceptibly to naked vision.

She scrubbed, but there was no moss on her. Maybe inside her? Oh by the sweet smell-taste of honeygrass! Hopefully not *inside* her.

"I'm not glowing," she snapped at Mlhlh-af. "It's just reflected light from these . . . things."

Mlhlh-af waved his antennae in alarm. "What are those? Did you bring them in your luggage?"

She groaned. "I told you, I only brought you gifts. And they screened us thoroughly. Made us go through decontamination and so on."

"You don't think it's coming from you?"

"I—" She hesitated. "I can't discount the possibility. I need to make some calls."

She shut out her environmental senses, leaving herself in the dark—but mercifully away from the inquisitive Mlhlh-af. She called Anayāun first, looped her into the room sensors.

"Why are you glowing?" Anayāun asked.

Hlaz-mlan buzzed with anger. "I'm not glowing! It's those blotches on the wall! At least I think so."

"I'm going to jump there. Have you called Dovber?"

"Not yet."

Anayāun seemed glad she was queried first. Securely in command. Hlaz-mlan let her do it; she was good at it.

"I will jump to you. And Dovber will jump with Mawu. If it's contamination, we're likely also contaminated, and it's best to have us all in one place. Keep your relative in the room."

"You're not glowing?" Hlaz-mlan asked with some resentment.

Anayāun furrowed her brow. "Can you see me glowing?"

Dovber was slightly wobbly after the jump, and he also looked different. It took Hlaz-mlan a moment to parse the change; she was still sleepy, and it was dark, besides the glow from the moss-like substance.

"Dvora?" she asked.

Dvora nodded. She looked much like Dovber: round, squat, curly reddish hair tied and pinned back, and a benign expression. But her face was hairless, the thick beard gone. There was a warm, cozy femininity to her. She was wearing a long black skirt with black hose and shoes, and a mauve pullover with a small brooch: a cluster of synthetic pearls.

Hlaz-mlan felt glad for a moment. She knew Dvora often didn't feel secure enough to assume her woman-shape, even when she felt woman. Then she reminded herself that Dvora probably didn't expect to run into any of her aggressive human relatives here on this out-of-the-way planet.

Mawu yawned, their jaw close to popping. "What's going on? I'm hungry."

Anayāun jumped in, displacing air. She also had to take some time to steady herself—as she sat cross-legged on the floor and rubbed her face. Mawu sat next to her.

Dvora stepped to the wall, leaning close to the glowing moss. Hlaz-mlan was about to tell her to be more careful when Anayāun held up a hand. "Hold on, I have a call incoming."

She looped everyone into it.

What followed was one of the more excruciating calls Hlaz-mlan had the opportunity to witness, throughout a lengthy counterintelligence career.

"No, we did *not* mean to abscond," Anayāun repeated over and over while an extremely angry hotel manager was shaking her abdomen at her.

Hlaz-mlan wasn't sure Anayāun could read all of the social signals of Hlaz-mlan's species, but *she* could, and it was mortifying to sit there in silence.

"We did *not* trash our hotel rooms and leave," Anayāun explained for the fifth time. "We will come back and scrub the walls. We had an emergency situation and had to jump away to meet our friend. All three of us will come back as soon as we can."

Anayāun tried to convince the manager not to enter the rooms or let anyone else enter them, but Hlaz-mlan frankly wasn't sure she succeeded. There was much angry vibration and abdomen-shaking.

Anayāun finally ended the call.

"So," she said. "All our rooms are turning green. It can be assumed that whatever it is, we have all been contaminated and are carrying around the contamination. But how did it get past the decontamination procedure?"

Mawu bit their lower lip. "I wonder if . . ."

Then the green patterns began to rise, away from the walls—what they had thought of as moss was starting to balloon and form large yellowish spheres.

Anayāun jumped up. Mawu also scrambled to their feet.

"They look like puffball mushrooms," Dvora said. "Don't touch them!"

The group formed a protective circle with backs against each other as best as they could. Hlaz-mlan didn't fit well. Where did Mlhlh-af go?

"Why? What happens if we touch them?" Mawu asked.

Dvora pulled out one of her hairpins. "I assume they explode. Or at the very least, they will release spores."

"We need to warn the hotel," Hlaz-mlan reminded them.

"I already told them not to go inside," Anayāun said through gritted teeth.

Mawu raised a hand, palm out. "I can try to deal with this."

Oh, the rashness of youth. "If you destroy them, we'll never find out what they were and what really happened," Hlaz-mlan pointed out as mildly as she could.

Anayāun lifted her left arm. "I'll make a protective bubble around us. Just in case . . ."

"But how much air will we have inside?" Dvora asked.

Air. That was it. Hlaz-mlan hummed with delight.

"Senior Operative?" Anayāun asked with caution edging into alarm in her voice.

"I think I figured out where—"

Then the quasi-fungal spheres began to explode with loud claps, splitting open and emitting clouds of what must have been spores. Despite all of Hlaz-mlan's training, she winced, her legs clacking.

"I told you so," Dvora said with more defeatism than triumph.

"Is this lifeform familiar to you from human planets?" Hlaz-mlan was wary.

Dvora shook her head. "Convergent evolution probably. There's only so many convenient forms life can take." She reached down and to her sides, and Hlaz-mlan recognized the gesture; she was about to pull on those strings, but she wasn't wearing them. She brushed her hand over her long skirt and sighed. "Operative, how much air?" She knew Anayāun liked the more formal terms. "How safe are we?"

The cloud billowed around the room, coming to a stop against the surface of the invisible bubble enclosing the group.

"I can, er, get clean air in from outside," Mawu offered. "And, like, swap." They were visibly shaking. This was definitely not what they'd signed up for. "It . . . it just depends on how long the bubble can be upheld."

Anayāun nodded. Repeatedly. "I'm doing all right so far. Don't worry. We've seen a lot worse." Hlaz-mlan was good at reading human social signals across all cognotypes, and she felt Anayāun was trying to convince herself as much as everyone else.

"We're still stuck," Hlaz-mlan added. "Should we hail the gunship?"

Anayāun tried. "They're outside comms range."

"Or eaten up by exploding space mushrooms." Hlaz-mlan kept her voice steady.

That left ATEF Dispatch, and Hlaz-mlan would rather not let them know they brought some kind of undisclosed contamination all the way planetside.

Dvora said, "I assume Dispatch is out."

"I'd rather not call," Anayāun and Hlaz-mlan said at the same time.

"Then that leaves us the scorched-earth option," Dvora said.

Anayāun grimaced. "I'm holding up the bubble. Mawu?"

Hlaz-mlan assumed Mawu would teleport the spores to some middle-of-nowhere corner of space. Or maybe to a safe ATEF containment unit, though at this point she had strong doubts about those.

Instead, raw māwal rushed out from the bubble, smashing against the walls in an omnidirectional tidal wave. The air shimmered with power, and Hlaz-mlan had to blink her eye filters into place just to be able to watch. Immense, destructive force that annihilated all living creatures—down to the microbial level.

Hlaz-mlan turned just in time to see her favorite hammock burn up and vanish in an instant. *Oh, but* that *would be inconvenient,* she thought.

Mawu dropped to all fours, gasping. "All . . . done," they said.

Anayāun released the bubble with a shrug.

The room felt oddly deserted—no hammock, no grass weavings. Hlaz-mlan assumed her hidden stash of sweets was gone likewise. The branches of the floors and walls were preserved and lacquered, and they did not seem to count as living for this purpose, so the room was still intact. But the moss, the balloons, the spores—they were all gone. It was a fair deal.

Anayāun looked around, her gaze moving beyond their immediate surroundings. "I don't think the contagion had time to spread outside. But we don't know that. It could be anywhere."

Dvora scratched her head. "I wonder if . . . were you all in bed?"

Assent all around. Mawu was trying to get upright but, in the end, gave up and just rolled onto their back on the floor.

"It probably waited until we were asleep. Or at least stationary. It might have been keyed to some simple physical process. I'd rather not . . . attribute sentience to it." Dvora hesitated for a moment.

Mawu said, "I'd sense sentience."

Anayāun sighed. "Not if it were entirely alien."

Dvora continued. "We can assume that, whatever it is, it probably activated once we were resting. But how did it get through decon in the first place?"

"I have an idea," Hlaz-mlan offered. "If you think about it, it started in my room before yours."

Anayāun slapped her thigh. "Ah! The two other rooms!"

Mawu said weakly, "I don't think I can do another jump."

"Can you do another room if I do the jump?" Anayāun asked.

"I'll just call the police," Hlaz-mlan said wearily. "They can deal with it." She would lose face. She had to get the local authorities involved on her holiday break? But both Anayāun and Mawu looked wrung out, and she would rather not risk her teammates' lives—not any more than she had to.

Mlhlh-af scampered forward from behind a dresser curtain.

"Grandson, you stay here until I come back. Don't leave the room. I'm sure you can find some way to entertain yourself."

He looked oddly grateful.

They all slogged back to the hotel, using entirely ordinary means of public transportation. Then they watched a team of three local māwal-users sanitize both rooms and erase the fungus out of existence.

"I still think we should've gotten a sample." Dvora sounded disappointed.

Hlaz-mlan shook her abdomen. "You trust those containment units still?"

Dvora shrugged.

"Do you have a moment?" Mawu asked, once the local team left.

Anayāun waved her fingers and leaned against a bland eggshell-white hotel room wall.

"I just, ummm, I remember that Senior Operative had an idea where it all came from?" Mawu looked hesitant.

"Oh yes. How does your respiratory system work?" Hlaz-mlan asked.

"We have lungs and inhale the air and—" Anayāun began but halted abruptly. "I'm sorry, was this a rhetorical question?"

Hlaz-mlan purred briefly but with great satisfaction. She went on, "I know how human standard respiration works. And I also know it works differently from mine." She pointed an antenna at Mawu. "Exhale completely. As much as you can."

Mawu did, looking perplexed.

"Now exhale a bit more."

They huffed sharply.

"This was your reserve volume. Not all the air leaves the lungs after a regular exhalation. But"—she pointed with the same antenna again—"roughly the same amount of air that you forced to exhale on your second try still remains in your lungs. You cannot empty them out completely." She paused. "You can breathe now."

Mawu gasped and frowned. "You mean it was hiding in our lungs? After decontamination? We literally breathed in the infiltrator when we—*owww*. This makes my head spin!"

"That doesn't work," Dvora said. "I changed shapes."

"You still had your lungs," Anayāun remarked.

"No, I didn't." Dvora sighed. "I didn't just change to my woman-shape, all right?"

"You don't have to explain," Hlaz-mlan quickly added.

Dvora shook her head. "I showed Mawu some of the fun monster shapes I came up with, okay? We were just amusing ourselves."

Hlaz-mlan couldn't begin to imagine the secretive Dvora showing Mawu a *variety* of shapes. She let it drop; she understood she wouldn't ever be privy to everything. It took maybe two hundred years for her to reach that point, and she wouldn't concede it. "You were in the same room though. Even if you somehow destroyed the material in your lungs, it still remained in Mawu's lungs," she said.

Mawu looked queasy but also oddly fascinated. They winced and coughed briefly, and a single poofing sound came from their chest. "Okay, I think I dealt with whatever might remain inside my lungs. Operatives Anayāun and Hlaz-mlan? You probably also should."

Anayāun coughed too. Hlaz-mlan tilted her head, unsure how to go about this. Mawu noticed.

"And um, how does your respiratory system work by contrast? I mean it started earlier in your room—"

That was when the alarm from Hlaz-mlan's family came in.

They dashed out of the hastily procured shuttle. The police commander onsite, an unfamiliar insectoid man, was yelling through comms.

"Floor four, sunny side, has been entirely compromised. We are detaching the main building from the wings! Explosive mite units standing by! Wsf-naf, check in. How are the evacuations going? What is the quarantine status?"

"Sitrep," Anayāun yelled back and sent over the required credentials. "We are with ATEF!"

"The eruption seems to be centered on the top floor restrooms. We are working hard to contain it. The lifecycle seems to be moss, puffballs, spores, walkers, and right now, the walkers are coalescing into insectoid forms."

"Walkers?!" Anayāun and Hlaz-mlan said simultaneously.

"The restrooms?!" Mawu and Dvora said simultaneously.

"Did you go to the restroom after lying down?" Dvora turned to Hlaz-mlan.

"I don't remember. If I did, I must have been half asleep!" Hlaz-mlan was both trembling with irritation and terrified for her family. Had she endangered Mlhlh-af by making him wait in her room?

"Quiet!" Anayāun shouted both of them down. "We're going in! Mawu, you stay here and sit tight because I'm *not* going to explain this to Dispatch if something goes wrong."

"Something?!" Dvora chuckled, her voice wavering as she transformed into an incredibly threatening and armor-plated shape.

"What is that?" Hlaz-mlan stepped back. "A combat mech?!"

Dvora popped open her hatch. "Mawu can pilot me if they want."

Hlaz-mlan was certain Dvora didn't need to be *piloted* in any way, but if the two of them did not want to separate, she could understand that. She'd been against involving Mawu in the mission itself, but after all that happened with the capture of the infiltrator, it was too late for second thoughts.

Anayāun must have had the same thoughts because she urged them on, her face set tight.

Despite herself, Hlaz-mlan was glad for Mawu coming along. She remembered the vast sweep of power. And *walkers*?! She rushed ahead, almost knocking Anayāun to the side.

"Wait! The bubble!" Anayāun yelled at her. Hlaz-mlan slowed just a fraction. All of them dashed into the house.

The vast front gates, decorated with espaliered trees, were gaping open, and one of the planters had been broken, the trunk of its tree cracked and with several of the branches affixed to the door surface splintered off. A century of work wasted. Before this, Hlaz-mlan only felt fear and anger, but now, she was also positively vindictive. Her daughter Lll-mhan had spent so many years getting those trees just right, the branches bending at just the right angles!

"You mess with my daughter, you mess with my house, you mess with *me*," she buzzed.

The contamination hadn't yet spread to the vast entrance hall as far as she could see, so the people who brutalized the front gate had probably been the police. She would have a few choice words with the regional brood-head!

She rushed up the climbing wall across from the entrance, putting her legs into the gaps between the carefully woven branches. Her legs were tense and sore. She wished for the severalth time that her nephew Bmmm-hy would finally install that elevator hammock that he ordered—what now, three years ago?

Anayāun climbed after her, hissing every now and then, and Dvora activated . . . a jet pack? Hlaz-mlan would have been fascinated if she hadn't been crushingly angry—with the invaders, with the lack of an elevator, with everything.

On the second floor, she could already see the walkers. They were round, flexible sticks about the length of a human leg but much narrower—like one of Hlaz-mlan's legs. They bent in the middle in both directions. They looked like a pair of yellowish sticks and walked in an oddly humanlike, doddering fashion.

Hlaz-mlan stopped climbing to watch, Anayāun right behind her. Dvora held onto the climbing branches too.

The walkers moved around erratically. Occasionally, they slapped one of their ends into the floor or the walls forcefully, cracking the glazing and making holes in the thickly woven material underneath. Dust from the centuries-old remainders of building-pods inside the walls wafted on the air. These walls were grown, bent into shape in the time of her great-grandparents, carefully preserved and periodically reglazed. This was the first time someone would lash at the walls violently, cause destruction.

A walker right in front of her hooked one of its ends into the floor, found purchase, and ripped up the thatch. A long gash opened in the hallway.

"We should climb farther," Anayāun said, her voice reaching Hlaz-mlan as if through a curtain. "The epicenter is on the top floor."

Hlaz-mlan climbed on.

Anayāun was still speaking.

"I'm sorry, could you repeat that?" Hlaz-mlan was too distraught to look through her sensory logs.

"Yes, I was saying there might still be people trapped on the top floor. They might have been caught in the initial burst. I'm trying to get some sense of the situation, but the puffballs put out a lot of mental noise. Still, I think there are at least three of your relatives up there and probably unable to come down."

Hlaz-mlan moved as fast as she could. On the next floor, she saw the walkers bumping into each other and intertwining, forming larger creatures. They scraped, scrabbled on legs of uneven lengths, seemingly proceeding by trial and error, but there was a kind of unfathomable intent underlying their apparent randomness. The next step of the *lifecycle*, Hlaz-mlan assumed. What was that cop saying about what would come after that?

The climbing wall was already beginning to detach from the top floor, and she had to swing her abdomen to jump across the gap. The branches and vines groaned. She turned around to see Anayāun make a māwal-assisted jump and Dvora touch down next to her.

"Let me know if you need a big bang," Mawu said from inside Dvora's attack mech shape.

I'd prefer a big bang that I could aim myself, Hlaz-mlan thought but remained silent.

Two kids ran up to them, buzzing and chittering in terror. Aubyy and Ymllh, some of her great-grandnieces who'd been introduced to her last evening. They had been some of the especially annoying nagging ones, but all Hlaz-mlan could feel was relief upon seeing them.

"Quick, Dvora will help you to the climbing wall," she shepherded them toward her fellow operative. "Dvora is a very nice person."

"Why, thank you!" Dvora snatched up the two kids in thickly plated arms, deposited them gently on the wall. The kids scrambled down with record speed.

"And wait outside! Find a nice policeperson!" Hlaz-mlan yelled after them, though she had more doubts about the niceness of the police—traditional police-counterintelligence rivalries aside.

"Do you think there are more people farther ahead?" she asked Anayāun.

"I . . . think so?" the operative offered vaguely.

"I can also look!" Mawu was really trying to help. Hlaz-mlan tilted her head toward Anayāun, who shrugged.

Any tries were preempted by an ear-splitting shriek, coming from the end of the corridor.

Mlhlh-af sounded like he was molting. It was definitely not the season for that nor his turn so soon after another molting.

Anayāun spun her combat staff forward and rushed in. She yelled something that might have been an Ereni curse and then, "I'm taking point!"

She kicked an oddly puppy-like entanglement of walkers out of the way as it aimed itself straight at her legs. She fought off another with a swing of the staff as it dropped onto her from the ceiling, even before it could hit her bubble.

Dvora moved ahead with Mawu still yelling something about how helpful they could be. Hlaz-mlan matched pace with everyone, so Anayāun wouldn't have to expand the bubble overmuch.

Just around the corner, where the walkway split in a T-shape, the walkers were everywhere—hanging from the walls, breaking open the skylights and climbing to the roof, popping out from the cracks they themselves had inflicted on the floor.

Bmmmm-flh's horizontal wall hangings, so carefully extruded, were in tatters. Hlaz-mlan remembered the wedding, the young bride beaming with joy, thorax painted with sweet syrup in intricate patterns.

Sound broke and fractured oddly. Where was Mlhlh-af? She turned around.

"Left, left!" Mawu screamed.

"Are you sure?" Anayāun shouted back as another tangle-like creature bounced off her bubble.

"As sure as I can be!" Mawu responded.

It had to be good enough.

Beyond the corner, the walls themselves were covered entirely.

"Like a cavern of bones," Anayāun said, and Hlaz-mlan was confused for a moment before she realized the Ereni must have referred to *human* bones.

The walls rippled forward. An invitation? Peristalsis?

Anayāun held out an arm. "Wait."

They ground to a halt in treacherous terrain. The floor lacked solidity to it.

"I don't think it's malevolent," Anayāun said.

But then Mlhlh-af screamed again, and Hlaz-mlan pushed herself past the other two operatives.

"What are you doing to my dearest grandchild?!"

She kicked in a door—a large jab of pain. Her front legs would protest later.

Mlhlh-af was fighting a creature quite like himself, their legs intertwined—except the creature's carapace was an eerie orange, the color so sharp as to hurt the eye.

"Whatever that is, it's surely not what I was about to turn into back with the infiltrator," Dvora muttered.

It looked like the orange monstrosity was trying to give Mlhlh-af a hug. That or peel off his carapace. Possibly both.

"Cease your attack," Anayāun shouted at the creature.

Hlaz-mlan didn't wait for any potential cessation. She jumped, trying to tear the fighters apart.

"Wait—" Anayāun yelled, something about protocol and procedure. Hlaz-mlan was kicking in all possible directions.

"Get off my grandson!!"

She finally managed to push them apart to maybe a lower leg joint's length, and she struggled to keep the assailant off Mlhlh-af.

The walls shuddered, fell forward like giant curtains of human bones, snapped in a whipping motion.

The room around them was spitting out more attackers, their bone-yellow turning into the same mind-numbing orange as they re-formed, solidified. Dvora leaned into the original attacker to push it away, and suddenly, Anayāun's bubble was aiding her so that she almost lost her balance. But then another creature crashed into her from behind, and she fell in a confusion of legs.

There were bursts of projectile weapons above her head—Dvora?

"We must get out of here! Anayāun?"

Hlaz-mlan grabbed hold of Mlhlh-af, the young man whining softly, half insensate. Dragged herself on top of him while who knows what piled on her.

"Jump?! I can jump us out, I can jump—"

A giant boom, one wall flowering out to the sky.

Hlaz-mlan rolled out through the newly created opening and fell with Mlhlh-af. She expected Anayāun to catch them as the two of them had done in training many times before—and a few times in live situations too—but instead, it was Dvora grabbing ahold of them, slicing through the air.

They landed on the soft grass, Dvora already back to her woman-shape, Mawu looking dazed.

"I'll need to eat soon," Dvora said. "That took a lot of body material."

"You grew a *rocket* out of yourself?" Anayāun touched down, groaning. "I'm running out of energy to fly."

Dvora shrugged. "Just a cannonball. Fling it fast enough and anything goes boom."

"I could have jumped us out—" Mawu restarted.

Anayāun pointed at their surroundings, the giant rectangle scraped into the ground around the main building. Hlaz-mlan saw that the walkways connecting the wings had been demolished—and she had a sudden incongruous memory of chasing a younger Mlhlh-af along a walkway, telling him to bring back the dessert pods *immediately*. Everything had been demolished. The wings were standing lonely and bereft, disconnected from the main hall imploding upon itself, the roof coughing spores into the air.

Hlaz-mlan dug her feet into the ground, half-expecting it to shake. After all, the world was ending.

"Come," Anayāun said mildly, "we need to be outside the perimeter." She led everyone outside the rectangle, nodded to the people standing on one corner. "Now that everyone is safely out, they're about to try to teleport the house to a safe location."

"The entire house?" Mawu asked what Hlaz-mlan was too shocked to ask. Anayāun nodded assent.

"Wow, that's a lot of people," Mawu said cheerfully. "That takes a lot of māwal. A lot of . . . stuff. Where are they taking it?"

Hlaz-mlan buzzed. She wanted to tell the small pilot to go quiet for once. Even though no one died, some part of her was already mourning.

"To space," Anayāun responded. "Some deserted quadrant. A place where they can store evidence safely."

"What are those boxes?" Ever so curious.

"Atmosphere generators. Once the house is secured, we can go back to investigate."

"If anything is left of it by that time," Hlaz-mlan added sourly, the first time she'd spoken in a while.

"We will go and see, all right?" Dvora reached out to touch her. Humans always felt like they were running too hot. "I know it must be hard on you."

"Thank you," Hlaz-mlan snapped. "At least *you* have some vaguely empathetic cognotype."

Dvora looked hurt. "Oh come on, Anayāun and Mawu are also trying to help."

"I spent the past hour trying to help more!" Mawu protested. "But Dvora wouldn't let me!"

Dvora shushed the young pilot. "Sometimes all you need to say is that you feel for someone."

Mawu stepped back and crossed their arms in front of their chest. "Well, I totally feel for her! This was a really cool house!"

Hlaz-mlan winced at the past tense.

Anayāun sighed and stepped next to Mawu. "I think this is not helping."

"I'm sorry," Mawu whispered at the ground and let Anayāun lead them off.

Hlaz-mlan glared at Dvora. "I know that was unfair. But . . . I really didn't need this." She buzzed, her voice scathing. "It's my home, not a fun exercise in large-scale māwal use."

"I hear you," Dvora said and turned around. "Hey, do you want to sit down somewhere for a while? Get a drink or something, eat a snack?"

"But Mawu and Anayāun—"

"They can take care of themselves."

"And my family—"

"You can tell them you're going to get a bite." She paused. "A slurp. A poke? Sorry."

Hlaz-mlan resisted the urge to shake her abdomen. She was conversant enough in Alliance idioms; they did not need to be adjusted to her body template. But she was glad for the offer to get something.

She sipped her savory fruit juice and leaned back in her hammock. Dvora also gave the juice a try and made a face that had no analog in Hlaz-mlan's lengthy archive of human faces.

"I take it you don't like it?" she asked Dvora mildly. Her immediate stress was fading, and what remained was only a great, hollow, house-shaped sense of loss. The small restaurant was built mercifully in a different style, its walls made of colorful plastics imitating seedpods.

"It doesn't quite agree with my metabolism," Dvora said. "And no, I don't know enough biochemistry to adjust myself just right, though maybe I could try." She grinned, leaning closer to Hlaz-mlan.

"You could do it, in principle?" Hlaz-mlan couldn't resist asking.

"I could, yes."

Despite herself, Hlaz-mlan was intrigued. "How does it work?"

Dvora shrugged. "I have no idea how it works, and neither does anyone else. Leftover technology from the Old Empire."

"You think the infiltrator might have also gotten ahold of something like that?"

Dvora bit her lip. "That's exactly my guess. We'll probably know more once . . . well." She stopped.

"You can say it. Once we go investigate the house again." Hlaz-mlan shifted in her hammock. "It won't be a house anymore. It will probably be a tiny planetoid of . . . fungus, floating in space. It will be easier."

"Everyone is safe. We can think of that," Dvora said. "And you rescued your great-grandson."

Hlaz-mlan buzzed. "Grandson. And my great-grandnieces." She paused. "They'll probably build something more . . . modern. More up to date. I will have to have a few choice words with them." She drank rapidly. "Though truth be told, coating the roof was always a massive pain."

"Life goes on," Dvora said and took a bite of her human food.

"Provided we find the source of the contagion," Hlaz-mlan added.

Dvora said something in a human language—blessing, curse?—and then, "Hopefully we will."

"But I'm not giving up on the house," Hlaz-mlan said. "It can be decontaminated. Scrubbed. Four generations of handiwork went into it. A bit more—what is that to a large family like ours?"

Dvora furrowed her brow. No additional eyes appeared. "Hey, do you want to check up on the house? I'm sure the space perimeter has some kind of display option. You will be able to see it floating there, waiting for us."

Hlaz-mlan was wary but also grimly curious. She sent a command, pulled up a video feed.

"See? It looks so peaceful," Dvora said.

"It's just a speck." She zoomed in.

Floating calmly in a deserted quadrant of space, the house was starting to resemble a cauliflower with what looked much too like legs, sticking out in all directions.

"Dvora," Hlaz-mlan said quietly, her legs aching all of a sudden, "I'm not sure this was such a good idea."

CHAPTER THREE: HAILING MUSHROOM ROCK

ANAYĀUN TURNED OFF THE VIDEO STREAM AND TILTED BACK IN HER CHAIR so abruptly that it transformed itself into a bed. She shut her eyes tight.

She wished she could make the world go away, turn it off with just a gesture. It was comforting to remain in the tiny enclosure of the ship, but people had a way of intruding. She had nothing against people, but this density of them was overwhelming. And all of them had a cognotype not only different from her own but rather badly clashing with it, she felt.

In order to get to the impounded evidence, she needed to speak to the chief evidence officer, the assistant evidence officer, at least five kinds of Alliance liaisons each with mysterious job descriptions, her boss, *her* boss, Dvora's boss for some unfathomable reason, and a badly rendered avatar of a talking cat.

She gritted her teeth and began composing her report to be sent back to Eren. A *written* report. With no need to speak to anyone. She tilted the bed up just a little, so she wouldn't fall asleep right away—though by that point she had reached that state of exhaustion where she felt too tired even to sleep.

The Ereni Security officer on duty responded immediately and chirpily.

Thank you!! Much appreciated. I hope you're having a good time out there in space! Let us know if you need anything. We're here for you.

She sent back something vague and tore off the silver-embroidered black cap of her uniform and rubbed her bare scalp. She felt a sudden rush of . . . anger? Envy? Everyone back on Eren could relax and have fun surrounded by people of the Ereni cognotype. Yet she was out here alone and having to *liaise* with all these slightly annoyed strangers who did not quite understand her. Over and over and over. Having to present herself as acceptable, typical, compliant.

She realized she was still grinding her teeth and forced herself to relax. She could talk to Mawu, the young pilot, who not only had the Ereni cognotype but was in the process of applying for Ereni citizenship. But Mawu was maybe half her age and seemed permanently confused.

The talking cat had informed her that the person to approve their access to the evidence was only back in office the next day. She could just spend that time in her room. It was, shockingly, too early to sleep—

Ermmmmm, do you think maybe possibly I could come in?

Mawu put hesitation markers even in text messages.

Anayāun sighed. Still, if Mawu felt lonely enough to ask her, maybe they could . . . do what? Read together in silence? Go out and race floaters around the evidence storage?

. . .

That actually didn't sound half bad.

Come on in, Anayāun messaged back.

There was little space. This was a small ship. The two of them sat next to each other on the bed, Mawu just a little bit jittery. They pulled anxiously at their curls. Their skin was light enough that their blush was not only visible but striking—much lighter than Anayāun's.

"I um, ermm. I'm kind of worried," they began with no preamble. "I really offended Hlaz-mlan, did I? I apologized to her again, but I'm not sure . . . like . . ."

"It might be best to just stop pestering her and behave as you regularly would with her?" After hours of dealing with people of another cognotype, Anayāun really did not want to advise Mawu on how to do the same. "You look all wound up. Maybe try to relax a bit?"

"But . . . but my citizenship committee will ask everyone I worked with for an opinion, and—"

"And we will say you were just fine." Anayāun sighed. "Look, Hlaz-mlan's species lives for hundreds of years in huge families. Everything you can say, she has heard a worse variant already. You only made an insensitive remark about her house."

Mawu didn't appear convinced.

Anayāun tried a different tack. "Just try to get it out of your mind. Do you know anything about floater racing?"

Mawu knew nothing about floater racing and was perhaps a little too eager to try.

"Out here, there's nothing save for the evidence storage," Anayāun said through her comms. "We can set up a track, but it's as safe as it gets."

Mawu adjusted their helmet and stared at the giant blob floating in space. What used to be Hlaz-mlan's family home had changed into a roundish planetoid of frothing organic material: the evidence. Mawu nervously yanked at their suit, and Anayāun had to remind herself that these fabrics could not be torn so easily.

Anayāun passed Mawu a floater board. They turned it around in their hands. "This just looks like a piece of plastic. How do I ride it?"

"There are variants with all kinds of propulsion, but this one is just a piece of plastic." Anayāun grinned at Mawu. "You hop on and propel it yourself."

Mawu gingerly pushed themselves away from the surface of the ship, taking care not to kick Kheinu. Anayāun hadn't known anyone before who was symbiotically bound to a spaceship, but she noticed and felt the care.

Mawu held onto the board, pulled themselves to their knees while grabbing the front, trying to imitate Anayāun. "What do I do now?" they asked.

"You use your māwal!" Anayāun leaned forward and pushed ahead. She was all out of patience for the day. Mawu would either get it or—

"Wheeeeeeeeeeeeeeeeeeeeeeeeeeeeeeeeeeeeeeeeee!" Mawu streaked full speed ahead.

"Wait, watch the perimeter of the evi—"

Mawu banked sharply right, immediately getting the hang of it. Anayāun grinned. This might actually be fun.

"You haven't tried this before?" she yelled at Mawu's back.

"I flew other things!" Mawu laughed in delight.

"Is this like flying the ship?"

"Kheinu flies themself," Mawu chuckled.

Anayāun quickly threw some pointers ahead. "Race to the end?"

"I'm in!"

The two of them raced around the giant rectangular space, which was off-limits, in curves and loops defined by Anayāun. She made sure not to make the track overly three-dimensional; Mawu had plenty to get used to without having to worry about that. Both of them hooted and laughed.

Anayāun leaned into the motion but didn't push herself overly hard. Mawu was trying to catch up, understeering at almost every corner but slowly getting the finer details.

"You're letting me win," Mawu yelled once the two of them were finally side by side.

"Am not!" Anayāun pushed more power into her flight. The roiling planetoid of *evidence* seemed such a tempting choice to draw power from, but who knew what would happen? She shook her head. Mawu would eventually win just on the basis of raw power, now that they could take a curve more or less properly.

But Anayāun would not give up without a fight. "Battle for position!" she yelled, trying to block her inside curve to prevent Mawu from overtaking her. Mawu would surely not be able to go for the more complicated outside, fly all the way around her.

Mawu grunted as they understood the maneuver. "Can't we do this in three dimensions? I'm a pilot, I get it."

"We can tr—"

As Anayāun stopped paying attention just for a moment, Mawu already pushed into the gap. Anayāun had to yank her board out of the way, but she quickly corrected. She gasped, realizing she would need to draw on some outside source of māwal soon.

The planetoid burped—soundlessly but with a resonance she felt in her bones—and a protuberance of organic material aimed itself right in the path of the two of them. Iridescent grayish curlicues of mush, flowing at incredibly high speed, passed through the perimeter of the enclosure with no apparent slowing, and Anayāun dodged just in time.

"Aaaaahhh!!" Mawu broke off at a tangent directly along the vertical, if the racetrack was the horizontal. Definitely no problem thinking in three dimensions.

The protuberance solidified into a sphere and slowly floated back to its origin. The planetoid reabsorbed it without any difficulty.

"BY THE LIVING VOICE, WHAT WAS *THAT*?!" Mawu screamed.

Anayāun cleared her throat. "I think it wanted to say hello."

Hlaz-mlan clacked her legs against each other as she sat, her insectoid body filling a shapeforming seat. Anger radiated from her, filling the small central room of the ship. "What were the two of you thinking?"

"I'm so sorry! We wanted to relax and have fun!!" Mawu looked on the verge of tears.

Anayāun sighed. "It was my idea. I take responsibility."

"But I wanted to do it!"

Just stay quiet for once, Anayāun thought.

Dvora brushed a hand on her skirt. "What's more interesting is how the burst managed to leave the enclosure. I thought these evidence containers were supposed to be thoroughly warded."

They *might be more appropriate,* Kheinu said. *Rather than* it.

"Excuse me?" Dvora's hand froze mid-motion, as if she'd forgotten about it altogether.

The planetoid appears to be sentient, Kheinu said.

Then the ding of an incoming message: they have been given access to the evidence room. Mawu shuddered, and even Hlaz-mlan stopped clacking her legs.

"It's the middle of the night on Alliance Central," Anayāun said, frantically pinging all her contacts who might have more information, coming up short. "The protuberance must have tripped some alarm."

"But wait, *sentient*?" Dvora was coming out of her shock.

"I think this is a false notice," Anayāun said. "No one's responding. Maybe the burst broke the systems in some way, and they issued an automated permission."

"We could still go in to investigate. Isn't this what we've been trying to do all day?" He grinned drily.

"My house. It's sentient?" Hlaz-mlan whispered and then chirped. "I must see this for myself."

It's not your house any longer, Anayāun thought but realized it would not be politic to say. The team had decided that only Hlaz-mlan and Anayāun would venture inside at first, and if something went disastrously wrong, Mawu and Kheinu could still take Dovber back to Alliance space. He had just shifted into his man shape, and Anayāun was wondering if it was in response to stress. When Dvora was more relaxed, she seemed to prefer her woman shape.

Hlaz-mlan held onto a floater that Anayāun had reshaped into a disc-like shape with grips and hooks along the sides. Anayāun dragged her along through an opening in the transparent force fields of the evidence enclosure.

"I'm glad they don't store anything else in this one," Anayāun said, trying to break the silence, even though small talk was not one of her strengths.

Hlaz-mlan simply ignored her. Mourning the loss of her family home?

They approached the planetoid slowly, gingerly, trying not to cause another protuberance.

Hlaz-mlan buzzed sharply and said, "I think that used to be the front gate."

Anayāun strained her eyes. It took her a while to find the spot, but she eventually noticed what looked like the remnants of the espaliered trees, the geometric pattern of their branches flat against the planetoid as if they had been painted on the surface.

Then the entire area crunched inside, leaving only a dark passageway. The trees vanished, digested in the constant churn.

"What could possibly go wrong?" Hlaz-mlan said, her voice a mixture of sadness, anxiety, and jest. Anayāun always felt a twinge of awe at how expressive Hlaz-mlan was, even in a language not her first, probably not even her second. She reminded herself that the question must have been intended as rhetorical and remained silent.

Hlaz-mlan softly buzzed. "Generations of pruning and adjustments to get those trees just right. What will my offspring inherit?"

Anayāun had no answer to that. "Are we going in?" she asked. Hlaz-mlan agreed after just a moment of hesitation. Anayāun felt she would not have noticed the pause had she not been already so closely focused on her fellow operative.

"I would try to communicate first," Dovber said through their comms.

Anayāun brought the floater to a halt. "You try."

"No response," Mawu said. "I also tried."

"Then could we get a move on?" Hlaz-mlan complained. "My legs are getting all cramped holding on to this floater."

"The protuberance might not have been a communication attempt." Anayāun felt they were all wasting their time. "I understand why you are hypothesizing sentience. Up close, I can sense it quite clearly." *Now that I'm not busy racing circles around them,* she thought. "But it seems to be a sentience focused entirely inward. I'm concerned our actions might be interpreted as an attack."

"They built themself from *my* house," Hlaz-mlan said. "I used to live in them. If that doesn't bias them favorably, nothing will."

Anayāun decided a snarky comment wouldn't add anything of value.

The two of them floated into the opening.

It was dark inside, and Anayāun quickly generated a helmet light.

"Of course, why would there be light inside?" Hlaz-mlan offered. "It's not as if there is light in the inside of an animal."

"I wouldn't assume they're an *animal*," Anayāun said. As they floated into what looked like a giant, ribbed esophagus, the walls began to glow—gently at first and then stronger and stronger until Anayāun had to invoke a filter. She considered dialing down her visual input, but the house-animal around them twitched, and the brightness began to recede to a level more comfortable for both of them.

"I think they noticed that we are uncomfortable," Hlaz-mlan said.

The exhaustion hit Anayāun again. What was she supposed to say? That she hoped that wasn't the case? She was sure the house didn't have access to her thoughts—and as a member of Ereni Security on loan to the Alliance, she had some of the best warding in Alliance space.

She stopped and looked around at the clearly body-like walls. Maybe the house noticed other measures of discomfort: tense muscles, a quicker circulation of air inside her suit, faster heartbeat . . . she wasn't sure how much her suit shielded that information and reminded herself to look into it in detail later.

Maybe the house simply paid close attention to the way their bodies moved, and that would be hard to shield unless they wanted to engage with the outside world from inside a perfectly spherical bubble.

"Do you think we should have brought in our ship?" Hlaz-mlan asked.

Anayāun gestured at the ribbing. "This looks like an esophagus, so I'm assuming the stomach must be up ahead. Better not risk the ship getting digested."

Hlaz-mlan buzzed tensely. Anayāun propelled the two floaters along.

The esophagus seemed too long. Were they circling around just under the skin of the creature? She could not think of being in a house any longer.

"I don't recognize anything," Hlaz-mlan said, leaning closer to the wall-surface and away from her floater.

ILLNESS, the house said.

Hlaz-mlan lost her balance and scrambled with her many legs to hold onto the pallet still, her suit glinting with odd highlights.

ILLNESS, ILLNESS, the house repeated. ***TRANSLATION.***

Anayāun stopped abruptly and had to reach out with the māwal and adjust so that the pallets would not topple on top of each other.

Did you hear that?! Mawu yelled in their comm link.

It was impossible not to hear. We felt it in our bones, Anayāun responded.

I don't have bones *in a mammalian sense,* Hlaz-mlan noted wryly. *But yes, it was rather hard to miss.*

ILLNESS, the house said again with what seemed to Anayāun like longing in their voice. Longing and desire. As if illness was a beautiful thing. She wasn't sure she was interpreting it right across what must be vastly different cognotypes. She reached out to Hlaz-mlan and initiated a gentle, loose groupmind with her; maybe the two of them together would make more sense of the impressions. It was good practice for first contact situations when isolated from a specialist team.

The disconcerting feeling at the outset was so familiar that it had long since ceased to be disconcerting in itself. Hlaz-mlan's mind was sharp and angular yet soft and welcoming against her own. Then there was a pop as if the surface tension dissipated when they merged.

Now one, Ahnlaayz-āmulnan listened.

ILLNESS, DISPATCH, the house said. Almost trembling with a desire to communicate. Then gingerly, tentatively, ***TRANSLATION.***

Ahnlaayz-āmulnan reached out with their minds—slowly, with a care matching the house's own. "We are listening."

They felt the mental impression of the house inching closer, reaching with what seemed like tendrils braided together, disentangling and entwining again. Ahnlaayz-āmulnan made contact.

ILLNESS IS DESIRE. TRANSLATION IS GLORY. EATING IS CONSUMPTION, NEGATED.

Hlaz-mlan was so jolted, she almost detached from their temporary groupmind. "That's . . . that's a paraphrase of one of my talking wall hangings," she said and helped Anayāun smooth her back into their groupmind.

Ahnlaayz-āmulnan remembered the poem.

Desire is glory, negated; the raw filaments
honeysharp-sweet. This illness of need,
this entanglement eating away at me with
a feverous joy—

It was a translation of a Nesker classic, a love poem that went on for many paragraphs, a long, embroidered strip that had been hanging in one of the little decorative alcoves. If you touched it, you could hear a simulation of the poet himself, reading it out loud, roaring and rumbling—a simulation, of course, because the poet probably didn't have any languages in common with Hlaz-mlan.

A favorite. Repeated many times, her thoughts resonating with the walls.

Ahnlaayz-āmulnan reoriented themselves from the Hlaz-mlan-memories, comforting as they were. Comforting and tinged with the pain of loss.

Ahnlaayz-āmulnan reminded themselves that the poem was not lost, simply incorporated. They tried to reshuffle the words to echo them back. They weren't sure how much syntax the house understood.

"Entanglement, desire? Need?"

EATING, the house said—less ominously, more wistfully.

"Are you hungry?" Mawu asked via the commlink. Ahnlaayz-āmulnan wished they could in-group them to the mind, but the young pilot was not an Alliance operative, and data leaks would have been a problem.

The house still responded. **EATING IS NEED, NEGATED. ENTANGLEMENT**

IS DESIRE. A small pause and then, *PLEASE HOLD ON TO THE HANDLE TO ADJUST THE TEMPERATURE DIAL.*

A remnant of the heating-cooling system. Maybe the house was just repeating random fragments of language at them? Ahnlaayz-āmulnan pushed back against what felt to themselves as overmuch a Hlaz-mlan-thought. Repeating previously stored pieces of language was how many Ereni kids communicated, and some adults too; it was purposeful more often than not. The consensus was more Anayāun-weighted.

Ahnlaayz-āmulnan spoke up. "You don't need to eat, but . . . you'd like to?"

EATING IS CONSUMPTION, NEGATED. ENTANGLEMENT IS DESIRE.

Ahnlaayz-āmulnan thought the house was maybe speaking of a more metaphorical eating. Which words were there still in the poem that could come in handy? Or in the heating system?

"To be incorporated; the ocean opens desert-wide / and your antennae, nearing—" Ahnlaayz-āmulnan recited. An idle thought that the poet must have meant *whiskers* originally, being Nesker. Or possibly *paws*? The more erotic a love poem, the harder to translate across different body shapes.

TO BE INCORPORATED, PLEASE CONFIRM SETTINGS CHANGE. TRANSLATION IS ILLNESS. A wariness trembled in the walls around them. *TRANSLATION IS ILLNESS. RAW, FEVEROUS INCORPORATION. CONFIRM THAT YOU ARE AWARE OF THE OVERHEATING RISK FOR SYSTEMS OVERRIDE.*

"Hold on," Ahnlaayz-āmulnan raised a set of hands, antennae, and legs across their two bodies. "You want to incorporate us in order to talk, but this carries a certain risk. Is that correct?"

A long, long wait. Digestive motions rippling through the esophagus. The house was struggling—either with understanding or with speaking. Ahnlaayz-āmulnan reached out a bit further, offering their language, trying to undergird the house's thoughts.

CHOICES ARE HARD, the house said.

Ahnlaayz-āmulnan sighed, recognizing the quote. A different poem. Hlaz-mlan hated that other hanging, but she had to put it up because one of her sons insisted, having spent a very long time making the lacework for her. But she disliked the poem, written by some kind of blockhead from Alliance Central. Ahnlaayz-āmulnan refocused from the Hlaz-mlan-memories and tried to disentangle the meaning. "Can you clarify? Rephrase?"

Another pause and then, ***THE PRINCIPLE OF SUBSIDIARITY.***

Ahnlaayz-āmulnan laughbuzzed. The house must have eaten some kind of Alliance report too. Subsidiarity was one of the organizing principles of the Alliance, at least in theory: everything that can be tackled by an organization must be tackled at the simplest possible organizational level. They decided the house must be asking the groupmind to detach so that only one of them would be put at risk.

Anayāun exhaled. The disassociation process always felt a bit sad to her but also a relief in some ways. Hlaz-mlan let out a forlorn chirp.

"Which of us should try to reach out?" Anayāun asked. She had intended the question for Hlaz-mlan, but the house was also attempting to respond.

Mawu gasped over their commlink. The house was trying to reach out to them.

"No, you can't choose Mawu," Anayāun said a bit louder than necessary. "Mawu is bound to Kheinu, our ship, and if something goes wrong, we can't get out of here."

Then it was her turn to gasp, feeling the vast closeness.

It made sense to her. Anayāun had the Ereni cognotype, like Mawu. The house's cognotype probably did not match any of theirs, but maybe this offered the most compatibility. The house chose her.

She panicked. They clearly did not think this through. But there was no time to wait who knows how many days for the Alliance to put together a First Contact team, not when their Counterintelligence team was in hot pursuit.

Well, semi-hot pursuit. Lukewarm pursuit? Her thoughts spun out of control. *There are some situations where no training is sufficient,* she thought. Some circumstances that are entirely unforeseeable.

Sometimes there is nothing to hold on to.

PROCEED, the house said, and the light increased ahead—at the end of the esophagus?

Anayāun floated onward, shielding Hlaz-mlan with her body, aware that she was making her way into a chamber that still reminded her of a stomach even now that she was inside it, not merely peering in.

Walls grew inward, curlicues corkscrewed toward her. She let go of her floater and kicked herself in the direction of the surface, pulling up a shielding bubble around Hlaz-mlan, who floated in the middle of the space.

She reminded herself of the prime directive of Ereni contact protocols: assume cooperation. But people were cautioned against assuming *friendliness*. She instructed her biosystems to deal with her panic, but it seemed the alternative was the crushing exhaustion. She chose the latter. They should all have rested before going in. Lukewarm pursuit, right?

She flew into the embrace of fast-growing tendrils that reached out, tethered her to the wall.

The surface was soft and wheezing, as if breathing oxygen.

Comforting.

Relaxing.

REATTACH VENTILATION DUCT TO RESUME COOLING, the house said.

Anayāun fumbled around, trying to reach her oxygen tube. The tendrils loosened to allow her to move but still held her close.

She wished she could sleep.

The house was asking her to do something with her breathing apparatus?

Dovber screamed through the commlink.

"ABORT, ABORT!" Dovber yelled. "Don't touch your suit! Move away!"

Anayāun shook her head, as if resurfacing from water, and kicked at the soft, squirmy wall to propel herself away.

The tendrils detached.

Anayāun dove back in the direction of the bubble shielding Hlaz-mlan. The bubble admitted her soundlessly but with what still felt like a loud plop that resonated in her head. The presence in her mind receded, and she was able to think more clearly. Or was she? She was still inside this creature, and she understood that this in itself might bias her thoughts.

"What's the fuss?" Hlaz-mlan said mildly. "The house wanted you to breathe them in. That's how we got here in the first place, by us carrying the spores down planetside in our tracheae, lungs, what have we."

Anayāun shuddered. They had been supposed to have some fun R&R and visit Hlaz-mlan's family. Instead, they ended up with Hlaz-mlan's ancestral home becoming a giant sentient glob impounded as evidence. "I am not sure that's worth repeating," she said slowly.

Dovber sighed so loudly that Anayāun's comm system was momentarily confused by the signal and tried to sharply downregulate the input. She had to manually adjust it to hear him again. "I'm glad you're away from the wall," he said.

Anayāun stared back where she'd come from. The tentacles wavered—invitingly? Tentatively? Forlornly? She wasn't sure.

"We still need to communicate somehow," she said.

"I'm sure we can do that without breaching your suit," Dovber said.

"Do you think the house wants to hurt us?" Hlaz-mlan asked with sadness in her voice.

"You only ask that because they used to be your house!" Dovber was growing more frustrated. "But your house was only used as raw material. Incorporated. And now this . . . this being wants to incorporate one of your fellow operatives!"

"'Translation is illness'," Mawu repeated quietly. "There must be a tradeoff. The house knows there is a tradeoff, no? And is trying to warn us . . . there is always a tradeoff."

Anayāun wished she knew more of the nature of Mawu's connection to Kheinu. "You're probably right. I wonder if I can ask for more information." She wasn't sure it was worth a try. The house was barely making sense. Maybe all the sense they extracted so far was an illusion, seeing patterns where none existed. But she could feel the sentience.

She sent out a request for a Contact team. Then she loosened the bubble just enough to admit the house's words.

THE HARD PRINCIPLE. THE HARD PRINCIPLE! PLEASE SIGN OR STAMP IN THE TEXT BOX.

Three hours later, Anayāun was jittery from trying to push wakefulness on her biosystems, Hlaz-mlan nodded off, and based on the sounds coming via the intercom, Dovber was nervously smoothing down his beard so frequently that Anayāun wondered if any parts of it still remained.

"I knew I should have gone into linguistics," Mawu said with an edge of annoyance.

Even the house seemed aggravated. They weren't getting anywhere.

Anayāun yawned. "We can't keep this up. We're not getting enough information."

"I think the house also doesn't really know the risks?" Mawu said. "It's not just that they can't communicate very well. It's also that they don't have an answer for us . . . kind of?"

"We should request a Contact team from HQ," Dovber yawned too. "Even if it takes forever for them to get here. We're wasting our time."

"I put in a request"—Anayāun checked—"one hundred twenty-seven minutes ago. It was denied one hundred eight minutes ago. Alongside an angry reprimand to solve the situation ourselves or don't bother coming back."

"Why?" Mawu asked.

"Information encapsulation, they said. There was also something in there about the principle of subsidiarity." Anayāun shrugged with sudden anger. "Just a boilerplate response. They are worried about leaks? If they don't know how to keep their own linguists from babbling, why don't *they* request a psych team from Eren?!" She slapped a palm on her thigh. "I'm going back in. If I'm eaten, let Ereni Security know."

She pushed out of the bubble, jolting Hlaz-mlan awake.

She braced herself.

She reached out toward the wall, and a wordless song blossomed in her head.

The melody all too familiar. The words?

[I-[NEG-[[the one]ascending]]] [[[I-[the ascension]]EMPH—]

Anayāun stopped herself with the māwal and floated, hand held out, not making contact.

The house was gently parsing through her mind, her language—Eren-sā. Pieces fell into place. Anayāun forced herself to relax, allow the process to run its course—and it did with a single great swoop.

I am not the one ascending; lo, I am ascension itself.

The morning rites of the Ereni Way.

Workers laboring in unison; raise the mighty towers

She had never been particularly observant. Hadn't done the morning contemplation in years.

But they carried a resonance of home.

Not the one ascending; I am the ascension.

The motto of the Free State of Eren if there ever was one.

Anayāun reached out. "We are both far from our worlds, aren't we?" she muttered, more to herself than to the house.

Tendrils reached out toward her breathing tube, and she guided them gently with her fingers, clicked open the clasp.

For a brief moment, she thought that maybe she should have just resigned on the spot once they denied her request for a First Contact team. But then who would have gone ahead? Once Counterintelligence, always Counterintelligence . . .

She took a deep breath.

Breathing in light. Smoothness and then rasping pain. Her lungs protested. Her nerves—she wasn't sure what was going on. She suppressed the defensive reactions of her biosystems as best as she could. It was difficult.

She didn't know whether to trust the relief.

The understanding.

Was this how Mawu felt, bound to their ship?

Coughs racked her entire body.

Blood on the inside of her visor—the material digesting it, shunting it away. She watched the smear dissolve.

It felt like she was being gently but insistently pulled apart at the seams. Tearing like thin layers of fabric. Then a massive kick in the solar plexus, and she doubled over. Her spine—she could not distinguish between separate sensations any longer.

"This is not how it feels." Who was saying that? Mawu?

Was Mawu still connected to her in some way? Where was anyone? What was going on?

There was always a tradeoff. Was this the tradeoff?

"Bindings are always imperfect," Mushroom Rock said. The house? The house did not think of themselves as the house; it was a purely external viewpoint, and her own viewpoint was now at least partially internal. "The bindings are always imperfect," Mushroom Rock repeated. "We have not found a way. But we made a good choice. With you it is easy."

Anayāun wasn't sure how her body was situated in space, and she couldn't see anything but golden light, but she attempted to nod.

"The young one would have been well-suited," Mushroom Rock said. "But we do not wish to act against your interests."

Anayāun shuddered. Something that felt like a giant, leathery blanket wrapped around her like the wing of a bat?

"Translation is an illness," Mushroom Rock went on. "As the young one said, there is always a tradeoff. I'm glad you understand."

"I was just impatient," Anayāun thought loudly, her mouth not quite obeying her.

"You understood the risks, as much as anyone could . . . reactions are always idiosyncratic. This time, I aimed to preserve essential autonomy."

Anayāun wondered about the previous time and remembered the infiltrator. Where was he? Inside the house in some way?

She was shivering. She tried to reach out, but she had very little access to the giant mind around her. Even the interior viewpoint had dissipated.

"We are trying to be cautious this time. We need to be certain of essential autonomy. Now your body needs to reach a new equilibrium," Mushroom Rock said slowly, and Anayāun felt herself drifting away into a dreamless but finally restful sleep.

When Anayāun woke, she felt energized. She would have done anything for sleep, she thought. That's why she'd agreed. She wanted something to happen as quickly as possible so that she could then sleep. Force the issue. Sleep deprivation had probably biased her more than being inside a giant house-being ever had. Now, she could think clearly again, though she checked herself: she could not be entirely sure she wasn't influenced by Mushroom Rock more than she'd realized.

She peeled herself out from what seemed to be a giant chrysalis. Hlaz-mlan was still in the bubble she'd set up—Mushroom Rock must have aided in maintaining it—and she was sound asleep.

Anayāun reenabled her comms that had turned off at some point, possibly in response to the onslaught of awareness. Dovber was softly breathing in and out, dreaming the dreams of the just.

"Eeeeeeh?" Mawu yelled. "You're awake? Sorry, I was reading!!"

"Hold on a moment . . ." Anayāun mentally inventoried her body.

It felt different. Her biosystems gave her a visual on which her body appeared shot through with veins of gold. She was awake and more cheerful than any time in the past few cycles, but her limbs ached all over.

She was reminded of more Ereni ritual, seemingly streaming at her from outside herself. From Mushroom Rock?

No transformation is ever without pain—
I call pain into me to transmute and sublime.
Open for me the gate, the gate inside myself—
the gate opens, and I can pass through.

She wasn't sure she was ready to be linked to a giant mound of evidence that quoted her own traditions back at her.

Hlaz-mlan stirred. "Operative? Are you alive in there?"

Anayāun nodded and kicked out to launch herself back at the bubble—only belatedly realizing that this was not the best course of action. She grabbed onto a tendril and whipped back toward the wall, the impact jolting her, pain lancing through her ankles.

Her self-repair definitely wasn't operating as designed.

"What's going on?" Hlaz-mlan asked. "Why the startle? Hop back on, and we can get going."

"No, I can't. I've been compromised."

To Anayāun's horror, Hlaz-mlan was trying to use the thrusters of her suit to boost the floaters toward the wall.

"No, don't approach! I'm contaminated! I'm—"

Hlaz-mlan buzzed, a low, droning sound. "You forget. Whatever those spores are, we all breathed them in already. We took them planetside. That's how we ended up with this . . . *evidence*," she said with more than a little exasperation.

"We're in this together," Dovber said through comms. "Don't worry about it. You talk to the house. We can worry after we're done with the assignment."

That sounded prophetic, Anayāun thought.

"Can you talk to the house better now?" Hlaz-mlan asked.

Anayāun nodded. "Mushroom Rock. That's their name . . . at least as best as I can translate it."

"And what do they want?"

She had no idea.

"You need to release me from the enclosure," Mushroom Rock said. "I would rather not push my entire mass through it. A small tendril was difficult enough." Anayāun dutifully repeated the words to the entire team. "We need to go back to our quadrant of space, and you need to accompany me. This is exceedingly important."

Anayāun sighed. "I'm contacting headquarters and summarizing the situation."

This time, she managed to hail someone right away—only to be told again to proceed. "We cannot spare anyone right now," Dispatch said, leaving much unsaid: *You have already been compromised. You might as well go ahead.*

Anayāun felt acutely aware that she was seen as an asset whose value had just been depreciated to zero.

She dangled her legs off her floater and wondered if she should reach out to the System back on Eren, the massive groupmind englobing the planetoid, even though this was a circumvention of Alliance protocol and technically illegal. You should not directly contact your member state behind the Alliance's back. But the System would treat her like a sentient being, not like a string of numbers.

She took a deep breath, closed her eyes, and reached out. She maintained most of her warding—clinging to an operations security that had just been shredded. She shared just enough of her mind with the System of Eren to avoid having to verbally summarize the situation . . . and she made absolutely certain that her mind was interposed between the System's and Mushroom Rock's. No need to make the situation worse than necessary.

Don't be discouraged, the System said with warmth. *You have been entrusted with an important task by sentient beings you are just getting to know.*

Anayāun hadn't thought of it like that. Now that she turned the concept around in her head, she reflected bitterly on how she was in Counterintelligence, not First Contact. Mushroom Rock had repeatedly asked them for help—had asked specifically *her* for help. She had agreed; why would she turn back now?

Do you wish to go ahead with this? asked the System. *You are not obliged.*

Maybe she wasn't obliged to the System, but she felt she was obliged to Alliance Counterintelligence. Then again, she was quite certain they had already put her on a casualty list. She couldn't be obliged if she was nominally dead.

She felt obliged to Mushroom Rock, and she told the System as much. The being was in great distress and had caused much trouble in Alliance space already. She herself was the only person who had so far managed to communicate with them.

Would you like us to send our own contact specialists to aid you, given the Alliance has turned you down?

Anayāun bit her lower lip hard. Yes, yes she would. But . . . it would cause a diplomatic scandal with the Alliance to go behind their backs. But if Eren offered a contact team to the Alliance . . . the last time that happened was with Earth, and that did not go well at all. That resulted in the first armed conflict Eren had been involved in since the War of Independence.

She could not risk diplomatic trouble, let alone a declaration of war. She shook her head, turning the offer down. The System understood. She suspected they only offered to make her feel better, and they knew well that she would say no.

But it worked. It did make her feel better.

She was a representative of her people . . . and now, of Mushroom Rock. People trusted her on both sides.

She grinned. She might as well go for it.

"'We need to negotiate. You need to understand the context'," Anayāun quoted. "That's exactly what Mushroom Rock said."

She felt more comfortable once they were back aboard Kheinu, even though they were slowly orbiting Mushroom Rock. Dispatch finally got someone to release the planetoid from containment, and they were all about to head out— but still waiting.

Mushroom Rock is holding back information, Kheinu said.

Anayāun raised an eyebrow. "Can you feel it, or is that just common sense?"

I can feel it. And *it's just common sense,* the ship responded with faint amusement. Anayāun paced the control room, though it was barely large enough for the purpose. "Don't hurt the messenger, all right? I can only convey what they are telling me."

"You could make a point about, um, informed consent?" Mawu said, chewing on their fingers.

"This is not a medical ethics textbook," Anayāun said with more aggravation than Mawu's comment warranted. "This is a first contact situation. They are well within their rights to withhold information, just as we do, and we're all aware of this. I didn't even let Mushroom Rock talk to the System of Eren directly." *Maybe I should have,* she thought. But it didn't seem safe, and the System didn't request it either.

"Bythelivingvoice," Mawu jumped up. "The . . . the thing!" They were speechless but projected an image of the outside as seen in Kheinu's perspective.

The edges of the evidence containment were beginning to glow with a malevolent, scouring light. A light that could evaporate all of them in an instant—Kheinu, Mushroom Rock, everyone.

"We have to get out of here," Anayāun yelled at both Mawu and Mushroom Rock. "Move! They're clearing the containment!"

"They have to know we're still inside," Dovber gasped.

Hlaz-mlan was already belting herself into her seat, securing all her legs. "I believe that's the point. Getting rid of all the . . . 'contamination' in one fell swoop."

"Sublight or jump?" Mawu asked.

Anayāun gauged the distance to the perimeter. The lights already turning in their direction. The wards still unlocked. How much time until sudden, painless death? "Jump."

"You can't possibly jump so fast, it's . . ." Hlaz-mlan was saying as the world curled around them.

"Let's hail the Alliance," Hlaz-mlan said.

"*Don't* hail the Alliance!" Dovber said and added something beginning with a guttural sound that sounded like a curse. "They tried to get us all killed! That wasn't a clerical error. You need to trigger the cleansing deliberately, and two evidence officers need to sign off on it!"

Anayāun was still trying to get back to baseline awareness. The sudden jump really messed with her māwal. Was the kid even conscious after that?

"Brtffffffcs," Mawu said. "Another?"

Anayāun dragged her seat back to upright position. "Sitrep?"

"Yes, Operative," Mawu muttered and rubbed at their face. Smearing snot? "The thing has imploded. We are out. Do I move, uh. A jump? To get us further? Where?"

"Where is Mushroom Rock?" She still felt their sentience.

"They jumped. I, ah, grabbed, and they propelled themselves? Themself? Themselves."

"Did you make the jump with them?" That was incredible mass.

"Nono," Mawu shook their head, curls flying in every direction. "They. Jumped themselves. I just helped." They got to their feet, wavering. "I think I need to lie down . . ."

Anayāun quickly unbelted herself and was already halfway to Mawu when they lost their balance and fell. Anayāun caught them with ease despite still feeling woozy. Something was wrong.

It hit her the next moment. "You didn't connect yourself. Physically to the ship."

"There was no time," Mawu said and coughed, a wet cough. "I . . . I can do it without, I can do the jumps, it's just . . . easier." Another cough. They rubbed their hands into their tunic, which absorbed the transparent liquid.

Anayāun blamed her wooziness. She should have remembered sooner. "Your blood, it's transparent. You're bleeding."

She eased them back into the chair, tilted it back.

"I'll . . . be all right, I just . . . my self-repair needs a bit of time."

"And rest." She put her hands on their shoulders. "Listen. Just how much did you help Mushroom Rock?"

"It's . . . it's okay," they grimaced. "It was fine. We're out."

Anayāun shook her head. "I'd prefer to see you alive at the end of each jump."

Dovber stepped to the two of them. "Ssh. If they hadn't done the jump, you wouldn't see *anyone* alive."

Mawu flashed a pained grin. "I once took down a . . . an orbital bombardment platform."

Anayāun chuckled despite herself. "For your sake, I hope that was *before* you made a run for Alliance space, not after."

Kheinu moved forward on sublight under their own power. They were in a quadrant just as remote as the one with the evidence containment and entirely deserted.

"The Alliance doesn't even seem to care enough to check whether we made it out," Mawu said, feeling better and cheerful to an unseemly extent. "But that works in our favor."

Anayāun was still uncomfortable. Mawu didn't lie . . . did they? But what had been the extent of the help they had offered to Mushroom Rock? Ereni had a custom against lying but not against equivocation or misdirection. Anayāun herself observed the custom, and after a lifetime of practice, it came easy to her even in a Counterintelligence position with the Alliance. She was very, very good at misdirection.

But Mawu wasn't even a citizen yet. Were they lying? Exaggerating? Misdirecting? Anayāun didn't want to pry, but she needed to know what to expect from Mawu—especially given that they were now stuck with each other with little communication to the outside world.

The System of Eren had advised the operatives to proceed without contact and claimed they would advocate for them with the Alliance. Knowing the System and the Alliance, this advocacy might take extremely convoluted forms—but Anayāun knew better than to intervene.

They could all go ahead while waiting it out. While waiting to see if they even had a place to return to.

The more Anayāun withdrew into her mind, the more she brushed up against Mushroom Rock.

It wasn't a comforting sensation.

Anayāun locked her sleeping enclosure and tilted back and forth on her bed, which could not decide whether to change back into an easy chair. It finally gave up and produced a cocoonlike shape around her body, open only a crack. Anayāun sighed but did not issue an override.

She focused her attention inward. Some part of her wanted this desperately—there was a solace in the closeness to Mushroom Rock—but she also immediately drew away. Where did her loyalties lie? With Eren certainly. But she spent so much time away from Eren that it was hard to relax into a similar feeling of being *welcome*. And now, she wasn't even supposed to reach out to the System anymore.

She couldn't put it off any further. She reached out to Mushroom Rock.

I have a question, she began, not sure what would be appropriate. *May I?*

Mushroom Rock felt faintly amused by her formality.

She wished the cocoon would close around her entirely, but she was afraid she wouldn't be able to breathe.

Just how much assistance did Mawu give you?

We jumped ourselves. They just helped, Mushroom Rock responded. Anayāun relaxed a fraction, but then she realized that the foreign sentience had simply repeated Mawu's words. And was still withholding information from her.

Instead of figuring out how much she should trust Mawu, she had to figure out how much she should trust Mawu . . . and Mushroom Rock.

She had a very unwelcome thought that Mushroom Rock was covering for Mawu, knowing that she would disapprove of both their actions. But Mushroom Rock and Mawu weren't even able to talk directly, or were they?

Anayāun strode out into the main area. "We need to prepare. I talked to Mushroom Rock about our route. They would prefer us to continue flying at sublight to the jump point in this quadrant and then jump to Point Purple Blue. It's one of the outlying nodes in the jump point network. Then proceed again at sublight from there. They will show us the way."

Mawu scratched their head. "Um, I can jump us directly anywhere if I have an idea of the destination. We don't need to follow the network. I mean, that's why you brought me?"

Anayāun realized Mushroom Rock didn't particularly trust Mawu either. They were all dancing around each other instead of working together. At least she could still trust Dovber and Hlaz-mlan—or could she? They had all been exposed to the spores. This didn't bode well for the mission. If it could still be called a mission.

"We will follow the instructions for now," Anayāun said firmly.

Mawu nodded and took a sharp, hissing breath. "The Jumpship Pilots Union will sue the . . . the everliving daylights out of Counterintelligence if we ever get back."

Mawu connected themself to Kheinu without any comment but hesitated. "Operative? If I may?"

Anayāun nodded.

"It will be easier for all of us if I help Mushroom Rock jump again . . . ? It will be all right. I'm prepared."

Now that they were all proceeding at a more measured pace, Anayāun had a moment to think it all through.

She realized that, if Mushroom Rock could jump directly anywhere under their own power, the spores could spread all across Alliance space in a matter of hours. Certainly, the more central locations were well-warded against intruders jumping in, and even some of the peripheral ones—Eren had the Barrier, a māwal structure guarding against this—but there were many smaller, outlying settlements, planets that were just in the process of joining the Alliance and, in general, a wide variety of potential security breaches.

Who knew how many beings like Mushroom Rock there were in the location they were approaching? And Anayāun knew all too well that the Ereni Barrier wasn't impenetrable either. She would never disclose this to the Alliance, but she herself had once witnessed a breach.

A terrifying vista opened before her: the map of Alliance space overtaken by contamination, giant chunks breaking off and losing contact with the network. Nothing was safe. Was this how the Old Empire had vanished?

She took a deep breath. "Hold off for now." She addressed both Mawu and Mushroom Rock, simultaneously talking inward and outward, her mind looping around to accommodate. "I need to know something. I understand we are all entitled to our secrets. This is a first contact situation. But this is mission-critical information." She paused. "Exactly how much did Mawu help

Mushroom Rock to get us all out of the containment? Can Mushroom Rock jump to any desired location under their own power?"

"Probably yes," Mawu said.

"We can't," Mushroom Rock said at the same time.

Anayāun was perplexed. "Which is it?"

Dovber sighed and messaged her privately. *I think the kid just has trouble estimating their own power. I wouldn't read too much into it.*

Her entire job was dependent on her reading too much into everything. Her jaw clenched from the tension.

Mawu looked apologetic. "I thought I didn't help them that much . . . ? I'm sorry . . ."

"Don't apologize. You saved our hides," Dovber said.

"I would like to remind you that I don't have a hide," Hlaz-mlan added mildly, but the tension lifted somewhat.

If Anayāun had to choose, it was better to have someone on her team who had trouble estimating their capabilities but was telling her the truth than the reverse. Especially since there was still a long way ahead . . .

"All right, go ahead with the jump," she said to Mawu. "Help them as much as they need."

She leaned back in her chair but expanded her awareness through the māwal. This time around, she would pay much closer attention to what was happening.

She knew that next time, her knowledge might save them all.

CHAPTER FOUR: SPHERES WITHIN SPHERES

THE SPHERE OF THE JUMP POINT SLOWLY FILLED THE FRONT DISPLAY, ITS smoothly interlocking segments rotating in the ship's direction. Mawu asked Kheinu to stop at a safe distance, and the sentient spaceship came to a gentle halt. Space was quiet all around, and Mawu felt the power that steadily radiated from the jump point and warmed Kheinu's hard, puckered skin. The ship was like a globe, floating across from another, larger globe—the similarity oddly striking despite the difference in texture. And behind the ship, a big lump waited obediently: Mushroom Rock, the foreign sentience. A whole set of spheres, like ornaments, hanging in space. Mawu refocused on their own body in the pilot's berth and quickly stretched. Their limbs felt crampy and stiff.

But Mawu's attention was drawn back to the external because Mushroom Rock started moving and almost crashed into Kheinu from behind. The pilot was frustrated. *This would all be much easier if Mushroom Rock was linked to me like Kheinu,* they thought.

"Why are we stopping?" Dovber asked, still twiddling the ends of his beard. Mawu was wondering if only his shapeshifting capabilities kept him from destroying it altogether; he'd been twisting hairs around his fingers for hours, ever since the team escaped from the evidence containment closing upon them like a deathtrap.

An Alliance vessel is coming through in the other direction, Mawu responded through the ship, Kheinu's mind a scaffolding for their own, keeping their words smooth and their sentences steady.

"This is an out-of-the-way jump point. I didn't expect traffic," Operative

Anayāun said and leaned as much forward as her safety harness let her, her black Ereni Security uniform crinkling against the straps. Sweat trickled down her face. She took off her cap and rubbed her bare skull and then stared at her fingers with the same scrutiny that she had focused on the jump point. "Should we be worried?" she asked.

"Always," Hlaz-mlan buzzed mildly. All three of the Counterintelligence operatives were unsettled—Mawu could tell through Kheinu, sensing their surface biosignals—but the insectoid Hlaz-mlan appeared to be the calmest. Dovber's heart was racing, and his face was blotchy red. Anayāun's usually warm brown skin had a grayish cast, though her systems controlled her bodily reactions tightly. Hlaz-mlan's legs twitched, but that was all; she didn't even wave her antennae.

The Alliance ship popped into existence. It was a non-sentient tug, barely one step above scrap metal. It quickly moved away from the jump point, dragging something large, spherical, and sparkly green behind it. It ignored them altogether.

"I *don't* want to know what that is," Dovber said.

Kheinu remarked to Mawu through their symbiotic connection that it wasn't like Dovber to be incurious. The ship seemed not only concerned but outright worried.

He must be very shaken, Mawu responded. *I am very shaken! Is that fair? I think that's only fair. We almost died.* Then they raised their voice and spoke over the ship's public channel.

This jump will take us to Point Purple Blue, and from there, we continue at sublight. It will be a long way to Mushroom Rock's home. A pause. They had to ask. *Are you sure you don't want me to jump there directly?*

"Mushroom Rock doesn't allow it," Anayāun said.

Mawu could sense the connection the two newly shared but didn't force their own mind into it. Their own and Kheinu's—it would be too dangerous. If anything went wrong, Counterintelligence wouldn't have a pilot to get the operatives home.

Except things were already going wrong, and there was no way home. The Alliance had assumed they were all contaminated by Mushroom Rock's spores, and this was probably true.

The question remained whether Mushroom Rock was *dangerous.* The intruder from beyond Alliance space had eaten Hlaz-mlan's multi-story family home without so much as an apology, following the operatives to their well-deserved R&R. Yet Hlaz-mlan was oddly relaxed. *What does she know that I don't?* Mawu wondered but decided it was better to focus on the jump.

There was little to do this time. The entire purpose of jump points was to allow passage without a jump pilot personally transporting the ship. Mawu and Kheinu reached out to get permission and sent the public endpoint request, the universe unsteadied, and—

There was no jump point on the other side, just the silky darkness of space.

No planets, no stars, no stations anywhere nearby. No spacefaring vessels. Just Kheinu and Mushroom Rock.

"This is not the right location," Anayāun said with a vibration in her voice— Mushroom Rock speaking through her?

Mawu was ready to scream. *I followed the procedures,* they said as calmly as they could. All the operatives started shouting at the same time, the barely restrained tension finally breaking out like a river, pushing past the floodgates. Mawu's spine arced back in the pilot's berth at the outburst, and the connection tentacles of the ship strained. Mawu worked through the steps of a relaxation exercise, apologizing to Kheinu, and refocused on the ship's main chamber.

"I knew it. I knew it!" Dovber paced. "One in a million chance for a jump point to malfunction, and here we go!"

I can still jump us directly to the target location, Mawu said. It didn't help. Mawu tried to detach from the sensory input from the inside of the ship as much as possible, let the operatives yell at each other while they sorted out the situation.

It took a while. Mawu cautiously ventured to pay attention again.

Hlaz-mlan was speaking, slower, as if trying to talk the others down from doing anything rash. "We just tried to move a giant chunk of . . . alien material through the jump point—no offense, Mushroom Rock. Maybe it's just not possible. The Alliance team didn't get Mushroom Rock to the evidence enclosure through a point either. It was a direct jump."

"Mushroom Rock says they got to Alliance space as a spore," Anayāun said. "Then they incorporated more material. There might be a mass limitation."

Mawu considered if there was a complexity limitation instead. But sentient ships of Kheinu's kind were connected to each other in a vast groupmind— the net of pearls—and they could use jump points without any trouble. Mawu wished they could call upon the pearls in this situation, but they had

had to disassociate from the net; that was one of the preconditions Alliance Counterintelligence made upon hiring the ship to transport the operatives.

It should have been a warning sign.

Then again, how many people in Alliance space had ever been in a first contact situation? Besides the specialized first contact teams? Probably very few.

Mawu was more and more certain that they should take up linguistics after surviving this mission.

Mawu disconnected from the ship, braiding their own connection tentacles against the small of their back. The operatives wanted to see Mawu face to face. More yelling? Mawu waited in the connection berth for a moment before opening the enclosure. Their curls were plastered to their face, and they tried to brush their hair away, rubbing their cheeks. It was always difficult to disconnect from Kheinu, even though the two of them remained in mental contact, but it was a more nebulous connection without the strength of the physical merging backing it.

And the net of pearls was no longer accessible to Kheinu. The System of Eren was also unavailable; Anayāun had disallowed reaching out in that direction for security reasons. Mawu adjusted their loose pilot's clothing and staggered outside, still dizzy from the disconnection.

"If we ask Mawu to get us back to the original jump point, then we don't know if we'll be able to use the point again either," Dovber said mildly. "What if the same thing happens? We should ask them to get us to Point Purple Blue instead and proceed from there at sublight."

"But why are we here?" Hlaz-mlan asked. "Out of all possible locations? Maybe there's something we need to find . . ."

"There's nothing here," Anayāun said with finality.

Mawu felt resigned. The operatives couldn't even decide whether to jump away from this place. Was there anything out there? Vast lifeforms were hiding in the cold darkness of interstellar space, but one didn't just chance upon them. Those creatures either needed to be laboriously located, or they came right away to eat you.

Eventually, the consensus tilted in favor of asking Mawu to jump to Point Purple Blue. Mawu thought this option wasn't much better or worse than any others, but at least, it would let them jump under their own power, their own control. Mawu had wanted to do this in the first place, and Kheinu had agreed. Both of them were confident they could get it right, and that way, no mysterious force could push them away from their destination. Mawu could almost believe the fringe theory that the jump points were sentient; their sentience was just too complex to be detectable. But that was an untestable statement and thus for the most part useless.

Mawu went back to their berth to reconnect to the ship, coughing softly. They felt like their self-repair hadn't run its course yet after the last-moment escape from the evidence containment. Mawu and Kheinu both agreed that one more jump should be doable, and from there on, it would all be a lengthy sub-lightspeed slog. Easy and boring.

Mawu hadn't been to this particular jump point before, but Kheinu had, back in the days of their first pilot. Mawu assimilated Kheinu's memories to aid with the jump. Purple Blue was an out-of-the-way jump point with little to recommend it. In safe distance, what looked like the material residue of an exploded planet circled the sun, smeared out over its orbit; maybe it would coalesce again into a planet over astronomical timescales. They both thought it had to have been an inhabited planet once and that that's why the Empire had set up a jump point nearby. But the Empire was long gone, and in its place, only myriads of riddles remained.

Kheinu's previous visit had been as a warship, but the area was now supposed to be silent, incorporated into Alliance space after a protracted territorial dispute. Mawu wished either of them had a talent for precognition, an ability to read the trendlines. Some people could do it, but Mawu felt at every try that the future was too malleable, that the act of observation itself changed it. Maybe Mawu didn't have a light enough touch.

Both of them steered their thoughts away from the future. They merged with each other a bit closer and initiated the jump process. Now that they weren't escaping from certain death, they could afford to go slower, but the ramp-up was always fast by necessity. Around them, power cascaded upward and outward until the moment of transposition, instantaneous yet producing a gap, a discontinuity in awareness—

Anayāun cursed loudly in Eren-sā. Mawu struggled to reorient. The area looked just like it had in Kheinu's memories, but a ship was approaching from the direction of the debris. It was unmarked but clearly armed—a non-organic and human-staffed war dart of a ship. Armed and shooting at them? Indeed. Mawu's immediate instinct was to jump away, but they couldn't get a handle on Mushroom Rock, who was already attempting some kind of breakaway maneuver. Even if they could do one jump so rapidly after another—and in their current state—the foreign sentience was still actively trying to get away from them, and to compensate for that would be much harder.

I can't do it, I can't do it safely, I can't jump away, Mawu sent over comms, their thoughts warbling with desperation. *Can Mushroom Rock stop moving and—*

"Target the spikes!" Anayāun yelled back. "I'll help!"

Mawu reached out to the incoming projectiles. Mass driver spikes with no load. At these speeds, one didn't need a warhead since the impact itself would be bad enough. Mawu bent the space, pushing more māwal into the action than necessary, and the spikes slid away on a hyperbolic arc with little time to spare. Mawu winced.

What is Mushroom Rock doing?! The frothing lump curved back, its trajectory projected to intersect with the attacking ship if both kept on course.

"Prepare! If they have mass drivers, they might also have—" Anayāun didn't manage to finish the sentence because something spherical appeared right next to her, floating: "*That.*"

Mawu's innards squished together as they teleported out this new weapon that had just been teleported in, their power snapping in a reflex motion just like a throw with pure muscle, brute force. Anayāun's mind gently steadied their aim as they hurled the bomb out—away from the ship and from Mushroom Rock. They could feel the heat of the explosion on Kheinu's skin. Doable at a safe distance outside, but it would have been catastrophic inside.

I can't keep this up. Mawu could barely get the words out. *Can someone ward us from those, can Mushroom Rock do a THING, SOMETHING, ANYTHING, instead of MAKING NO SENSE—*

Mawu hadn't meant to shout. But thinking was hard enough—keeping it straight who got which thoughts, impossible. Mawu was making a last-ditch attempt to fend off the second wave of incoming spikes, and they could already feel the energy prodding at them as someone on the attacking ship was trying to teleport another weapon inside Kheinu; it was as if someone was repeatedly kicking Mawu in the stomach, and they doubled over in the connection berth—

Before their awareness blinked out, the last impression they got from Kheinu was of Mushroom Rock, soaring toward the attacking ship and changing shape, hollowing out in the middle like a giant maw.

Mawu was coming to in someone's arms. Anayāun? Mawu's eyes wouldn't focus, but they tried to reach out with their mind. They had to know. Did Mushroom Rock counterattack, or had that been a fever dream, a hallucination brought on by—

"Ssh, ssh, just rest. We're safe for now." Anayāun was fiddling with something around their back. Mawu tried to turn around but failed, muscles spasming. They retched and passed out again.

Mawu was coming to inside Kheinu's mind. They realized Anayāun had to have been trying to reconnect the tentacles. Mawu could rest here, safely enveloped. Their body was a small, painful knot inside Kheinu's vast bulk. They relaxed into that bulk and impossibly, implausibly, slept.

Mawu awoke. Kheinu was moving steadily away from the jump point. Their attacker was gone, and Mawu could not sense them anywhere in the nearby space.

Mushroom Rock trailed Kheinu. Something didn't quite fit. Was the giant spherical lump bigger all of a sudden?

"Is the young one awake?" Hlaz-mlan said, somewhere down and inside. Anayāun must have said, "Yes," but Mawu still couldn't quite understand. They tried to turn their attention back inward. Hlaz-mlan continued: "Take your time. We're safe for now."

Did . . . did Mushroom Rock eat the enemy ship? Mawu didn't mean to say it out loud, but their thoughts were like little frogs, jumping all over.

"Yes," Dovber said, his muscles tense with . . . resentment? Frustration? "Wasn't it you who asked them?"

It took an effort to remember. *No, I just told them to do something, anything.*

"Well, this was what they chose to do."

Definitely resentment, Mawu decided.

Anayāun sighed. "You can't blame anyone for defending their life against deadly force."

Mawu thought that Mushroom Rock was defending *other* lives. Mushroom Rock had already been doing an evasive maneuver and potentially could have gotten away. This thought remained unspoken as the boundaries of Mawu's mind reasserted themselves. *Who were the attackers?* Mawu asked out loud.

"Scavengers, fortune hunters," Anayāun said. "Here to find something amidst the ruins of empire."

Armed so well? Both Mawu and Kheinu were suspicious of that.

"Some of the scavengers are ex-military. And there's a cutthroat world out there." Anayāun got up to pace. "We'll soon know more, but Mushroom Rock is still in the process of"—Mawu caught the moment of hesitation—"incorporating them. Eating is a lengthy process across species, it seems. In the meanwhile, we are headed in the direction of"—she stopped moving as if listening—"Mushroom Rock's family."

"No, we're not," Hlaz-mlan said into the silence that had suddenly ballooned inside the ship. "We need to reassess."

Dovber let go of his beard. "What do you mean?"

"The three of us, we are with Alliance Counterintelligence," Hlaz-mlan waved her antennae in the direction of Dovber and Anayāun, shifting in her seat to clack her artificial legs loudly together. "We signed up for danger. We signed up to fight if the need arose . . . the kid didn't."

The two other operatives opened their mouths simultaneously, but Hlaz-mlan didn't leave a moment for them to speak. "The kid was hired to get us from place to place fast, and that's it." She made a very loud chittering sound that Mawu hadn't heard before. "No one expected us to get into space battles! It was supposed to be investigation, bureaucracy, an arrest together with local police . . . with the ship safely in orbit!"

"So what do you propose?" Dovber was close to yelling again. "Do you want us to contact the Alliance and surrender?"

"They'll quarantine us, but we'll stay alive," Hlaz-mlan said. "It's unfair to ask either the kid or the ship to take us into *this*."

"The Alliance won't quarantine us." Anayāun's voice was hoarse. "The attackers were fortune hunters indeed. But Mushroom Rock now knows that they got an anonymous tipoff."

"Well, that junkheap of a tug saw our endpoint request before the jump point malfunctioned, but surely the Alliance wouldn't send *fortune hunters* after us?" Dovber's voice edged up.

Hlaz-mlan buzzed at him. "I understand. We cannot go back. I still think this is wrong. The kid—"

Mawu lost their temper. *I am not a kid! I'm an adult, even if I'm young. And you know what, I don't want to fight, I-I ran away from my home planet because I didn't want to fight, but you know what, I don't have a solution either! I don't want to be killed! I am not one of you operatives, and I would not sign up in-in a million years, but can we worry about that after we stop RUNNING for our LIVES?!*

"Mushroom Rock will fight for you," Anayāun said slowly.

Mawu had a sudden desire to disconnect from the ship and stride into the main area to yell at the operatives with their own voice. Still, they did not hold back. *Mushroom Rock has already fought for me! Killed for me! You think I don't realize?!*

"Incorporation is not the same as death."

Tell that to the fortune hunters!

Anayāun sat back in her chair, coming full circle. "I just might."

The four of them landed smoothly on Mushroom Rock's surface. Mawu pushed down the craving to lie down on the ground and be incorporated. They wavered on their feet, the soles of their spacesuit digging into soft chunks of grayish material shot through with glimmering, colorful veins. They took a steadying breath and refocused their thoughts on Kheinu. Mawu had already been incorporated into Kheinu and did not need to merge with anyone else.

"Mushroom Rock wishes you hadn't come this close," Anayāun said. "It's dangerous for you."

Mawu gritted their teeth. Their connection tentacles twitched. "I know. It makes me desire to be eaten, even when that makes no sense? But I want to see this for myself."

"We all do," Hlaz-mlan buzzed.

A vaguely humanlike shape began to emerge from the surface, arising as if from deep underground.

Hlaz-mlan tottered forward, and Mawu wondered if something in her suit didn't quite agree with her legs in the low gravity. "Wait," she said, "could you also do this with my *house*?"

"It's not funny," Hlaz-mlan glared at the giggling operatives. Mawu wanted to rub their eyes but couldn't figure out how to do it in the suit, even though there must have been a way.

"But your voice!" Anayãun chuckled. "Such desire! *'My house'* . . . would you really want your house to be made of *this*?" She kicked at the ground, her foot bouncing off from the suddenly even springier surface.

"My dear fellow operative, it's not only the *young pilot* who can desire something," Hlaz-mlan said, taking a step back. Mawu grimaced, but at least, she didn't call them a *kid* again.

The figure arose, but it didn't become more humanlike nor seem more aware of the environment.

"It's too early," Anayãun said. "All that information still needs to be processed."

"You mean digested," Dovber groaned.

Anayãun shrugged forcefully. "Mushroom Rock didn't eat me altogether. We just linked. I'm not sure how this goes." They all waited in uncomfortable silence after that as the figure gained more detail.

Mawu set the legs of their suit to rigid because they were struggling with the need to crouch down while waiting, to sit even, to sink into—

Hnf, the humanoid shape said in their minds.

A thought projection in the absence of an atmosphere to speak in, Mawu thought. It wasn't a very coherent projection, not yet.

"I must say, it works faster on my home planet," Dovber remarked with a casualness that Mawu couldn't decide was forced or spontaneous. "The mechanism might be different. I didn't consider that."

Mawu couldn't follow. "Your home planet?" they asked with effort. "Where you were . . . ?"

Dovber blinked and smoothed a hand down the front of his suit, his beard out of reach. "No, I didn't go through the transformation on my home planet. It was after I'd joined Counterintelligence. There are these barrels left over from the time of the Old Empire," he gestured to indicate the considerable size. "They put you in the barrel, and you end up like me. Alas, it's single-use. Or half the population of Alliance space would be shapeshifters by now."

"So how does it work on your home planet?"

"The planet eats you, and you reemerge. You become part of the planet, but you do retain your cognitive autonomy. But it's done only with a handful of people, so they can mediate between the rest of the inhabitants and the planetmind. Halachically, it gets very complicated, very fast." He tilted his head sideways. "In religious law, I mean."

Mawu was trying to understand. "And you say that transformation, which some people do on your planet, is the same kind as your transformation in the Alliance? But this one is different?"

Dovber turned again to look at the shape. "Yes . . . so instead of one mechanism we don't understand, now we have two." He cleared his throat. "What joy."

Was that sarcasm? But Mawu suddenly had a much more important thought.

"Wait, Operative, um, Dovber?" Mawu flailed their hands in excitement. "This does tell us something! That we, we don't necessarily have a link between the Old Empire and Mushroom Rock!"

"And how is that helpful?" Hlaz-mlan asked.

"We can't use our preexistent strategies," Dovber said. "For instance, we do know that Imperial-style shapeshifting has a countermeasure, a certain device, and this new type of shapeshifting might not have such a countermeasure. We might not have a way to disable it."

Anayāun stepped to him. "Did you just threaten Mushroom Rock?"

Dovber chuckled. "I'm only speculating, *Operative*."

Mawu thought that maybe the operatives weren't on such good terms with each other as it'd seemed at the outset. Or was this situation bringing out the worst in everyone?

Pffflup, the humanoid shape said and puffed out a tiny cloud of spores.

The shape started waving its upper appendages, scything through the vacuum of space, joints bending both ways. Small chunks of grayish material detached and floated back to the sphere, reabsorbing. The shape projected a variety of mental impressions, none quite clear but all carrying a sense of distress.

Dovber took a step back to avoid being hit. "Definitely not the same process as on my home planet . . . or my own transformation. And I thought that was rough."

Mawu really wanted to be somewhere else. The shape was clearly in pain, tremors running up and down the structure roughly corresponding to the spine, the raw matter spasming.

Anayāun crossed her arms. On the defensive? "Remember, their whole ship was consumed very abruptly."

"This is not very appealing," Hlaz-mlan said. "For future reference."

The shape heaved as it turned inside out, gaining definition as if a human body was dragging itself out from treacle, straining against resistance. Glimmers of multicolored light threaded increasingly through the gray mass.

Fuck me sideways, the shape said, toppling forward and onto all fours, weaving for a moment and then crashing to the ground. Spores billowed up like golden dust.

Hlaz-mlan moved closer. "Are you alright?"

Mawu stepped to her. "Um? Senior Operative? I, I don't think they can hear you. They don't have suit comms. You have to project your thoughts . . . like . . . I can help?" They made Hlaz-mlan's thoughts carry.

The shape groaned back in response. *No, I'm not alright. I'm not alright at all. What is this fucking faerie wonderland?*

Mawu did not miss that Dovber reached for some kind of weapon. Couldn't he make projectiles out of himself? He probably wanted to spare the material.

"They're referring to the interior landscape of Mushroom Rock," Anayāun said.

I'm a proper man, a man of Earth, the man said and was abruptly reabsorbed into Mushroom Rock, the ground smoothing down with a gentle wave.

Just as Mawu was stepping closer to investigate, the man emerged again, struggling to stand. His shape rippled as he surveyed the small crowd, as if his attention being directed outward used up all his mental resources to maintain consistency. The folds on his body imitating clothing also shifted.

He made a face—halfway between a grimace and a grin, Mawu decided. *I didn't consent to being eaten alive,* he said.

"We didn't consent to being shot at," Anayãun snapped back at him with so much force in her thoughts that Mawu shivered.

The man spread his arms. *Fair enough.* Mawu wasn't sure if he was mocking them.

Dovber moved closer. "Where is your companion? You weren't the person teleporting the weapons into our ship."

She's somewhere in there. She doesn't want to talk to me anymore, he said and frowned. *I am the captain of this ship!*

He made an angry wave with his right arm, but it detached at the shoulder, slowly floating toward the ground. He stared and reached out to retrieve it, though it had already lost its shape. The scintillating grayish blob tied itself around his fingertips. He swore, waved around the blob, and then smeared it into his thigh and pulled at his right side. Another right arm emerged.

"Can Mushroom Rock release the captain?" Hlaz-mlan asked. Still wondering about her house maybe?

Anayãun shook her head. "No, incorporation is a one-way process." She looked away into the distance. "For what it's worth, the other person is having fun."

"These types of transformation do not seem to be reversible in general," Dovber said. "I will never not be a shapeshifter. You can block my changes using countermeasures, but that won't change my internal makeup."

"This is ethically difficult," Hlaz-mlan said, her voice deepening. "You are autonomous and not tied to a planet. The captain, on the other hand . . ."

Will any of you pay attention to me?! The ex-captain yelled in their minds.

Mawu zoned out during the ever-lengthening back-and-forth, but when they reminded themselves to pay attention, they could immediately understand that the conversation was definitely not going well.

"This has gone on long enough. I will make a promise to you," Anayãun said.

The Earth human cocked up his chin. *Go ahead. I'm listening.*

"I know you got the message anonymously. But if you're inclined to make a guess about the sender, I will be inclined to help you break free. I don't know how to do it. But I promise you I'll do my best to find it out."

Why would I need to tell you? You can just make the alien *tear it out of my mind,* the ex-captain said.

"I would rather maintain your cooperation," Anayāun told him. Mawu noted that Anayāun simply assumed cooperation, and by saying so, brought it into being. The ex-captain snarled but didn't protest.

We work with the Alliance sometimes. On the edges, you know? They scratch my back, and I scratch theirs. You know the deal. They want to keep the peace. And Minather is good at keeping the peace. He used male forms.

"Minather. Is that your name?" Hlaz-mlan asked.

The ex-captain spat. *I would never tell you my name.* His spit circled back to reattach to his face, the errant material as much a part of Mushroom Rock as anything else. He made an angry gesture to ward it off but was unsuccessful. *I'm done talking to you,* he said, and his body sunk back into the surface.

Anayāun resumed her pacing immediately once inside the ship. Mawu went back to their berth to connect to Kheinu—all the pacing making them feel queasy. It was as if Anayāun kept on circling around in their innards. Mawu tried to adjust their own biosystems to downregulate sensory sensitivities, but everything seemed off-kilter; once they adjusted for one problem, another one sprung up. They really needed to rest more.

Everyone was running ragged. Dovber changed to Dvora, saying that it felt more restful. Hlaz-mlan clicked her artificial legs against each other so much, Mawu wondered if they would wear away. And Anayāun was pacing, her gait tight as if she was in pain. An issue from merging with Mushroom Rock? Probably, Mawu concluded.

"The Alliance works with smugglers, fortune-hunters, small-time criminals all the time. They can be a great asset in the outer regions," Hlaz-mlan said between two clacks. "Especially from a counterintelligence perspective."

"I know! But I've never heard of this Minather, and our knowledge base for this region has nothing about this topic." Anayāun stomped around.

"Dispatch would surely be able to inform you in a different situation." Hlaz-mlan added. "If we were still on . . . speaking terms."

"I always make sure to update our knowledge base before leaving on a mission," Anayāun said.

"Maybe they just haven't told us," Dvora chimed in.

"What, because I'm Ereni and this guy is from Earth?"

"Eren does have a turbulent history with Earth. You must admit," Dvora said.

Anayāun raised her voice. "That's because they declared war on us!"

"Listening to you, one would think the war was still ongoing," Hlaz-mlan added mildly. "It lasted less than a day."

"Yes, but—"

Mawu tried to ignore their arguing and scout ahead instead, see what lay ahead of them out in space. There was a structure in the far distance, but it had a jagged, technological nature to it, entirely different from Mushroom Rock. It didn't broadcast any signals. Deserted or just running dark? Mawu wondered whether they should try to look closer, seek out any sentients inside. They reached out and sensed some kind of ward—flimsy or just graceful? The only way to tell would be to push against it. But if there was a ward, and such a subtle-looking one, there must be at least someone on board to maintain it. Just a quick touch—

No! Mushroom Rock spoke to them directly. *Stop that!* Mawu curled up in their connection berth, withdrawing from the awareness of the space surrounding Kheinu.

"What happened?" Anayāun was pounding on a wall. "Mawu, what happened?! Why is Mushroom Rock angry?"

If they don't tell you, why would they tell me? Mawu responded, more bitterly than they'd intended.

But Mushroom Rock spoke, through Anayāun but in all their minds simultaneously, with overbearing force.

I have come to seek your help against the inflammation, the conflict. But if you incite it further, you will not understand. I cannot explain—I could not bring so many memories across the size barrier. I only know that you must see.

"You're not in communication with your family?" Dvora asked.

I must rejoin. They will decide.

"Decide what?" Anayāun yelled.

Merge, ignore, destroy, cooperate, the words resonated like loud strikes against a bell.

Anayāun waved her arms in the air. "With who? Us? The Alliance? The fortune hunters?"

I come home carrying this distinction, Mushroom Rock said and fell silent.

Mawu showed the operatives the jagged structure in the distance, but this only produced more strife.

"Are we supposed to infiltrate this place? Is that what Mushroom Rock is saying?" Dvora was growing redder and redder by the minute.

Anayāun shrugged. "I am afraid that's why they've brought us here. This is some kind of smuggling outpost, and it seems to be directly between us and Mushroom Rock's family. We could go around it, but we need to know why this outpost isn't on our maps, why this Minather is unknown to us . . . I think this is the source of the 'inflammation.' It's some kind of clash with intruders. This is why Mushroom Rock was sent into Alliance space to begin with. We can't quite understand their conflict unless we take a look at the people provoking them. At least a brief look."

"We're Counterintelligence, not Intelligence," Dvora pointed out.

All the aggravation was rubbing off on Mawu too. They snapped. *I'm from the Jump Pilots Union!*

Mawu lost track of who was saying what in all the yelling. They took a deep breath and another. It was hard to work with these people.

". . . we want to dock with it, we need a ship! A plausible smuggling ship!"

". . . enough material! Mushroom Rock swallowed a ship, and we can disguise . . ."

". . . a ship and a captain, if only he would cooperate. They must know him . . ."

". . . well, YOU are a shapeshifter!!"

". . . if they've already detected our approach, then it's all—"

This at least they could answer.

I'm sure they haven't detected us yet, Mawu said through the ship's comms. *I drew back from the ward. We have huge sensory range: Kheinu is very skilled, and I have a lot of power to back them. I can hide us to an extent. But if we move very close, they will see us?*

Dvora stood. "This means we still have enough time to disguise ourselves. Mushroom Rock could cover Kheinu and produce the shape of the ship they swallowed. The dimensions should be right even if the details are very different. The densities wouldn't match, but I don't think they would be on the lookout for that. They are smugglers, not border guards. The same for a distribution of cavities and the like. They might notice if they specifically looked. I don't think they'd specifically look."

So they'd be smuggling themselves into a smuggling lair? Mawu was increasingly confused.

Hlaz-mlan protested. "Kheinu and Mawu can stay here, outside the station's sensory range. And the rest of us can board in a new ship entirely made of Mushroom Rock."

Mawu shook their head but realized the people would not see that from the main area. They drew on Kheinu's help to speak more effectively, to smooth down the jagged sentences. *You need me close by in case of any emergency, to get people out. You remember what happened early on in your mission. Even if I don't board the station, it's better if I am at the very least in the docks with Kheinu.*

Hlaz-mlan buzzed wordlessly. She looked up at the ceiling and addressed Mawu. "Then I can stay on board Kheinu with you. We don't have a good excuse why someone of my species should be with the captain anyway."

This plan was finally agreeable to all.

Mawu disconnected and wandered out to talk to the operatives. Dvora had assumed the shape of the smuggler captain. Her voice was low to match the captain's, scratchy and coarse. But Dvora didn't seem satisfied.

"I can imitate his body and his voice but not quite his verbiage," she said. "I know this type of Earth extremist, but I've never had to infiltrate their groups." She added something in a language Mawu didn't understand.

Mawu tilted their head. "I think you look very . . . captain-y."

"It will have to do." She shivered. "I don't feel very masculine today. But I've done this a lot. I just need to get in the right mindset. The rugged individualist out here on the frontier . . . every man for himself . . ."

Mawu didn't quite understand it. The operatives were also out here but working together as a team. A loud, shrill, constantly disagreeing team but a team nonetheless. For all they were so unbearable sometimes, Mawu liked them. "I should start getting ready with Kheinu and Mushroom Rock? I think you look very convincing," they said.

Dvora smiled at them with the bristly face of the captain. "I'm sure the ship will come out great too. Go, prepare. I'm going to quickly say my afternoon prayers."

Mawu perked up. "Can I listen again, would that be okay? Just for a few minutes?"

"These are mostly quiet. And short," Dvora paused. "You know my religion doesn't proselytize, right?"

Mawu sat down on a storage crate. "I'm okay with my religion, I think. I just find it interesting when other people have theirs. I think it's cool." They shifted in place. "Yours actually doesn't seem all that different from mine. I looked it up. We have the Living Voice, which is the manifestation of the divine in the world. And we have the Powers, which serve the Living Voice. But they mostly just do what the Living Voice wants, a bit like your angels?" They remembered they wanted to ask something. "So do you have, like, mandatory daily prayers?"

Dvora held herself like Dvora in the captain's body, entirely unlike when she was practicing impersonating the captain. "Hmm. Well. We have prayers three times a day, but in . . . my denomination, it is mandatory only for men."

"But you're still doing it?" Mawu stopped themself. "I'm sorry, was that rude?"

She chuckled and her voice shifted back to Dvora's warm alto. "Not at all. I'm a woman *and* a man, so I try to do both sets of observances. Which is sometimes rather difficult."

"What do intersex people do?" Mawu really wanted to know. Maybe they would not survive this day. They felt a need to ask all their pressing questions simultaneously, but they knew there was only time for a handful.

"Mm, I think it varies? It is kind of a mess. I looked it up because of the parallels with my embodiment. Jewish law talks about intersex variations, all the way back . . . I mean in the time of sticks and stones, not spaceships. So that's really quite early. But for almost two thousand years, people mostly just ignored those bits. I mean"—she frowned—"if they weren't intersex themselves, I guess. Now, it's a bit more known. But mostly in less . . . traditional denominations."

This sounded familiar to Mawu. All too familiar. "Have you thought about changing your, er, denomination? I have, you know!"

"And have you?" Dvora laughed, softly but with an edge of bitterness to it. "I haven't either. I'm always considering it though."

"It's not that easy."

"So what was your issue with your denomination, if you don't mind saying?" Dvora tilted her captain's head sideways and Mawu realized they were earnestly curious.

"Oh, it's . . ." Mawu sighed deeply before being able to continue. No one in the Alliance had ever asked them this before, and they felt more shaken by that than they would've expected. "It's mostly politics. My father's a priest. And the priesthood supports the Isolationists, on my planet. I'm like, I'm good with the Living Voice, but I want . . . the more decentralized version, I suppose."

"I hear you," Dvora nodded. "Well, it's time to pray. You can stay as long as you want. The really long ones are the morning prayers, so I'll be done soon."

"I'll just sit and be quiet," Mawu said. "Thank you. And thank you for . . . talking to me. I feel like you understand."

Dvora smiled at them, her eye color shifting from the blue of the captain to her own dark and back. Mawu almost missed it. "That's mutual," she said.

"*It's dangerous,*" Mushroom Rock said through Anayāun. Anayāun herself shook her head: "Dangerous but doable."

Mawu was back inside the connection berth, concentrating on making sure Mushroom Rock fit around Kheinu just right—not covering any openings but still in the shape of the fortune-hunter ship. It wasn't quite working.

This would be really much easier if we could connect somehow, Mawu grumbled to Mushroom Rock. *The operative can mediate . . .*

When no response was forthcoming, Mawu pushed away their apprehension and tried to focus on the technical challenge instead. Kheinu was slowly being surrounded as Mushroom Rock melded around them, the giant mass faintly glimmering with an iridescence. Mawu and Kheinu tried to relax, and Mawu attempted to be as open to impressions as possible without actually merging with Mushroom Rock. Something would need to be done about the new ship's surface to make the color and texture just right.

Mawu could feel Mushroom Rock's mind slowly closing around them. *No, you leave that open, you only need to incorporate us with your physical shape—*

Mushroom Rock stopped. *We're not sure we understand the distinction.*

Mawu was already enveloped in Kheinu, and Kheinu could potentially be enveloped in Mushroom Rock—and the feeling drew all of them closer. Mawu took a sharp breath.

"... and it shouldn't be a major danger. You're not physically linked," Anayāun was saying somewhere, a faint, barely audible voice on the edge of distraction.

I can connect to Kheinu while not physically linked, Mawu said, *and besides—*

Far behind them, the jump point spiked with energy. Mawu startled. Kheinu startled. Something slipped.

Mushroom Rock closed around them in a pure defensive reflex, resonating through all of them as Mawu's awareness expanded through and into Mushroom Rock, the vastly different minds clashing together, a giant mental vista expanding inward and unmatching, unmatching—

Mawu gasped for breath—then again, then again—together with Kheinu, and Anayāun was dragged into the fray and hastily attempted to mediate across the gaps being scrunched together. Mawu had been incorporated into the net of pearls before, and that was vaster, if vastnesses could be compared, like infinities, countable and uncountable.

Mushroom Rock was one entity, if manifold. Not connected to their family yet. This should have been more manageable.

Yet Mushroom Rock was like a planet, having eaten houses of rooms upon rooms, people, the renegade ship, all manner of detail carefully preserved but reassembled in an all-new whole; a whole that was also dynamically changing at any point, pulsating, fluctuating. Unmatching to Mawu's mental shape and scraping, slashing against it like a thousand knives.

Mawu reoriented. Sobbed. Screamed. Reoriented. The world stretched into myriad glittering filaments. Reoriented. The ship. The other ship.

I cannot connect without having merged, they thought at Anayāun, the words not quite reaching. *I haven't merged with them like you.*

Anayāun was so far! Mawu reached, reached, reached.

I have to make it through this alive.

The faces of people left back in Alliance space.

I have to make it back.

They expect us to return.

In the distance, a ship passed through the jump point.

The disguise, Kheinu remembered.

Mawu's thoughts clenched upon Anayāun's thoughts of Mushroom Rock's memories of the ship's surface and molded, molded, time slowing with the effort. The process helped, a distraction, a setting apart. Mawu slowly disentangled their mind from Mushroom Rock as they formed the sharp edges of the warship, adjusted the planes of its surface.

"I'm guessing this wasn't the original plan, but *wow*, that looks great," Dvora said, somewhere in a little air bubble contained in a ship within a ship.

Mushroom Rock wanted to eat the outpost.

Mawu strained to withdraw into Kheinu's mind, their own mind. Some connection had been established after all: the desire to merge with Mushroom Rock had been replaced with Mushroom Rock's desires.

Chiefly, to eat.

The outpost. A hot lunch from the fabricator. The craggy trees surrounding Hlaz-mlan's home. Ïsyasun's latest novel and the prequel novella that just begged to be inhaled. Vegetable balls with blue pasta salad. An introductory linguistics textbook. Kheinu. *Wait, what?!*

Mawu managed to produce some distance, and they could feel Anayāun attempting to rein in the giant mound now in the shape of an unaffiliated, mechanical warship with many angles and protrusions. *We are investigating, not consuming*, Anayāun thought at Mushroom Rock with force.

Mawu steered them all toward the outpost. *Let's dock. Before that other ship reaches us.*

The remaining flight gave them all time to re-sort their minds and reorganize the information flow. Mawu and Kheinu finally disentangled themselves from Mushroom Rock, only maintaining whatever connection was necessary to preserve the disguise. Anayāun kept Mushroom Rock in check and mediated with Mawu and Kheinu. It was easy for Mawu to connect with Anayāun; while

Mawu hadn't gotten Ereni citizenship yet, they already had their systems set up to do it with ease. Thus the confused mental tangle gave way to something more ordered.

Dvora was shaken, even on the outside of the clash, but still inside the ship. She kept on rubbing her face, the captain's bristles. Only Hlaz-mlan was calm, the least māwal-active of them all.

But they were all alive. Alive and unharmed so far.

And Mawu understood, finally, in the stark light that comes from a sense of self-assurance, that they wouldn't need to laboriously search the outpost.

It's not necessarily about physically eating, Mawu realized. *It's about incorporating the information. Mushroom Rock latched onto me reading a book.*

Mushroom Rock doesn't quite distinguish between mind and physicality, but we do. Even if the separation is only on the surface while down below it's all the same substrate of māwal. The separation can be leveraged.

Mawu set about to organize.

Kheinu had the skill and grace borne out of experience, the most experience of them all with the māwal. Kheinu could survey all of the outpost rapidly with clairvoyant clarity once they were inside its wards, if Mawu themself supplied the raw power—and maybe even the brusqueness if there were further wards inside to be crossed.

Anayāun could then transfer the information to Mushroom Rock without creating another hopeless tangle. And Mushroom Rock could be satiated for now and in turn discuss the results with Anayāun. Finally, they would all head out to Mushroom Rock's family, hopefully understanding the conflict better.

If only Dvora could keep up the pretense long enough for Kheinu's survey to run its course.

The docking codes were all good, routed through a complicated pathway from Mushroom Rock to Anayāun to Mawu to Kheinu and Dvora.

Dvora shuddered. "Keep the rest of the information to yourselves. I know enough to bluff my way through."

"If worse comes to worst, I can always create a distraction," Hlaz-mlan said. "You just need to get on board, do a quick handover of . . . whatever it is that you're supposedly delivering here, and then get out because whoever is māwal-active enough on board will certainly notice what we are doing. Your cover won't last long, but we only need a few minutes for the survey. Then we can analyze the results at our leisure and discuss them with Mushroom Rock's family even."

Dvora pulled at her grimy slacks. "These people have enough resources for self-cleaning clothes, but they wear this because of the grittiness of it all. I can't believe it. The sooner we're done here, the better." She dragged out a crate.

"Just one?" Hlaz-mlan asked.

"Yes. Hopefully this one is similar enough. I'd rather not ask Mushroom Rock to recreate the one they ate from their own material."

"I'm having enough trouble keeping them from releasing spores into the station," Anayāun said.

Dvora tilted her head sideways—her own gesture, not one imitating the captain. "Also, the box will be filled with ballast. I'd rather not break about five non-proliferation treaties today."

Hlaz-mlan chirped. "You mean they are smuggling weapons?"

"Of mass destruction, yes." Dvora sighed. "Whatever conflict they have been having with Mushroom Rock's people, it's escalating quite rapidly."

Mawu watched through Dvora's comms as a fellow smuggler came out to greet Dvora, the presumed captain.

"Temel? I haven't seen you in a while. *Damn* you haven't changed at all." The smuggler spat, and the floor obediently swallowed the organic material for reprocessing. *If not self-cleaning clothes, at least they condescended to this much cleanliness,* Mawu thought.

"I have the goods," Dvora said, slapping a hand on the rolling crate. She cleared her throat. "What a fucking shame I can't stay. But I have something else to pick up in the ass-end of the galaxy."

The cussing from Dvora's mouth felt entirely unreal to Mawu. But she was a good actor, a good Counterintelligence officer. She was playing her part as the hidebound fortune hunter.

"Oh, man. Say hello to Eliin from me?"

"Aye, I shall."

Mawu wondered if Dvora was overdoing it a bit—*Aye?*—but the smuggler was entirely taken in by the performance.

Dvora reopened the airlock. The smuggler began thumbing at the crate.

"Now," Hlaz-mlan said.

Mawu reached down and inside, toward the substrate of the universe, the power rising within them. Kheinu shaped it and directed it outward, a wave of māwal sweeping over the station from their point inside the docks. Pure awareness mapping every nook and cranny. Anayāun braced herself, guiding the information transfer to Mushroom Rock.

"What's in this, cucumbers?" the smuggler said.

"Fresh produce is the best disguise," Dvora responded nonchalantly, already cycling through the airlock. The lights overhead flickered, and the smuggler fell silent, probably listening to some station transmission. From the person on warding duty who had just let them through?

"Let's get out while we still can," Dvora wheezed, and Mawu redirected the power into propulsion. Kheinu broke away from the station, unhindered by the wards, and the other newly arrived ship was too slow to give chase.

Dvora sat down heavily in her chair, already changing back to her woman form. "My goodness! Even when I'm a man, I'm not like that."

"You don't smuggle weapons of mass destruction, for instance," Hlaz-mlan said.

"As they've just found out," Dvora chuckled.

A smaller ship broke away from the station. Mawu quickly ran a projection and shared it through comms.

"They're not going to catch up with us," Anayāun said. "They either don't have a jump pilot or need that person to maintain the station wards. And accelerating at this rate . . ." The projection shifted. "That doesn't look good. Can we go faster?"

We certainly can, Mawu responded. *Or a direct jump?*

"We agreed not to do that," Anayāun said.

Not even if we are being chased? Mawu wondered but said nothing. They leaned into their power, the speed, the acceleration, gently adjusting the countermanding so that the operatives wouldn't flatten out inside the ship. The smaller ship couldn't quite keep up—or could it?

Mawu felt the first touch of something immense, waiting for them in the distance ahead, a mental impression of a vast fortification, a city sprawling in all directions, floating in space. Reaching out toward them and brushing against their thoughts.

Dvora gasped. Mushroom Rock slowly began to melt and re-form into their original globular shape while still maintaining their hold around Kheinu. They seemed smaller than before. Where did the material of the smuggler ship go? Mawu figured the eating must have involved some process of compression. Physical compression or data compression? They weren't sure which was the more intimidating thought.

"Mushroom Rock's family welcomes you," Anayāun said, her voice echoing, doubling back upon itself inside the sphere within a sphere.

CHAPTER FIVE:
WHEN IT ALL WENT BOX-SHAPED

HLAZ-MLAN WONDERED IF THEY WERE FINALLY AT THE END OF THEIR ROAD. The alien sentiences that had invaded Alliance space, destroyed her family home, and made Alliance Counterintelligence attempt to get rid of its own operatives to prevent "contamination" spread out in front of them, sprawling in the emptiness of space.

The three former Counterintelligence operatives were taking turns to negotiate. Would Mushroom Rock be able to rejoin their family and share their memories with the main mass? *Their memories about gallivanting around on the periphery of the Alliance, causing chaos and eating everything,* Hlaz-mlan thought bitterly. She would miss her poetry scrolls.

It was Anayāun's turn, and Hlaz-mlan was frustrated, pacing in circles around the main area of the ship and having little to do. Her legs hurt, and she found herself contemplating how every part of her was aching in a different way. She wondered if people with a humanoid body template had this too; they must have, for they sometimes complained, but did it really feel the same? And did shapeshifters like Dvora have it, or could they just shapeshift their aches away? Hlaz-mlan wondered if she could somehow ask her without sounding rude. The negotiation went on and on.

She tuned into the outside view to keep her mind away from her aggravation. Outside, around Kheinu the sentient spaceship and Mushroom Rock surrounding them, more of the alien sentiences were gathering.

They did not have a well-defined shape. From a distance, the small team of operatives had seen giant castles floating in hard vacuum, odd fractal crenellations, a city in space tinkling in shades of crystalline blue and purple. But all the seemingly rigid curves would shift and move at a moment's notice as if giant crabs were massing around Kheinu. Buildings that had come to life.

Dvora said, "Could you please stop running around? You're making me dizzy."

Hlaz-mlan refocused on the interior of the ship and morosely came to a halt. She'd always thought she was good at having her attention in two places at once, but she'd missed Dvora's frown, her shifting uneasily in her shapeforming chair. "My apologies," Hlaz-mlan said.

It was Anayāun's turn to lead the negotiation, but despite her bond with Mushroom Rock, the intruder to Alliance space, she could not get either Mushroom Rock or their family encircling them to agree on anything.

"Mushroom Rock will not rejoin their family until they get a guarantee that all of us won't be harmed. Their family is not willing to provide a guarantee, considering we share a body template with their attackers. And both sides are worried what will happen to the data Mushroom Rock gathered if they merge again with their family. They are carrying a lot of information, and this is not frequently done," Anayāun said. "Even if everything were to remain intact, the new data would still need to be processed and be inaccessible in the meanwhile."

"While the fortune hunters might be planning another attack." Dvora nodded.

Mawu, their young pilot, spoke up through comms. *Can the data be analyzed before the merge?*

"Not by them," Anayāun made a hand gesture, indicating something along the lines of *everything out there*. "They would need to use my bond to pass all the data, and I don't think that's feasible." She glanced up. "No, Mawu, don't even offer to help."

Hlaz-mlan didn't quite understand what was going on between those two, and it wasn't just because her insectoid species had different ideas about family ties. Anayāun acted increasingly protective of Mawu but also frustrated by them in turn. Hlaz-mlan wanted to keep Mawu out of trouble; they had not signed up with Alliance Counterintelligence and were only hired together with the ship, Kheinu, to transport the operatives. Before the Alliance tried to summarily murder them all, to rid the universe of the alien contamination.

She wasn't quite ready to think of herself as an *ex*-operative. But what had happened went beyond a simple misunderstanding.

"I am wondering . . ." she began slowly, not entirely sure where her train of thought would lead her. "We could analyze the data on our side before passing it on."

Dvora sighed. "At this point, Mushroom Rock is carrying information on everything that was in the fortune hunter base. The piece of lint stuck to a doorframe? The location of every little knickknack at the time of scanning? Where would we even begin?"

Where indeed. Hlaz-mlan just wanted to rest, but she was too agitated. To rest, drifting off slowly into sleep . . . to dream . . .

Indeed.

"Can we create some kind of projection of the base? Something we can walk around in? Then we could explore it." *Like a dreamscape,* she didn't add for fear of sounding ridiculous. Other species had really strange ideas about the process of dreaming, at least the ones that dreamed. Humans did for once.

"Oh yes! That's GREAT! I can help!" Mawu's enthusiastic yelling made Hlaz-mlan wince so hard one of her artificial legs slipped, and she had to readjust her stance.

"This might work." Even Dvora seemed encouraged. "We'd only need to transfer the information from Mushroom Rock to us that would be relevant to describe our immediate surroundings, and Mawu could work together with Anayāun to facilitate that."

Anayāun nodded. "This is definitely more workable than the previous plan. But do you want to walk around in a smuggler base?"

Hlaz-mlan switched to private messaging, worried that the conversation might somehow be detected by the giant crablike buildings gathering outside. *It beats other options like waiting here for the data to process until we get attacked by the mysterious Minather, waiting here until we run out of food, waiting here until Mushroom Rock's family gives up and eats us all, and other charming possibilities.* She was cranky, and she decided that for once she would own it.

Everyone seemed to be in agreement.

"Where is Mawu?" Hlaz-mlan said, looking around. The docking area of the smuggling outpost was much like she'd imagined it, based on Dvora's complaints: rugged with crates of who knows what piled up in corners. It was all very lifelike, even including the somewhat uncomfortable smell-taste impressions, save for one small detail. "Where is Mawu?" she repeated.

Anayāun shuddered. Her representation gained more detail as it drew on her own self-awareness. Her Ereni Security uniform was always spotless, thanks to ample technology to keep itself that way, but now she also looked less ruffled herself. Her warm brown skin was smooth, the beads of sweat gone from her face, and even her frown evened out. The cap covering her bare head was no longer askew, and her eyes glinted with alertness unmarred by a chronic lack of sleep. She reached up to rub her face. "Mawu chose not to instantiate," she said. "They offered to take over most of my tasks in running the space so that I could investigate more freely."

Hlaz-mlan nodded. That made sense; Mawu wasn't an operative at all and had no investigative training.

Dvora looked just like herself, and Hlaz-mlan was surprised at first, but she realized that as a rapid-response shapeshifter, Dvora could look like herself anytime she wanted and the circumstances permitted. Still, she was surprised that Dvora looked tired and rumpled, her pullover sliding up her hips and her pale skin blotchy.

Dvora followed her gaze and tugged her pullover back onto her hips and belly. She chuckled. "I have a very precise self-image," she said. "Comes from my increased body awareness." She laughed. "The way I look is exactly the way I feel, trust me."

Hlaz-mlan was tempted to ask if that was because she was a shapeshifter or because she was trans, but she did not want to be tactless. "Let's start looking."

As they sifted through the crates, Hlaz-mlan wondered how she would appear to others. She knew they called her their giant insectoid grandma, but she suspected that the way she imagined herself to be beautiful would be entirely different from their own perceptions. And how did Mawu imagine themself? Was Kheinu a part of their self-image and vice versa?

"Here we have five crates of proximity grenades with fissile charge in stasis containers," Dvora said over her shoulder. "And three more of some kind of conventional fusion bomb. Unarmed, of course." She added something in her own language, which Hlaz-mlan did not speak, but she was startled there was a certain amount of crosstalk between their minds in the simulation. Dvora thought something that roughly meant "mercifully" with an invocation of a specific deity not familiar to Hlaz-mlan but comparable to the Ennihar Allseer.

For all they had been working together, Dvora barely told her anything of her religion. Why didn't Dvora trust her? Hlaz-mlan remembered with unease that Dvora talked to Mawu about prayers and some kind of special religious food, and they'd just gotten to know each other on this particular mission.

Maybe she should also show more curiosity. Mawu was both outgoing and somewhat clueless; they would simply ask Dvora, even if the question was inappropriate.

The questions seemed to be inappropriate more often than not.

"By the Ascension!" Anayāun yelled. "Scattershot-4A?!"

"Does this qualify as a weapon of mass destruction?" Anayāun said, her voice still shaky. The operatives crowded around the box.

"What, you mean fission and fusion charges do *not* qualify?" Dvora snapped.

Hlaz-mlan bunched up her legs and lifted her torso higher so that she could see, but the box contained components entirely unfamiliar to her.

"Scattershot-4A is an order of magnitude worse than a fusion charge," Anayāun said. "It rearranges molecular structure, and it can *spread*. In an environment like this? Almost indefinitely."

Hlaz-mlan buzzed. "You mean a so-called *contamination* like the one we were accused of carrying?"

Maybe the Alliance had more than one reason to get rid of them.

Anayāun put her hands on her hips and took a step back. "Look, we all know the Alliance likes to arm vigilantes on the outskirts. The captain of that attacking ship also said as much after Mushroom Rock ate him. But this is extreme. This could ravage entire border regions."

Dvora licked her lips. "Get rid of two problems in one fell swoop, you think? The alien intruders *and* the smugglers. Wipe the slate clean . . . would the Alliance seriously do that?"

Anayāun tilted her head sideways, still staring at the box. "I note that the deactivator is missing."

The docks did not harbor more surprises, but the three operatives were still moving around gingerly, afraid not of the simulation of a box but of what it portended.

"Do you think these vigilantes know what it is?" Hlaz-mlan posed the question that had been bothering her.

"Most definitely not." Anayāun said. "This is a recently developed Alliance weapon."

Dvora pushed a box back into place. "So how do *you* know about it?" She asked nonchalantly, but Hlaz-mlan knew Dvora better than to assume that.

Hlaz-mlan also figured it was time to distract the duo before they began to bicker. But before that, she asked, "Did the System of Eren think there was a non-negligible chance you would encounter this weapon on your mission?"

"The answer is obviously yes. And before you ask your next question, no, I don't know their reasoning." Anayāun sighed. "The System would not set us up though. I wish I could say the same of Alliance Counterintelligence."

Hlaz-mlan turned away and pretended to busy herself with a set of smaller containers. If any Ereni ever learned about this weapon, the System could in principle also know about it . . . and share the information with any other Ereni. But the Alliance understood that. Hlaz-mlan was bitter: for all the Alliance had accused her own species of having some kind of groupmind purely on the basis of their insectoid shape, it was the Ereni who had a massive groupmind right in the middle of the Alliance. Well, on the periphery of the Alliance to be precise—but still.

Despite that, Hlaz-mlan had more trust left for the System than for her own employer, Alliance Counterintelligence. Ereni were often painfully earnest. Their culture had a prohibition on lying . . . though not on misdirection. Still, they were honest to a fault. Surely, a groupmind composed of many of them would be the same.

She desperately wished that the groupmind out there in space and surrounding them with all its sharp edges would also prove at least vaguely similar.

Hlaz-mlan tamped down her fear, her instinctive response that they had to get the word out, they had to contact HQ . . . but HQ wasn't listening, and they'd barely escaped the deathtrap.

She would need to rethink her entire life. And right before retirement too—not that that was any longer an option. They were fugitives on the run from the biggest political entity near and far.

"Let's see what we can find in the offices next," she said, trying to imitate Dvora's casual tones.

"I don't think I can get their computers to work in the simulation," Anayāun said. "But they might have some other kind of evidence lying around."

Hlaz-mlan did not ever want to think of the word *evidence* again.

They did find out about the mysterious Minather. Dvora fingered a very imposing-looking metallic nameplate. "This must be his office." She rattled the door. "It's closed."

None of this is real, Hlaz-mlan wanted to lecture her junior fellows, but instead, she just chirped loudly and walked into the door, willing herself to pass through.

It worked.

She turned around and unlocked the door from the inside.

"Mawu is asking you to please let them know in advance if you intend to walk through walls again," Anayāun said, her frown back.

"Please convey my apologies," Hlaz-mlan said hastily. "And now for the task at hand." She poked at a massive wooden desk nailed to the floor. "This looks more like a status symbol than useful furniture on a space station. I think we've found the boss."

Fifteen minutes later, they were forced to concede that the boss did not have anything in his office besides expensive handcrafted trinkets, antique weapons, and a large painting of the station itself. Even the file drawers had only contained an assortment of etchings, art prints, and handwritten manuscripts—all very expensive-looking but not informative in the slightest.

"Everything must be on the computer system," Dvora said. "At least we know he has a keen eye for art, and . . ."

"I don't understand it," Hlaz-mlan interrupted her, driven by the fear of wasting time. "Where are the people?"

"I asked Mushroom Rock to remove the snapshots of people from the simulation," Anayāun said.

"Can they be put back?"

A man who must have been Minather appeared in front of the painting, frozen in a position of grimacing at it. He was pale, bristly and angular. His jaw was severe and his head balding, and Hlaz-mlan wondered if this was his attempt at indicating human masculinity. But there were more important topics at hand. Maybe the painting held a clue? She rounded the immobile man and determined that the expression on his face was characteristic of many humans of his cognotype while using a computer interface. No, definitely not the painting.

Dvora patted Minather down, turned his pockets inside out. "Ewwwww. Now I know what he had for lunch. Or breakfast. Or breakfast the day before."

"Let's try to look elsewhere," Anayāun said. "I also want to find the person who warded the station."

They left Minather's room and found themselves face to face with a stranger. A living, breathing, *moving* stranger.

The person tilted their head sideways, their long, wavy orange hair gently rustling. Their limbs were long and lean, but Hlaz-mlan guessed from the way their clothing moved that they were muscular in a wiry way rather than thin overall. Hlaz-mlan thought there was something in them that also reminded her of Minather, even though they were lighter-skinned; maybe they were the same ethnicity? They did seem to have the same grayish eyes.

Senses sharpen in the face of impending danger, Hlaz-mlan thought and reminded herself this was a simulation.

The person was pale enough to blush and lively enough to giggle. "I'm Zsa," they offered in Alliance Common, their dialect close to Central. "Thank you for saving me from Captain Jerkface. He was the most annoying traveling companion."

"Oh." Anayāun took a step back. "You must be the woman he complained about. 'She's somewhere in there. She doesn't want to talk to me anymore,'" she quoted with the captain's exaggeratedly gruff tone of voice.

"That's me," she grinned. "Thank you, this is great."

Anayāun raised a hand—more in warning than to offer a handshake. "You teleported the weapons onto our ship."

"I'm sorry about that! It's complicated . . ."

Hlaz-mlan slowly moved to the side. Could she subdue Zsa if the need arose? Most humans would just scream when Hlaz-mlan made a move to attack them.

Zsa turned to her. "Hi, great to meet you too! I'm sorry. I can't shake your hand in the absence of, uh, hands. I talk a lot when I'm nervous, which is right now. I'm sorry! But thanks again. Can I help you somehow? I'm sorry. I babble."

"You don't need to apologize that much," Dvora said when she could get a word in edgewise. "Why are you here?"

"I'm not *here*. I'm inside the giant blob. But when the giant blob asked me if I wanted to hop on over, I thought it could be interesting?"

"Let's make this clear," Anayāun said, and Hlaz-mlan was very aware of Anayāun getting ready to strike. "You are a smuggler." Slowly. Evenly. "You are a powerful-enough māwalēni to be able to teleport weapons into a well-warded ship. What are you doing here?"

Zsa blinked rapidly, taking in the sight of her uniform. "Wait, are you with Ereni Security?"

"Yes, delegated to the Alliance."

"Oh, crap, maybe you can help me. I wouldn't tell you if I weren't sure you knew already. Wait—"

"Tell me what? Hold on." Anayāun raised a hand, this time with a different gesture. Then as if reading off a display: "Zsuzsa Várdai Inárcsi, Officer Class U, Alliance Intelligence?"

She nodded. "That's me. Oh, what a relief. I suppose I can trust you folks with this?"

Dvora took a step forward. "What are you doing here?"

"I'm trying to embed myself into Minather's stronghold, or rather, I was trying to do that before I got, you know, eaten."

Be ready, Dvora messaged Hlaz-mlan.

"Mr. Jerkface got a message to take out your ship. I was trying to make sure he could trust me." An emotion passed through her face that Hlaz-mlan couldn't decipher for all her experience.

"Who sent the message?" Anayāun asked.

"That's what I'm trying to figure out! I talked to the blob! Okay, well, it was all really rudimentary. They said it was wrong to attack and something confusing about the Alliance being evil. But you are here now and will help me get this sorted out, right? I need to get word back to HQ so bad."

Never mind, Dvora sent to Hlaz-mlan. *Let's see how this plays out.*

They were all sitting on top of a hill, stone ruins to their back and a small town with tiled roofs and white-painted houses at the bottom of the slope. The weather was crisp but easing as the sun rose. They were no longer in a simulation of the station but in a simulation of some kind of place Zsa liked.

"This is ridiculous. I'm sorry. This is terrible," Zsa said. "Thank you for explaining all that."

"Do you always blurt everything out?" Anayāun leaned back in the grass.

"No, just the inconsequential things! I'm a marvel of neuroengineering." She laughed. "But I'm like this. I mean, this is not an act, this is my actual personality. It works great. Those louts underestimate me a lot. Because I'm bubbly? Girly? You know? They might've exaggerated it a bit, the good people in Intelligence Neuroengineering, but they didn't make it up from scratch, you understand? I would have said no to that anyway."

Hlaz-mlan clambered on top of a small boulder to be eye to eye with her. "If this helps any, Dvora here did not underestimate you at all."

"Oh, you were trying to jump me? From the side? I was wondering! And she"—Zsa pointed at Dvora—"was telling *you* to do that"—she pointed at Hlaz-mlan—"while she *here*"—she pointed at Anayāun—"was getting ready to blow my head off with the māwal, pretty much." She raised both hands. "Oh no, you're warded enough. It's just that you were so calm and steady. I was sure you'd attack any moment now. Life experience."

Anayāun laughed; Hlaz-mlan hadn't heard her laugh in a long time. "I would never underestimate anyone who can displace heavy objects." Anayāun paused, any trace of merriment gone. "Now we need to make a plan."

Hlaz-mlan did not trust Intelligence. At all. It went beyond facile interagency rivalries: Intelligence and her, they had a history.

Fortunately, Zsa didn't trust Intelligence either. Maybe they could build on that.

"Look, I'm honestly really sorry for trying to kill you folks," Zsa said. "I want to make amends for that somehow." She stood, gazing out toward the town. "This is not very easy for me. But I'm going to say it. The blob—sorry!! Mushroom Rock—knows everything I've ever known, after having eaten me. Which is not much because need-to-know is a thing. But certainly everything I've found out on this mission." She crossed her arms as if defending herself. "When Mushroom Rock rejoins their family, it will be shared. So I might as well use it as a bargaining chip, you know . . . I can share it with you. We're colleagues, after all."

Hlaz-mlan slid off the boulder in a way that she would have liked to be more dignified and walked up to her. "Are we colleagues? *Us?*" She waved her antennae at her fellow operatives. "We were set up by our own bosses in Counterintelligence." She found herself wishing Alliance Common had a distinction between inclusive and exclusive *we* like her first language.

"You don't think I was set up?" Zsa turned to her. She wasn't crying or steeling herself against something. For a moment, she just had a plain curiosity on her face, and Hlaz-mlan shivered. Someone here had a temperament well-suited for intelligence work. It took Hlaz-mlan a while to gather her words for an answer:

"If the weapon had gone off, you would have died. And someone in a position of power ordered your ship to fire upon our ship. But did they know *you* were on it?"

Zsa furrowed her brow. "I'm not sure. I don't think anyone knows where I am right now. They've probably written me off already. Maybe they knew at that point, and you know, now I'm wondering! But they certainly don't know right now."

Assets whose value had just depreciated to zero, Hlaz-mlan remembered. "We're in this together. Let's share what we have, and maybe we'll come out of this alive."

"Come out where?" Zsa shook her head. "I'm tied to Mushroom Rock now. If they merge again, I'll be tied to their entire family. Which isn't necessarily bad, but . . ."

"I'm also tied to them. In a different way," Anayāun said. "Let's make the most of it."

The operatives logged out, leaving Zsa on the simulated hillside but remaining in touch via Anayāun and Mushroom Rock.

Several hours and a large acyclic connected graph later, they weren't much better off.

Anayāun walked around the tree of nodes, floating in the main area of the ship. "You confirmed a lot of what we suspected. The Alliance seems happy with the out-of-control smugglers and the alien intrusion threat mutually annihilating each other. But what are we going to do?"

"Mushroom Rock and their family both think they would lose too much time with the merge, and it would leave them vulnerable. We need to get the weapon off the station first," Anayāun said.

"What, commando style?" Mawu blinked at the operatives.

"At this point, they're probably expecting an attack, and they know the 'captain' who showed up was an impostor. After Dvora left them a box of . . . human-edible vegetables," Hlaz-mlan said. What was it? Artichokes? No, cucumbers. "We have few options. At least the weapon is dismantled and in a box, so they can't handily use it in a pinch if we are fast enough."

"We could just jump in and out, but I'm . . . sure they beefed up the station wards . . . ?"

If even Mawu seems hesitant about a jump, that does not bode well, Hlaz-mlan thought.

Dovber bounced up from his chair, again in his man shape. He seemed so alert and agitated, making Hlaz-mlan even more concerned. "Correspondences!" he yelled.

The tree graph had vanished, and its place was taken by a wireframe drawing of the smuggler station. Dovber paced around it, the thin tassels hanging off his sides, flying in all directions. "The māwal is all about correspondences, right? Just think of the old example. After you cut your fingernails, you burn the pieces so that someone else can't gather them to use as a link to you. Or throw them in the fabber."

"I don't have fingernails," Hlaz-mlan added.

"I have never heard of this custom," Anayāun said. "But my fingernails are reduced to a desired size by my biosystems as needed."

"And mine don't grow anymore, not after the shapeshifting transformation," Dovber shrugged. "That's not the point."

Hlaz-mlan understood the metaphor but was perplexed by the example. Humans *burned* the pieces they cut off themselves? Or was that just Dovber? She'd have to clarify this, but the conversation was moving along fast—and she'd already missed something.

Anayāun nodded. "We have a detailed model of the station. We can draw an exquisite set of correspondences."

"But it's only a simulation. How will we jump from a simulation to a physical space?" Hlaz-mlan asked, still not quite following and just a little resentful of the human-centric anatomy reference.

Anayāun pointed outward. "It need not be a simulation."

"I'm not sure how this works physics-wise," Hlaz-mlan buzzed. "And with this much effort, we could get my house back."

Outside in space, Mushroom Rock detached from Kheinu and twisted and turned like some kind of puzzle—looking increasingly technological, hatches and panel seams proliferating and receding, airlocks popping out. They turned into the smuggler base. Hlaz-mlan wondered how Mushroom Rock managed to budget enough material. Maybe some rooms were replaced by air bubbles?

"Um, we could just show up like this to the station, scare the crap out of them with their own duplicate," Mawu giggled.

The operatives were soon ready to board.

"We should've done this first, not bothered with the simulation," Hlaz-mlan remarked, waiting for the airlock to vent.

"It took a lot of convincing Mushroom Rock still," Anayāun said. "This was a lot of effort for them. There'd better be some eating at the end of the line. I made an argument about Scattershot-4A being tasty."

Hlaz-mlan froze. "You promised to give them Scattershot-4A."

"I did not, per se? But it would level the playing field," Anayāun shrugged. "Nothing like mutually assured destruction."

Hlaz-mlan shuddered, tremors going along her torso, all the way down her legs. "You—!!"

Dovber jumped between the two of them, Hlaz-mlan already poised to pounce. The airlock finished venting, but the operatives were busy getting at each other.

"You can't just *give* them an Alliance weapon of mass destruction!" Hlaz-mlan's voice edged into chirps. Mawu crouched in a corner, terrified.

"Look, the only thing that won independence for *my* people was exactly that!" Anayāun yelled back.

"What do you mean? Eren is a member of the Alliance"—Dovber started and then—"oh."

Anayāun was referring to the Ereni War of Independence over three hundred years ago. Hlaz-mlan was shaking but no longer in anger. In fear.

"The only thing that stopped the genocide was us erasing the Imperial Court of Emek from the face of the planet, and we live with that knowledge *every single day*," Anayāun said, gritting her teeth. And slowly, with pauses between each word, "I do not want it to get to that point." She turned to Mawu. "This is the history you'll live with. Are you sure you want that citizenship?"

Mawu nodded, trembling, barely managing to speak: "I . . . I guess I mean yes, I . . . where I'm from . . . we also have things like that in our history? This makes sense??"

Hlaz-mlan wasn't so sure about that. "Are you sure you're not just saying this because you're bound to Mushroom Rock?"

Anayāun shook her head. "This is not about me as a person or any of us. This is about self-determination and power imbalance. We all thought the intruders could destroy us with their spores in the hypothetical. It turns out, *we* can destroy *them*—we the Alliance—and have already made preparations to do so!"

"The fungus destroyed my house. That was not *in the hypothetical*!" Fear again gave way to anger.

"They were trying to communicate." Even Dovber took the side of Anayāun. "They saved our lives when we were being attacked."

"They just like to eat," Hlaz-mlan grumbled but stood down. "Still, you should've told us you'd make this offer."

Anayāun shook her head. "I was trying to think on my feet, and besides, I did not actually make a promise. In any case, we need to get that weapon away from the fortune hunters. Regardless of what else might happen. Do we agree?"

People murmured yes. Anayāun continued, "For that, we need Mushroom Rock's help. It was just a stray idea, but they liked it. I can't quite hide my thoughts from them."

"We can't just destroy the weapon?" Hlaz-mlan asked. She wasn't ready to give up yet.

"I don't think we know how," Anayāun said. "These things have defenses against being thrown into a fabber. But probably no defenses against an unknown, shapeshifting sentience."

Hlaz-mlan chirped a slow, mournful chirp. "We say the Alliance would destroy a sentient species just because it was less hassle than trying to communicate with it . . . but I can't wrap my mind around that. Has this been someone's policy decision at Central? Or just a set of small decisions on the margins of Alliance space, adding up to something beyond what anyone could have foreseen? But what—"

Dovber rubbed his face, pulling at his beard. "Folks? If we can't get back that Scattershot-4A, all this discussion is in vain."

Mawu popped open the airlock, and they all filed out in silence.

"This is very realistic visually," Dovber said. "And breathable air . . . with the smells just right," he made a face. "But"—he knocked on a bulkhead—"the textures and densities are wrong."

"There is a difference in mass," Anayāun said. "Some allowances needed to be made. Mawu? Let's start setting up. Mushroom Rock will have to help too. This will take a lot of power."

Hlaz-mlan would leave the work to them. She'd be busy enough as it was. "Let's consider this once again. Mawu jumps us in with the help of Mushroom Rock. Dovber stays here with Kheinu, and if anything goes wrong, they can try to get us help. Anayāun jumps us out with the help of Mawu, which should be easier. I will be the only one not dealing with the jumps, so I'll just grab the box. And off we go. I can also scare any fortune hunters who might show up."

A shape detached from a bulkhead with a loud, wet pop. "I'm not asking you folks to take me with you," Zsa said, more humanlike with each word. "I've seen enough of that terrible station. I'll do my best to help. I'm not quite separate from Mushroom Rock, but I have experience with matter displacement."

"Yeah, awesome!!" Mawu jumped into the air, waving their arms. "Come over here!!"

These two are quite alike in some ways, Hlaz-mlan thought. *Maybe this could work.*

Mawu was scrambling around on all fours, drawing a complicated assortment of lines on the floor. Anayāun occasionally stepped in to straighten a line or smooth out a curve, make small adjustments. Zsa puttered with the finer details, occasionally asking Mawu something.

The whole figure reminded Hlaz-mlan of the acyclic graph of the information they had gathered. She looked away; this wasn't her area of expertise, and she didn't want to interfere. It was enough for her to know that her teammates weren't worried in the slightest, working entirely absorbed by their task.

Then the jump, a discontinuity in consciousness—

"Go, go, get it," Anayāun was yelling.

Hlaz-mlan shook herself to clear her thoughts.

In front of her, someone twice Mawu's size was brawling with the youngster. Mawu was unsteady on their feet, but this seemed to confuse their opponent.

Hlaz-mlan scrambled to fetch the box. The entire docking area was in disarray, the storage containers thrown around haphazardly. Nothing was going the way it had been planned. She heard a loud thump behind her and Mawu gasping. Someone had clearly fallen to the ground, but who? Quick, the box. Where was the box?! What happened, why did she take so long to come to after the jump? Hlaz-mlan's mind spun.

A giant crash—

". . . have no idea what went wrong!" someone said.

Someone calmer said, "It's not that they were waiting for us. They were having some kind of problem too. Did you notice the containers?"

There was a dizzying perspective reversal. The two people weren't speaking; they were messaging each other. Over a private channel also shared with her.

Anayāun and Mawu?

Everything was blurry. Hlaz-mlan couldn't move, and she couldn't quite think either.

The containers? Mawu asked.

When we arrived, they were already in a heap. The smugglers must have been searching for something, Anayāun said.

And we interrupted them. Mawu sighed. *And they were armed. And angry . . . what's going on?*

I don't think it's fruitful to speculate. Anayāun seemed frustrated. *Maybe they finally realized what they had on their hands. Or did not have on their hands since they were actively looking for it.*

Hlaz-mlan opened her eyes, still not awake enough to participate in the conversation.

They all were in a small room, Mawu and Anayāun sitting on a cot and herself in a tangle of legs on the floor by the entrance. She carefully rearranged her limbs. She ached all over, but she had not been shackled. The walls were covered by convoluted scribbles of what looked like black marker. Hlaz-mlan assumed they were the physical anchors of the wards dedicated to keeping them inside. Was this the brig? Or whatever served as one on this station. She remembered looking into it briefly when they were searching the simulation. It had been empty then.

Anayāun and Mawu were having an increasingly animated discussion about how to break out and get back to Kheinu. The technical details went past Hlaz-mlan. Mawu was complaining about the separation being hard on them. Hlaz-mlan could finally offer a coherent thought. *We need to get out of here as soon as possible in case they come back and restrict us further,* she messaged them.

They startled and began fussing, relieved to see her awake.

How are you feeling? Anayāun messaged her. *I'll help you up. A whole shelf of smaller boxes toppled on you.*

I, I think maybe we didn't account for your body type well enough? Mawu added. *You seemed confused when we arrived, and—*

Hlaz-mlan was trying to reconstruct what had happened. *I don't think it would have changed much,* she said after a pause. *The box had been moved. I couldn't see it at all. Maybe it was buried under the other containers. I couldn't see the box we brought onboard either. Was that stuff edible, by the way?*

The door of the room slid open. "Well, well, you seem lively enough at last."

Three people filed inside: Minather, in a dress tunic and pants so light a blue as to almost be gray, and two of his cronies in armor.

Mawu shuddered—in fear? No, more like holding something back.

Wait, Hlaz-mlan messaged Mawu and Anayāun hastily. *We might be able to negotiate.*

"Glad to see you, Commander Minather," she said, hurrying to the front. Her legs twanged. "We have an important message for you."

"We can discuss that. But first . . ." Minather raised a hand, waved a guard in a face mask forth. The person raised a stunner at Mawu and then collapsed in a twitching heap.

Mawu blinked.

"Consider not triggering the active defenses of my colleague, Commander," Anayāun said, her voice icy cold.

Minather did not miss a beat. "Consider that I can remove the oxygen from this room."

Mawu shook their head. "I can survive in—"

That's ops info, Anayāun messaged them rapidly. *Don't disclose.*

Minather went on. "I can substitute any kind of gas mix. I can electrify the walls. I can introduce a wide range of environmental stressors. You can risk it, but I suggest you don't." He sighed theatrically. "We can discuss anything. With you," he looked square at Hlaz-mlan, "and *maybe* with the Ereni woman if I'm generous. But I want the kid in the pilot robes unconscious. This is not negotiable."

Don't risk it, Anayāun and Hlaz-mlan messaged each other simultaneously.

"I want a guarantee that no harm comes to our pilot," Hlaz-mlan said out loud.

"You're not in a position to dictate that." Minather coughed. "But I don't intend any harm. I'll get the kid back to the Alliance through my contacts."

Hlaz-mlan had no doubts the Alliance would pay the ransom. For someone highly exploitable, yes. And there would be strings attached. She felt more and more resentment—and increasingly, anger. Some things could not be justified. Maybe, she realized with a startle, she felt it was more unfair when other people were exploited or hurt than when it was about her own self.

Mawu looked about to burst out, *I'm not a kid,* but instead, they raised their hands, palms open. "It's fine? I mean, I get it," they said, their voice tremulous. "I can just lie down here and shut down my systems or something?"

Minather nodded, approval plain on his face. "Good. But I want the Ereni to do it. I trust the Ereni not to lie."

Can you do it? Go ahead if you think that's wise. We have few options, Hlaz-mlan messaged Anayāun.

Anayāun nodded. Stepped to Mawu. "Whenever you're ready."

Mawu pulled their legs up and lay down on the cot. Anayāun squeezed their shoulders encouragingly. "It will be all right." Mawu nodded, looking all the more childlike in their silent fear, Hlaz-mlan thought. They lay back, and Anayāun put a hand on their forehead. They twitched once, and their breathing abruptly slowed, deepened. Hlaz-mlan could not sense people's minds, and for once, she sorely felt the lack. Would any of them get out of this alive?

"It's done," Anayāun said.

"I want you to say it." Minather paused. "In detail."

Anayāun's jaw tensed, mirroring his. "I have shut down their conscious processing and put their biosystems on standby until the next override from me or from someone with the appropriate permissions."

"Well then. If there is a loophole in that, I don't see it." He laughed briefly with hoarse guffaws. "I'll take that. Now about that message?"

Hlaz-mlan wondered if negotiating was a mistake. Minather's remaining guard looked inexperienced, moving behind him rather than to the side. Together with Anayāun, she could easily overpower him and Minather as well. But then they'd still need to get out of this tightly warded room. She wished dearly for Dovber, always cunning Dovber . . .

Hlaz-mlan shook her abdomen. "The Alliance wants to kill you and destroy your station, Commander."

For a moment, she was relieved she did not have any kind of mental safeguards, preventing her from disclosing secrets like the ones Zsa claimed to have. Sometimes, one needed this flexibility, and she was senior enough to use her judgment.

Minather looked suspicious, considering his words before speaking. "And you're telling me this why?"

"Because they also tried to kill us," Anayāun said. Hlaz-mlan was surprised; she'd thought the Ereni would not be able to speak. But maybe her safeguards were flexible enough. Ereni psychotechnology was on par with the best the Alliance had to offer.

"You're not lying," Minather said. "Which offers a puzzle. You're betraying your employer."

Anayāun crossed her arms. "I would never betray my employer. What we're about to tell you is in the interest of all sentience."

Minather guffawed again. "Oh no, don't tell me this is about the space fungus!"

Hlaz-mlan decided to bluff. "Either the space fungus or the missing box, is that right, Commander?"

These types loved being called Commander, she knew.

He did miss a beat this time. "How do you know about that?"

Anayāun just smiled that annoying, all-knowing Ereni grin. She could bluff with the best of them, Hlaz-mlan knew. Lying or not lying aside.

Minather cursed. "My fence promised to take that damned box off my hands. But it disappeared."

"I tell you, boss, this station is haunted," the guard said in a low alto.

"It's the space fungus," Minather almost yelled. "After months of scrubbing. I'm sure it's still that." He turned back to Hlaz-mlan. "You have something to say about *that*, insectoid?"

She would not rise to the bait. "I can tell you all about my house . . . *human*."

"The Ereni doesn't leave the brig," Minather had said, and Anayāun acquiesced. "I don't want her to get a message back to her ship via the māwal."

After an only slightly exaggerated retelling of the demise of her ancestral home, Hlaz-mlan had to find the box of Scattershot-4A on her own.

The good part was that Minather finally understood the urgency.

The bad part was that she had no idea about the box's location.

She wandered around the station. The disorder was getting on her nerves, and it was only compounded by roving bands of smugglers, frantically turning the station upside down, shouting at each other. If they couldn't find the box on their own station, how could Hlaz-mlan stand a chance?

She did have more counterintelligence experience than everyone on the station combined, she reminded herself.

She decided to talk to the station māwalēni first—the person who was in charge of the general wards, who'd also set up the brig, who'd maybe have an idea how to locate a missing object. There were two options: the māwalēni could not find the box, or maybe he could but just did not want to. Both were equally enticing on an intellectual level. Hlaz-mlan tried to think of all this as a mental exercise and not as a situation of mortal danger.

His name was Peter, which her systems gave an 84% probability of being an Earth-human name. Unlike Minather, which was estimated at 76% Alliance Central. Minather had probably adopted a more prestigious name, Hlaz-mlan decided.

"You were looking for me?" Peter the māwalēni said. He looked much the same as on his profile and slightly less rugged than most of the others on the station. He had his straight brown hair tied back in a ponytail with sloppily dyed purple fringes, shading his face on both sides. It was an odd combination of rebelliousness and not caring for one's looks, Hlaz-mlan decided.

"Indeed, young man," she said as amicably as she could given the circumstances. He looked like a cousin of Minather's, not only the same race but probably the same ethnic group.

"Let's cut to the chase, ma'am. I have no idea about your box," he said.

"It's not my box, young man." She already felt her patience wearing thin, and they'd barely started.

He ignored the jab. "I swept the station multiple times. It's as if the physical object itself had disintegrated."

"You think the fungus ate it?" she asked.

He shrugged. "I don't know. We scrubbed everything after the latest breach. We haven't had an outbreak for months. The fungus kept on coming back for a while, but then it just vanished."

She wouldn't trust him, but she decided to offer him a morsel. "You know they're sentient, right?"

To his credit, he looked horrified. "What? No! I couldn't sense anything!"

"They have a . . . markedly different cognitive structure." Hlaz-mlan said. Only part of the truth. The fungus needed to develop, to grow into sentience. But the less these people knew, the better, at least for the time being.

"So you say we couldn't sense it."

The problem was, she couldn't sense them either.

"Anything and everything on the station could have been contaminated at this point," Hlaz-mlan said and stopped herself. She forced herself to use a different, more neutral word. "I mean *exposed*."

Her thoughts rushed ahead. If the intruders came here in spore form as they did to her home planet, they would not have had the sentience necessary to understand the situation at first. But they had been scrubbed before they had had a chance to grow to a significant size. They also would not have had a chance to communicate with the central mass, Mushroom Rock's family.

But Dvora also came onboard the station and could have carried bits and pieces of Mushroom Rock. Except she hadn't . . . or—

"What's wrong, ma'am?"

She waved her antennae at Peter to remain silent. She had to think!

The cucumbers.

Fresh produce is the best disguise, or what was it that Dvora had said?

Had she tried to smuggle something onto the station in preparation for a later strike? Then why hadn't she mentioned it? Why hadn't Mushroom Rock?

Hlaz-mlan had to get to the bottom of this.

"Where is the box of groceries that was brought onto the station by someone who looked like . . . ?" She realized she did not know the name of the captain beyond Mr. Jerkface.

"Ah, the surprise attack that wasn't really an attack?" Peter scratched his head. "I couldn't quite understand that. The box gave me weird vibes, so I put it into my tool cabinet. I figured I'd investigate it later, but then the other box vanished—"

"Where's your cabinet," Hlaz-mlan said all one word. *Wheresyourcabinet.*

The two of them broke into a run.

The rolling crate of cucumbers was there, shoved into the bottom shelf of Peter's tool cabinet filled with various occult paraphernalia. A wheel dangled sadly in the air.

The ordinariness of it did not reassure Hlaz-mlan in the slightest. Her legs were aching from the frantic dash.

"Don't touch it," Hlaz-mlan yelled at Peter. The māwalēni cringed, making the impression of someone who was often the target of yelling.

"This is not a box. If I'm right, this is an autonomous construct," she said more quietly.

"An autonomous construct of *what*?" His last word came out as little more than a squeal.

"I'll explain later." She thought to herself that the construct had been brought onboard, and then it waited for a while until the situation calmed down and ate the other box and came back here, reassuming its original box shape. She said out loud, "If it's heavier now, that would prove my theory. *Don't touch it!!*"

"Uff." He put the box back. "If we've been exposed anyway, it doesn't matter now."

He was right as much as this annoyed her. "So was it heavier?" she asked, trying not to be overeager.

"Yes, much more so."

"It didn't change shape while you were holding it?"

He looked at her, baffled. "You would have seen that. You were standing right here."

"Just checking. It must have a command to activate. But what is that command?"

"How smart can it be, you think?" A good question.

"Based on the ones I saw elsewhere, maybe . . ." She was trying to think of some Earth animal for the purposes of analogy. "A cat? The one with the eight legs. No, I mean an octopus."

He had the grace not to look amused. She reminded herself to never, ever underestimate māwalēni.

She had to speak to Dovber. Or Dvora at this point? But for that, she'd have to get Anayāun out of the brig somehow. If only she could control the construct . . .

It might have an override for all the team members. But what could her fellow operative have chosen as Hlaz-mlan's passphrase?

But of course.

She shook her abdomen and spoke slowly with feeling. "*My house.*"

The box made a remarkably artificial-sounding ding for an organic construct. "Approved. Command prompt," it said in Dvora's voice. "If you're getting this message and I'm not there, I'm assuming you're in really big trouble . . ."

CHAPTER SIX: LIKE DUST THAT SCATTERS

DOVBER LOOKED UP FROM HIS SEAT AND STARED AT THE CEILING WHERE Kheinu's ribs arced upward and met in the middle like a sea urchin turned inside out. Dovber wasn't sure how to talk to the sentient spaceship; the two of them usually talked through Kheinu's pilot, but Mawu had left to teleport the strike team in and out. The team jumped away and now it was just the two of them in this deserted quadrant of space . . . the two of them and Mushroom Rock. A giant, globular creature of unknown origin with a tendency toward both curiosity and hunger. And in the distance, the family of Mushroom Rock—more of the unknown, fungal sentiences—were floating in the hard vacuum of space.

Dovber wished he could be somewhere else. Maybe on a routine Counterintelligence assignment where he wouldn't have to chase down a weapon of mass destruction on the outskirts of Alliance space while smugglers and giant space fungi presented alternating threats . . . though his own department had attempted to kill them. This threat, that threat, this one again . . . wait, now you get them all together! He frowned, thinking of one of his cover identities—the traveling merchant, always adapting to new situations to do business, and he had the intonation perfect: *An amazing one-time deal! Three for the price of one! Handcrafted and artisanal, this one hasn't seen the inside of a fabricator!* He sighed softly.

"I can't contact the others, and I'm guessing you can't either," he said to the ceiling curving overhead. "Too much time has passed. They must've gotten trapped on the smuggler station somehow. We'll have to go help them."

This had been the plan. It wasn't a very good plan, Dovber reflected. But they had no way of getting the two other operatives and Mawu out of the station—at least, no way without mounting a full-scale assault. Knowing that Mushroom Rock would accompany Kheinu, that would just result in the station and everyone inside it being eaten.

Now, he would need to go and rescue them by himself. They'd planned this. He himself had planned it in even more detail than the others; he'd already seeded the station with a little surprise for the smugglers, even.

He couldn't talk directly to Kheinu or Mushroom Rock, but he could summon Zsa, the former operative of Alliance Intelligence, now merged with Mushroom Rock and having nebulously defined adventures on the inside. If it was really her still, Dovber wasn't quite sure. But they needed to talk.

He only needed to board the planetoid.

He scratched his head under his large black kippah. None of the humans were here right now, and his spacesuit never quite fit right. He was a rapid response shapeshifter though—so why would he need to change himself to fit the *suit*?

He sighed softly, evoked the right mental image, the right sensations from his body. He changed to a shape that'd been designed with great care and that he hoped he wouldn't ever have to use: a body shape designed to board hostile spacecraft. Even if Mushroom Rock wasn't hostile in the moment, Dovber wanted to be prepared for anything. The fungus ate Zsa after all.

The shape wasn't flashy—and not just because of the quasi-invisibility its gunmetal-gray surface offered as an option. (He tried to think of it as the *shape* rather than *himself*. The one part of Counterintelligence he disliked had been the combat training.) The *shape* was designed to get him from point *A* to point *B* across hard vacuum and probably also through several bulkheads as fast and as invulnerably as possible. It was smooth with just enough carefully placed sharp edges to make people think of a war machine. It was both utilitarian and a tool of psychological warfare. And it was chunky enough to remind Dovber of Martian-style Brutalist Revival.

Of course, there was a tradeoff between speed and invulnerability. He had been taught to opt for more of the latter, but now, he wondered: Zsa was in Intelligence, so she must have been trained in the exact opposite way. Less Brutalist Revival and more Art Deco, perhaps?

He shook his head. He shouldn't see Zsa as a threat. Interagency rivalries within the Alliance aside, both of them had been betrayed by their superiors and sent on a wild goose chase of a mission. Only, it turned out halfway in that they were the goose being chased.

Dovber tried to calm his mind as he cycled through Kheinu's airlock. Mushroom Rock was aware of his mind, but little if any information went both ways. They were too alien for each other. But Zsa was human—or at least had been before Mushroom Rock ate her. And Zsa was probably skilled enough with the māwal to take his mind apart, thought by stray thought. Surely just *talking* wouldn't be such a problem.

At the last moment, he grabbed a handheld thrust unit. He would rather not spend any more of his own hard-earned molecules on propelling himself.

Dovber landed on the slowly undulating, bumpy surface of Mushroom Rock. There was no sound in space, but the spray of spores under his feet made his brain assume that a soft hiss must have been heard. He vaguely remembered something from Intro to Psychology for Counterintelligence Operatives—what was this called? The jumping pylons illusion? He shook his head. Time to focus.

He emitted the Alliance standard radio communication signals that his suit was supposed to produce had he not left it in a locker inside Kheinu. For a moment, he was glad for the combat training.

"Zsa? Hi? I came over because the strike team's not responding."

A tap on his shoulder. He was infinitely glad that this martial shape suppressed startle reflexes, but the suppression itself was a very uncomfortable twisting sensation deep within him. He wasn't sure about his internal configuration in this version. In his nonexistent guts? He turned around.

Zsa was grinning at him, her form molded out of the material of Mushroom Rock so accurately that she had to have begun forming it while Dovber was still sitting inside Kheinu. He could see each individual strand of her flowing reddish-orange hair.

Yeah, I've been waiting for you, Zsa said in his head all too clearly. Dovber realized she was drawing power from Mushroom Rock. *But do you seriously want us to head over there now? Look, I know that was the plan, but I've been thinking. I don't want to create an even bigger mess.*

He nodded. "I've also been thinking."

You look like a chunky tabletop miniature without the paint. That's just my blurting-out thing, sorry. That's not what I've been thinking about.

Zsa was still entirely unbelievable to him as an Intelligence officer: someone who blurted out everything that came to her mind? But that probably worked in her favor; no one else believed she was an Intelligence officer either. He waved at her to go on, feeling it was best to wait for her racing thoughts to run their course.

See, approximately five thousand things went wrong. The Alliance almost killed us. Was that intentional, was that not, I have no clue. But what I'm saying is, a mess of this magnitude will eventually get noticed by Internal Auditing.

Despite his current lack of startle response, he almost did a double take. "You want to get help from *bookkeepers*?"

Zsa grinned at him. *The most badass bookkeepers in the known universe, sweetheart.*

Was she flirting with him? Everything was going downhill fast, as much as that was even possible in space, and here she was flirting with him. Or maybe this was just part of her personality. He decided to ignore the comment.

"I also have a plan," he said. "And we can keep Internal Auditing in mind too, though I'm skeptical we can contact them. I think I can get us some help from an independent source."

She tilted her head sideways. He wasn't sure if she looked skeptical or amused—maybe both. *Do tell,* she said.

"So"—he cleared his possibly nonexistent throat—"have you heard about my family?"

Strictly speaking, he didn't want help from his family. His family had no inkling that he was, one, a rapid response shapeshifter; two, a bigender trans person; and three, an operative of Alliance Counterintelligence. Each one of those items would have provoked a scandal in itself, let alone a combination of them. He imagined telling his family, "I went off to join Alliance Counterintelligence because they could make me into a shapeshifter, and this was how I was trying to deal with my unresolved trans feelings."

They still thought he was a traveling salesman.

With equal emphasis on the *sales* and the *man* parts.

But if he went home to see his family, he'd get to talk to the planetmind of Bayit Ledorot—and the planetmind could surely help them. Probably even jump him back into the smuggler station through whatever warding had been in the way. And then he could work on springing out the others. He was, after all, a reasonable approximation of a commando operative of Alliance Treaty Enforcement if the need arose—if in shape only, not in combat experience.

He could also reach out to the System of Eren, but he didn't know them, they didn't know him, and he was not looking forward to explaining the situation.

While family was family.

I see, Zsa finally said. *I've never heard of this planet of yours, but I know of similar arrangements. So basically, the planetmind allowed you humans to live there because they were . . . curious about you folks? I feel that—instant entertainment, a new episode every day. But why did you go live there? What did* you *get out of it?*

This was where it got tricky. He never knew how much explanation to provide. "We are Olimpianer Chasidim," he said.

He expected this to draw a blank, but Zsa grinned some more, nodding eagerly. "Yes, yes, Chasidic Jews? Chabad Lubavitch? I'm from Budapest! I know Chabad Lubavitch."

He wanted to bang his head into a convenient bulkhead. "No, not Chabad," he said as evenly as he could. At least, she didn't compare them to Satmar. "We split away from them a few generations ago. Theological differences."

And that was as much as he would say. He wouldn't get into the speculations about the Messiah, the move to Mars; he wouldn't get into the whole story with the Olimpianer Rebbe and how he made his entire community switch to speaking Hebrew from Yiddish so that he could fill out their ranks by recruiting from the Modern Orthodox crowd. With a lengthy, meticulous justification based on religious law.

It was the most controversial story in the annals of Chasidism since the Seer of Lublin fell out of a window on Simchat Torah, and he couldn't even begin to explain it to her.

Not the least because, while the Rebbe was generally regarded as a fringe figurehead on the fringe of an already fringe religious movement, Dovber himself read his writings and was convinced the man was a true genius, the most breathtaking intellect Chasidism had produced in generations. If the Lubavitchers had been able to keep him—

But they hadn't, and off the new Rebbe went with his followers to Mars, who then spread out to various planets across Alliance space.

"You see," Dovber began, trying to provide at least *some* context to his entire life, "we Chasidim believe that the world is full of sacred sparks that were scattered during . . ." Great, would he now have to explain the Kabbalistic creation of the universe? "Well, during Creation. It's complicated. And it is our task to gather them back together. Which we do by performing good deeds."

Zsa didn't seem amused. *So let me get this straight. Your group went off to live on this whole new planet, which was* already inhabited, *to what, gather sacred sparks? I'm sorry, but this comes across as pretty colonialist.*

Dovber sighed. "We asked if we could live there. We didn't invade the planet. We didn't convert the planet. We are in fact forbidden to proselytize. It's the planetmind's planet, and we do our best to be respectful guests." He chuckled sharply. "And we provide ample entertainment."

Zsa shrugged. *Fine, I guess I'll see what happens when you ask them for a favor of this magnitude.*

Dovber fumed to himself as he cycled back into Kheinu. *This is a diaspora like any other. We've lived in diaspora for generations upon generations. If we live here, that's a problem. If we live there, that's a problem. Somehow, we are always the problem.* He hoped Zsa wasn't paying attention to his thoughts anymore.

He didn't want to admit to himself that she'd touched a nerve. After all, "Bayit Ledorot" meant "a home for the generations" in Hebrew. And coexistence with the planetmind wasn't always easy for either side. That was different from colonialism, certainly. But still deeply difficult.

He wasn't sure the planetmind would grant him a favor, let alone such a big one: to expend an enormous effort to jump him into the smuggler station. He hadn't managed to reach the planetmind mentally; he would have to go there and be physically present. And he'd have to go alone, for Kheinu should not be in a different quadrant from Mawu while Mushroom Rock had to be kept out of Alliance space proper if possible. Not to mention the giant ball of fungus was still linked to Anayāun somehow, and he wasn't sure what the radius was on that connection. Kheinu would be hurt if separated so far from Mawu—for all he knew, both of them were hurting already. But he could do this alone.

Zsa had to ask Mushroom Rock who had to ask their own family. (Relatives were complicated, Dovber reflected.) But together, they could teleport him—if not to the planet surface itself, at least sufficiently close by that he could get to the orbital transport station in an escape capsule.

Dovber tried very hard not to consider what this meant about a potential invasion. He didn't trust them. But he had no other way out of localspace.

The jump was more disorienting than usual. Trying to convince the orbital station control to let him take the capsule straight down planetside without boarding the transfer station was even more disorienting. He didn't want to risk contaminating the station with whatever spores he might have been carrying from Mushroom Rock, and he figured the planetmind could deal with anything extraneous and undesirable.

He hoped he himself wouldn't be considered extraneous and undesirable.

"Yes, believe me, I'll be fine," he repeated to station control.

"It's going to get hot in the capsule during descent." The voice sounded bored. Dovber didn't recognize the dispatcher. Someone new? It was not time to indulge in his curiosity.

"I'm wearing special equipment," he said. No one here knew he was a shapeshifter besides the planetmind, and that was good that way. He also didn't want to use any of his Counterintelligence overrides in fear of being tracked. "Look, this is very urgent. I have to head straight down planetside," he repeated.

"At your own risk," the dispatcher gave in, but Dovber already wondered if he was being reported somewhere for suspicious behavior.

After all, he'd even had a fellow congregant complain to the rabbi once that he was reading secular literature and telling her kids about it. What did she say? *The other side.* The evil influence. He grimaced to himself—if only they knew . . .

He was having this thought all too often lately.

It indeed got very hot in the capsule. Hot enough that Dovber had to change back to his fearsome warrior shape. Hot enough to force him to rethink his life plans.

His life plans? *Her* life plans? In the context of family and home, she often felt the most woman—regardless of her physical shape—yet there was no way for her to show that. Dvora could feel her whole identity wobbling as she contemplated landing, interacting with various relatives, congregation members, acquaintances near and far. She tried to tone out the heat, the rumbling, her shape designed for space combat. She'd be planetside soon.

The planet allowed her to approach, to steer herself toward the landing area. Slowed her descent even. The landing wasn't desperately bad.

She had ample time to gather herself, before leaving the mercifully opaque capsule, and change back to . . . Dovber, not Dvora, which hurt her so much. She *was* Dovber, definitely, but right now she wasn't, and Dovber would be the only face of hers they ever saw. Shapeshifting aside.

Her feelings were clear. But there was no place for them on Bayit Ledorot, was there?

Dvora shook her head and clambered out of the capsule in her male form. Cheerful and chubby. She would look very similar if she could—

She couldn't. She shook her head to chase away the thought.

Her biosystems compensated for the sudden blaze of sunlight outside. Dvora didn't get blinded, didn't even need to squint. She could see the waving grass, the bushes and trees, the exuberant green dotted with flowers in all colors of the spectrum.

Bayit Ledorot wasn't a garden world. All its natural substance was made from the same material, shiny like quicksilver and protean. Dvora knew if she were to tear off a small branch, she would see the familiar metallic gleam. She wasn't sure why the planetmind assumed the form of trees, entire forests, blades of glass—but there must have been a reason.

After Alliance Counterintelligence had stuffed her into a barrel full of the same quicksilver substance to make her into a shapeshifter, she and the planetmind became akin. And Dvora certainly had many good reasons why she kept to her human shapes. She would be the last person to question the planetmind on this particular topic.

She slowly stepped into the ankle-high grass of the landing. The grass trembled. Dvora wasn't sure what that meant, for she was structurally similar to the planetmind, though of a different origin. They were not connected in any way; they were just sentiences implemented on the same substrate. She'd need to talk to someone who was connected to the planetmind—maybe young Shai now that he'd gotten over his own accidental transformation.

A small, quiet cough. Dvora's head whipped up, and she was frustrated with herself for letting go of situational awareness if only for a moment. She'd blame it on the descent.

Chani tilted her head sideways, her heavy dark curls hanging straight down. "The planetmind needs to talk to you," she said.

She hadn't said *Dovber*. She hadn't said *Dvora*. But Chani knew everything because Chani was of the planetmind.

Dvora nodded.

"You need to be decontaminated first," Chani told her. "Let's get you to a lake."

They headed out. Everything was refreshingly pastoral and heimish in the way only a Jewish neighborhood could be heimish. Spaceflight was still noisy, but landings were soft—enough so to keep the grass intact. The landing area was quiet, only two bachurim were unloading a kosher meat shipment. Some people were convinced real beef tasted better than whatever came out of the fabricator, even if the end result was identical down to every single atom.

Dvora avoided the young men. She could say hi later, but now, it was better if she didn't spread around who knows what kinds of spores. Even with the men's attention elsewhere and Chani knowing about her, she still didn't change her form. She didn't feel safe enough to do so. People were meddlesome, and she was sure there were security cameras covering the landing site.

The lake was conveniently—and entirely not incidentally—near the footpath into the town itself. Its surface shone metallic in the Earth-spectrum sunlight; one of the only places where the planetmind's substance could be observed in its most basic form.

"Get in," Chani said with an authority that belied her teenage form. Chani did not speak to her like someone her age and gender would have spoken. Chani spoke to her like the planetmind.

Dvora hesitated. This was the way the planetmind incorporated the people who would then go on to mediate between the planetmind and the settlement. This was what Chani had done—though Shai had been eaten by the planetary self-defense mechanisms by accident, so there were certainly other ways. But Dvora had no plans of getting incorporated, ever.

"I prefer to maintain my independence," she offered.

Chani groaned. "This is just to remove the material you are carrying. You have it even inside your body. Also, you can change your form. I can shield you from onlookers."

Dvora remembered what Hlaz-mlan had said about the spores spreading. Even if she had no idea how they'd survived her multiple recent transformations, Chani and the planetmind were probably right. Still . . .

Chani shook her head. "No one's listening, so I can tell you this. You probably cannot be incorporated. You are of the same material as we are already. And you work differently. You have much more conscious control of your shape." She grimaced. "I'm still trying. It's hard enough to maintain my consistency."

Dvora grinned back. "Well, for me it's easier. I'm not a part of a larger whole. At least, I don't think the Alliance counts—especially now."

"Hop in, and we can also retrieve your memories." Dvora was wondering if the allusion to a ritual bath was intentional, but neither of them commented on it.

Dvora waded into the shimmering fluid. She didn't undress—with the exception of her ritual garments, all her clothing was a part of her body. She simply stored her talit katan in a sealed internal pouch, like she'd done countless times before. It was like having the tzitzit fringes tickling your stomach from the inside, but she was used to the sensation. While she was doing this, she also changed to her woman shape. The first time in public on her own planet, though she wondered if it counted as public if no one else could see her. Still, the moment felt poignant. The change itself felt easier and easier each time, and she was accustomed to every aspect of it; her hips' shifting felt the most uncomfortable at first, but by now, all the sensations were familiar and welcome—in both directions.

She wasn't used to what came next.

It was as if all her molecules passed through something else's molecules. It was as if her body was slowly pushed through a giant sieve. It was like drowning—except it wasn't exactly like anything. It was uncategorizable, ineffable. She wondered if the people of the Old Empire had terminology for this. If they did, it had been lost after the collapse and the centuries hence.

It didn't hurt, unlike her transformation, unlike Chani's getting incorporated, unlike any of that. Dvora supposed Chani had been telling her the truth. The planetmind did not threaten her independence.

After a timeless interval, the substance receded around her. "Moshe rabeinu and the splitting of the sea," she murmured to herself. She moved her ritual garments around her body so that they were in the right place. Chani turned back to her when she was done, helped her out of the pond. Dvora hesitated before accepting her hand. "Are we even supposed to touch each other?" she asked. There were many religious prohibitions around men and women touching.

Chani shook her head. She looked sad—and angry? "Regardless of *your* gender, they don't consider me a proper woman," she said. "Not after the transformation. Not a proper man either. I'm something that doesn't fit. They've been debating it endlessly. They say, *If you can change your shape . . .*"

Dvora sighed. She knew those kinds of debates. "But you consider yourself a woman."

"So do you," Chani said, ferocity lining her voice.

"Well, not always."

"But right now." She paused. "I'm aware of your mind. I can tell even if you don't say anything."

This was the last thing Dvora wanted to talk about. But Chani and her, they had this in common: their families, their people, wouldn't see them for who they were. Chani had been assigned female at birth, and Dvora hadn't, but they had ample common ground. Dvora reminded herself she shouldn't be combative. Chani was also half her age, though now as shapeshifters both of them were quasi-immortal. In another few centuries, the age difference wouldn't matter, but it mattered at this point.

Dvora switched to Alliance Common. It was handier with gender than Hebrew. "I know someone, our pilot Mawu. You've seen them in my memories. They're intersex and undecided about gender. Their family is upset they haven't picked a gender. It can be complicated on other planets too."

Chani sighed softly, and for a moment, she looked like the teenager she was, not only an envoy of a vast planetwide consciousness. "I'd like to meet Mawu sometime," she said.

That was all the convincing it took.

Dvora stared at the town in the distance. She could put off a confrontation with her family for another day. The planetmind had agreed to help her. She turned back toward the landing.

"Your capsule will be consumed," Chani said. "It also carries the spores, and in any case, you won't want a record of having been here if you're not going to meet your relatives." She was speaking without reproach. She had had a hard time with her own family, Dvora knew.

But weren't the two of them family to each other in some way?

"You'll jump from the planet-surface to within the smuggler station," Chani went on. "You're not that māwal-active. Do you need weapons?"

Dvora shook her head. "I can assume some very aggressive shapes. And I've left something on board the station that can also serve as a weapon. Maybe some of the others have already figured it out."

But she doubted they had. She hadn't heard from them.

"When your task is done." Chani paused, visibly struggling to speak, "will you bring your colleagues? Your fellow operatives. And Mawu. And their ship."

"I . . . I don't know how that would go over." Dvora waved a hand. "With everyone."

Chani looked at her, her large dark eyes pleading. "I'm not asking you to out yourself to your family. You have your cover identities. You can pose as traders. I . . ."

The planetmind could know all their thoughts. How would that work with operations security? Dvora remembered with a deep ache in her bones that Alliance Counterintelligence had already written them off. If they survived all this, they might as well come visit.

"I would love to do that," she said. And she would.

She was finally finding fellowship, friendship, here and there in pockets of time stolen from work that involved mortal danger more often than not. She would hold onto it.

Dvora took a deep breath and sang softly in Hebrew again: from the Yom Kippur prayers, though with a modern melody—

"Humans' origin is from dust and their end is dust,
risking their soul, they work for their daily bread,
like a vessel that breaks, like the grass that withers,
like a flower that dries out, like a shadow that passes,

like clouds that lighten their load, like winds that move on,
like dust that scatters, like the dream that flies away . . ."

She fell silent.

"You know how it goes on," Chani said.

Then the two of them in unison, "But you are King, living and everlasting G-d."

They would have to draw their solace from that.

Chani broke the silence again in Alliance Common. "But aren't we the religion of good deeds rather than faith? Let's go and get you to do your good deeds. Rescue your fellows, get back that weapon, and help everyone. One who saves one life saves a whole world," she paraphrased the Talmud.

Dvora nodded, and she understood both of them felt the same way. She would go through fire and water and face the sword for someone who understood her, for someone who spoke the same way, someone who habitually quoted the same sacred texts as her.

Someone who was excluded just like her.

She should have come home sooner.

But now she had to leave, to help her friends . . . who understood her better than her own family. It was a relief for her to leave the planet without meeting her relatives, and she felt uneasy about that.

Who was family, really?

The jump was smoother than ever, even through the station warding. Just a clean cut in awareness, nothing jarring, and then Dvora was in an ideal location, even if cramped: in a small storage closet off the ship bay of the smuggler station. If this was possible for them, what could the planetmind potentially do? Dvora felt like an ant, scrambling along in happy or unhappy ignorance on the surface of something infinitely vaster. She felt . . . humored.

She would introduce Chani and Mawu to each other, but now, even more than that, she wanted to introduce the family of Mushroom Rock to the planetmind of Bayit Ledorot. *Helpful tips about how to coexist with billions of tiny sentients who call themselves the Alliance!* Even if she wasn't truly a trader, she could sell them on that. And all that before we got additional vast entities like the System of Eren into the mix, who would surely want to be involved even closer . . .

It was time to get things done. She needed to find Hlaz-mlan, Anayāun, and Mawu . . . and it was also time for her to retrieve that innocent-looking box of groceries. Had her plan to create chaos on the station worked? She gritted her teeth and allowed them to melt away, her shape assuming her hostile-boarding version. She didn't want this shape, but she knew it would probably save her life multiple times over before the day was done. It was designed for commando units, and it was simultaneously sleek, elegant, and lethal—fit for any gender, though extremely unfit for her in particular. She did not want to kill anyone, and she wouldn't. This was pure masquerade. She noticed something she'd never thought about: this shape was quite feminine, but now, she felt more uneasy about assuming it than earlier as Dovber. Maybe because earlier she just needed something that could withstand the vacuum of space, regardless of how it looked, whereas this time she needed to pose as a member of an Alliance strike team? Or maybe there was something else to it. She would have to think it over. Later.

She edged the closet open. Her thoughts raced. Now that she was inside the station wards, surely Anayāun or Mawu had to have noticed her already. But she could feel no minds reaching out to her own. They were either unconscious or inside a further ward.

At least no one *else* was noticing her. Her quasi-invisibility was working, but she wasn't sure her mental shielding would escape notice from someone with more skill with the māwal. Who was keeping up the wards?

Maybe that person was occupied too.

She jumped up to the ceiling of the corridor, turned on instant adhesion with a thought and stuck her limbs to the surface, and then began to inch ahead. Hopefully, no one would try to replace a light just now.

Someone ran along the corridor just below her, his head almost brushing her torso. A smuggler, screaming assorted obscenities. "WHERE IS THE BOX, THE BOX!! Minather will rip our guts out! The secret weapon!" Three more smugglers followed suit.

Dvora was confused. This was surely not about her box of groceries. It had to be about the Scattershot-4A, the Alliance weapon somehow in the smugglers' possession . . . but then why didn't they know where that went? Weren't they supposed to keep it under lock and key?

Then it hit her. Her plan had actually worked.

The box originally disguised as groceries—made of Mushroom Rock's material and kindly donated for the purpose. The box of limited sentience but at least some autonomy. The functionality she'd asked of Mushroom Rock with the kind help of Anayāun:

The box should wait a day after being moved. Then it should reassume its fungal nature, locate the most exciting object it can find on the station, and eat it. Then it should return to its original location and wait for Dvora or one of the other operatives to activate it. Just in case.

Eating wasn't a problem. And Dvora had designed a purely inorganic construct that would handle the activation, user verification, and command interface. She only needed to feed it to the box and convince it that it was worth keeping. But how the box would evaluate *excitement* was for the most part unknown. Mushroom Rock was sure the construct would be up for the task, but their concepts of excitement were different from humans'. Anayāun had been dubious. And Hlaz-mlan . . . she realized that she somehow amidst all the chaos *forgot* to tell Hlaz-mlan.

Something had to go wrong. The plan was a long shot, a plan *C* or *D* or something that wasn't even a backup plan. Just something to have in case. It wouldn't hurt. Would it?

Anayāun had told Mushroom Rock that the weapon of mass destruction must be *tasty*. Would that be the first thing the box sought out?

Dvora hadn't had a particular object in mind originally. The task of the box was merely to cause chaos. An *exciting* object, suddenly gone missing—surely that would sabotage the station in a relatively harmless way, and the time they won with that might be exactly what they would need.

She did this type of thing a lot. These gambits didn't have a high success rate, but when they worked, they worked spectacularly well.

She fervently hoped this would be one of those times.

In addition to Hlaz-mlan, Anayāun, and Mawu, she'd also need to find the box . . .

She moved slowly along the corridor, hanging from the ceiling, her attention focused in all directions.

It took her a while to hear a familiar voice.

"What do you mean, command prompt?!" Hlaz-mlan was yelling. "What commands do you even take?! Execute!"

Dvora didn't hear the reply, but she knew the box had to have said, "Command incomplete."

"Help!" Hlaz-mlan yelled. "Something . . . ! *Manual weird box!*"

That should have worked. Alliance standard command syntax.

Except Dvora hadn't had enough time to write the documentation.

She was now close enough to hear the box say, "Manual unavailable. Do you wish to search for a nearby network connection?"

She hopped down to the floor behind Hlaz-mlan and a stranger, muttering, "Now you can see why I'm a Counterintelligence operative and not a software engineer."

The stranger spun around. A young person from Earth, probably white, probably a man? Their hair brown with sloppily applied purple highlights, and they looked agitated. Dvora disabled her invisibility.

The stranger fainted.

"We-ell," Hlaz-mlan looked at Dvora as dubiously as only a giant insectoid could and waved one of her antennae in the direction of the inert body. "Meet Peter, the station māwalēni. I don't know how long the wards are going to hold if he's knocked out."

"You mean I should keep him under?" Dvora asked. This shape could produce just the right kind of injectables for that purpose, but she was hesitant. She didn't quite understand the situation.

"Commander Minather put us all in the brig, but he let me out to help locate the Scattershot-4A, which has gone missing," Hlaz-mlan said rapidly, but she still took the time to place great derision on the word *commander*. "This was our deal. Do you know anything about that"—gesturing toward the box—"by any chance?"

Great, now Hlaz-mlan would assume that Dvora hid the secret of the box from her on purpose. Dvora had somehow managed to outsmart even her own self. "Yeah, my box of groceries was supposed to do something. I forgot to mention that," she said. "It wasn't human food, not really."

The stranger groaned. Dvora decided on impulse to inject him. It would win them at least a little time, and surely, his wards wouldn't go offline right away if they hadn't yet. Peter fell silent again.

"Good move," Hlaz-mlan said mildly. "So what was in the box?"

"What was the box, rather. A chunk of Mushroom Rock."

"I suspected as much," Hlaz-mlan said but then buzzed anxiously. "What if the people on the station ate the human-looking food?"

"Gruff smuggler dudes who imagine themselves to be cowboys don't eat *zucchini*," Dvora responded all too fast. "Even if it's fresh. It's an Earth thing, a gender thing." Looking at the scrawny stranger who seemed the farthest from a cowboy, she was no longer sure she had been right to generalize.

Dvora nudged the young man lying on the floor. "I think our friend Peter here was considering eating it. Why would he have kept it for himself?"

Dvora clutched her head. "This is a mess. I'm glad he didn't. What do we do now?"

Hlaz-mlan chirped. "Is this fancy military shape of yours bulletproof? Because then we might have just gotten ourselves a hostage. Or . . . I don't assume you can break through the wards he set up for the brig?"

"I'm not a professional māwalēni," Dvora said, frustrated. Even her comrades would believe anything of her. Then again, she'd cultivated that kind of impression. "But we have the station māwalēni, and we have my box, which I assume has eaten *their* box, so we probably also have the Scattershot-4A. And if we only keep . . . Peter, we can outlast everyone else even if we can't open the brig yet." She lifted him to her shoulder. "Didn't you want to negotiate with Minather though?"

"I want to know about that," Minather said from a speaker somewhere.

Dvora would have rolled her eyes if her present configuration allowed that. They should've just talked through secure messaging. She felt she was growing sloppy—or just exhausted? Of course Minather had a keyword alert set to his name. Did he spend his free time going through everything his underlings said about him behind his back?

She decided the answer was probably yes. "Come on over, and we'd be happy to talk," she said, her cheerful tone entirely at odds with her martial appearance.

"Alliance Treaty Enforcement. I knew this would bring the marines to the yard," Minather grimaced. Dvora wondered if Peter was one of his relatives. She could see the family resemblance, even minus the purple highlights. Minather's jaw was wider, his face more openly hostile, but that was about it.

Dvora decided to leverage that. "Would you mind if I put him down somewhere?" she nodded at Peter's inert body. "He's unharmed, just sleeping."

"I'm assuming you'd rather not have this meeting in my office," Minather said and nodded at a crate half-blocking the corridor farther down. "You can put him on top of that."

They all ambled over, and Dvora lay Peter down on top of the crate, tried to arrange his gangly limbs just so. Minather seemed annoyed enough with Peter to be his relative.

Now, to make sure he believed there was a whole squad of ATEF in orbit.

Dvora said perkily, "Wherever one of us shows up, the rest are not far behind." Not a lie, per se. Anayāun and Mawu would like that.

Minather grit his teeth so hard Dvora was afraid for a moment they would snap. "Are you taking the box? The Alliance weapon?" Did he believe the bluff, that he was five seconds away from the Alliance crushing him in its iron fist?

Dvora nodded with as much eagerness as she could muster. "Oh, we would happily take the box."

"And what then?" He almost spat. At them? Dvora hoped not.

"We're not here to arrest you. And you've had enough trouble," Hlaz-mlan said, playing along with her game.

"We can take the Scattershot-4A and be on our merry way." Dvora added.

Minather looked back and forth between Dvora and Hlaz-mlan. He didn't quite understand. "I never imagined the Alliance would help me out better than my own fence. This box only brought trouble for us."

"We're not paying for it. Don't get us wrong," Dvora snapped at him.

"Just go. Take the box now that you've found it—you have, right? Give me back my crew, and we won't bother you anymore." Minather was deathly pale. "Will you deal with the aliens next? We didn't dare use the weapon." He looked ready to beg, though he would not quite condescend to that. "Will you do it?"

Dvora crossed her arms. Time to bluff. "You've been through hell here," she drawled. "Tell me about it."

Minather looked away from her. "The aliens. What are they made of? Ever since they first showed up, it was like . . . it was like reality destabilized. Nothing worked quite the same. *Physics* didn't work quite the same. And we couldn't get rid of them. A little wiggly thing would turn into a blob would turn into a whole chunk of nightmares. Ever clean anything with a blowtorch?"

Dvora decided this was not the moment to tell Minather about traditional Passover preparations. She nodded sagely. "I understand. We're here to deal with the situation. Let my people go."

Whatever his traditions, Minather did not recognize the Bible quote. Dvora thought of Chani, her insides churning with sadness.

But at least, finally, things were going her way.

Peter made hand-waving passes at the door of the brig, reminding Dvora of some kind of old-fashioned Earth mesmerist. "MMMMMMMMMMMMMMMMM," he said. If this worked for him, Dvora decided she wouldn't pass judgment.

He spat on the door.

Dvora groaned. Her resolve would only stretch so far.

"What," Peter turned back at them. "Body fluids have *great* magical properties."

The lock clicked, and Peter pushed the door open. A split-second to act— Dvora jumped forward and grabbed his arm. "No. I go first."

Peter blinked at her helplessly.

"Knowing my colleagues, you're walking into an ambush," Dvora said, fighting her instincts to shout.

"The marine is right," Minather said. Dvora was amused for a moment that he decided not to gender her. At the moment, her gender presentation was mostly "assault team"—and he'd never recognize her in either of her usual shapes. He wouldn't even recognize her voice.

Peter slowly stepped back and gestured at the door. "You first then."

Anayāun and Mawu definitely looked about to strike, but they recognized Dvora and stood down right away.

"You cheated me," Minather hissed at them. "I said I wanted the kid unconscious."

"I'm not a kid," Mawu said.

"You didn't say for how long," Anayāun said simultaneously.

Dvora wasn't sure what this was about, but there would be enough time later to figure out exactly what had transpired on the station in her absence. If there was a later.

"What am I going to do with all this māwal I raised?" Mawu asked.

"Get us back to the ship?" Hlaz-mlan buzzed.

"There's one more person than on the way in," Mawu blinked.

"I can help," Peter interrupted their conversation. Minather said nothing, just waved a hand at him to go ahead. Definitely a relative, Dvora decided.

"I can boost your jump, and then, you can certainly make it," Peter said. "But please exit the brig, I'd rather not have to take down the wards inside the walls."

"One moment," Dvora held up her palms and turned to Minather. "I need more information from you if we are to deal with the aliens." Start the bargain high. "I need your memories."

"How d—" He sputtered.

"Just the memories related to your interactions with the aliens. How you fought them." She kept her voice even. "You can keep everything else to yourself, including your little business dealing in weapons and who knows what else. This is an Alliance security issue."

It indeed was, but they didn't know she no longer had the right even to demand anything like that, being on the run from the Alliance herself.

"If that means you'll get the aliens out of our hair for good, fine enough," he grunted. "Peter, share your memories."

Dvora pretended not to notice how Minather outsourced the task to his—cousin? Younger sibling? She hoped they wouldn't notice how she'd outsource the task to Anayāun either. She could maybe pass as a marine on visual inspection but definitely not when it came to the māwal-active domain. She had some ability but not that much. And no training.

It only took a few minutes, and Anayāun nodded that she got what Peter had offered.

Dvora nodded in turn at Mawu and Peter to get started with the jump, and they launched themselves into the preparations.

"I'll do the targeting, and you do the setup," Mawu told Peter. "I know where we're going. And we can split the power-raising part, I dunno, two to one?"

Peter nodded, not disputing the division of labor. He was clearly practiced at doing this in groups, which was a relief to Dvora. Even she could feel as the power ratcheted up—

"Wait—all Alliance elite troops are māwal-active. This one is a fraud!" Minather pointed at Dvora with a shaking finger. "They're not with the Alliance!" he shouted.

"Don't interrupt me!" Peter screamed back at him. "I'm casting a fucking teleport spell for four people. You want the station to blow?" He swatted at the air, and Minather flew against the nearest bulkhead.

Weird Earth terminology and cussing aside, he was doing a good job, Dvora thought.

Then they were back exactly where Mawu wanted them to be, on board Kheinu, all safe and sound.

Together with Peter.

Dvora changed back to her comfortable woman shape and threw herself into a chair, which made an organic squishing sound upon contact. "We seem to be gathering Earth humans as we go." She glared at Peter. "You have *one* minute to explain yourself."

"She's right," Anayāun stepped closer. "I was saving *my* māwal just for a situation like this."

Peter hugged himself as if defending his torso. "I just wanted to get away from my brother," he muttered. "He's a jerk. And it's getting worse, you know— and he makes fun of me, he makes fun of my magic, he makes fun of . . ." He looked devastated. "I'm gay." Then he went on, now with anger mingling with tears. "They'll be fine without me—Jake can step in, they can recruit someone . . . all he needed me for was to have someone he could treat as his doormat."

"It's all right," Anayāun said once she could get a word in edgewise. "It's all right."

"From one bad situation into another though," Hlaz-mlan added mildly but with frustration lurking in her words. "You know we're on the run from the Alliance."

Peter rubbed his face. "I-I figured." Then he looked up at them and chuckled.

"You're much too ragtag to be a real commando unit. Don't get me wrong. That's cool."

Dvora furrowed her brow. "We in fact used to be an Alliance unit. Different department though. But then we met Mushroom Rock and their family . . ."

"The aliens? I know. They have that effect on you." Peter shook his head. "I know," he repeated.

"How about we eat," Mawu said. "I'm starving after this jump."

The three ex-operatives convened in the main area and asked Mawu and Peter to wait outside. Peter probably didn't know that Mawu could hear anything going on in the ship.

"We have the Scattershot-4A," Anayāun began. "I think we can discount the smugglers as a threat. Their māwalēni abandoned them, and their station is in disarray. But we need to deal with Mushroom Rock's family."

"If we give them the weapon as you proposed," Hlaz-mlan said, rubbing one of her legs with another, "they will greatly owe us, and they'll also see that not all sentients in the Alliance are hostile toward them. But it seems too large a step to take." She looked like she was in pain. Had she injured herself on the smuggler station?

"I don't want to argue against myself," Anayāun added. Dvora was sure she was going to do just that. "But we need to face it. They have no idea how to interact with others." She sighed. "Look. I understand that. I'm Ereni. We're a small cognitive minority in the Alliance. I know what it's like to deal with people not of your cognotype on a daily basis. I can now talk to Mushroom Rock, but I still cannot talk to the greater entity beyond that. And even this is difficult."

"We have gained enough time for Mushroom Rock to rejoin their family," Dvora said. "The fortune hunters are occupied for now. The Alliance hasn't caught up to us yet. We have time. Wasn't that our goal?"

Before the Scattershot-4A, before Peter nibbling on his food in a corner and trying to talk shop with Mawu, before the situation got even more complicated.

Anayāun nodded. "I can tell them to go ahead with the merge."

The merge took forever and was immensely uneventful for all but Anayāun, who retired to her sleeping berth. Dvora kept an eye on Peter, not willing to trust him just yet but, at the very least, willing to give him a chance. It was not like they could offload him just anywhere: he was probably carrying some of the spores himself.

Mawu came up to Dvora. "The System of Eren is a massive groupmind, right?" they began without preamble. "I'm sure they could help Mushroom Rock's family figure out how to interact with us with less frustration. And maybe *your* planetmind could do so too. There are plenty of really big entities in Alliance space."

"We'll need to ask Anayāun about the System," Dvora told the young pilot. "And in fact, the planetmind of Bayit Ledorot wanted to meet you."

"Me?" Their eyes grew wide.

"It's complicated. People can get lonely sometimes." Dvora wasn't exactly sure how to explain that.

"Like Peter?"

Dvora didn't have the heart to tell Mawu about Earth politics, about the gay white supremacists of Mars. She was still wary, and she didn't know how much Mawu understood about the context—maybe more than it seemed. But she nodded. "Yes, like Peter."

Mawu gasped, and at first, Dvora thought she'd said something wrong. But then they yelled, "Small courier vessel inbound on official business from the Alliance?!"

"Oh no," Dvora muttered. Did Zsa manage to reach her contact in Internal Auditing after all? She'd thought that wasn't a good idea.

Zsa was inside Mushroom Rock, who was busy merging with a vast interstellar entity. There was no way any of them could talk to her right now.

Dvora shook her head. Even if the vessel was small, it could still carry more of Scattershot-4A. "We are dust," she mumbled, more to herself than to Mawu. "Dust that scatters."

She had to remind herself of what Chani had told her.

CHAPTER SEVEN:
AN EXPLORATION OF SOLIDARITY

Mawu just didn't understand the three Counterintelligence operatives. They seemed so surprised that their own organization had turned on them and were still scrambling to deal with the "situation," running around in the cramped insides of the ship. Always calling it the *situation* too. *Sitrep! Opsec!* All the snappy abbreviations.

As far as Mawu was concerned, attributing beneficence to a massive political entity never went well. Then again, Mawu themself had run away from one only to find themself in . . . whatever this *situation* was.

Mawu tried to lay it out for themself. Mushroom Rock was re-merging with their family of giant sentient fungi after a prolonged separation. The Interstellar Alliance had tried to get these beings and a band of smugglers to annihilate each other to solve the *situation* on the Periphery with one fell swoop. Mawu had been hired to take the three Counterintelligence operatives to an investigation, but then they'd all been exposed to Mushroom Rock's spores, and suddenly, everyone was after them. Anayāun connected with Mushroom Rock, Dvora tried to seek help from her own sentient planet, and Hlaz-mlan still mourned the loss of her ancestral home to the space fungus on what had been supposed to be a fun visit planetside with some R&R. Then when they tried to prevent the smugglers from blowing up everything, they ended up with one of them on board: young Peter trying to run away from his brother. Meanwhile, they also ran into Zsa from Intelligence, who'd previously been eaten by Mushroom Rock but claimed to still maintain her essential autonomy.

Mawu shook their head. Could they get a break somehow? Now another ship was approaching. Who would want to meet them here, out beyond the Periphery?

"We discussed it! I said no!" Dvora yelled. "Zsa wanted to call Internal Auditing to ask for help *within* the Alliance, and I told her—"

"I can't *reach* her!" Anayāun yelled back. "Whatever Zsa did, we need to wait for Mushroom Rock to finish merging with their family!" *So much for essential autonomy?* Mawu wondered.

Hlaz-mlan made a raspy sound and waved her antennae. "You have to have at least an estimate—"

"I don't have an estimate!"

This was when the transmission arrived.

"Hailing the ship Kheinu of Downstream Clutch, pilot Mawu of Dahond, and presumably a Counterintelligence team on board?" The voice was melodious with a faint, chanting rhythm to it. There was no video stream attached. "This is Piekkat-dali-Nifar, Alliance Treaty Enforcement, Internal Auditing, Counterintelligence Oversight Section. If you would be so kind as to allow me aboard."

These Alliance identifiers from the ship can't be easily reproduced by outsiders . . . so if this person comes aboard, we'll have a hostage at least, Dvora messaged the little group back glumly.

Mawu wasn't sure what was worse: the operatives needlessly trusting the Alliance or not trusting it anymore.

This makes no sense, Anayāun messaged. *If they are truly with Internal Auditing, then they have to know about the spores, so why would they want to come aboard? But if they're misrepresenting who they are, how do they know about our situation?*

There's just one person. We'll overpower them if need be, Hlaz-mlan offered, buzzing.

"Can you speak in actual words? I have no idea what's going on!" Peter was growing agitated he wasn't privy to the messages.

Mawu sighed. "You can come help me connect to the ship. We might need a quick getaway." They didn't need any assistance, but this was as good an idea as any to distract Peter. He looked both anxious and frustrated, his fingers pulling on his loose clothing.

Mawu's whole body sagged with relief as their connection-tentacles merged them closer with Kheinu. Everything was clearer, sharper. Peter was saying something about how he'd never been on a sentient ship with a symbiotic pilot before. Mawu tuned him out.

The courier connected to Kheinu's airlock, and a large sentient passed through. Piekkat-dali-Nifar was shaped like a large wheel and had several sharp, protruding segments sticking out from their flat sides that looked as if building blocks from a child's toy had been pushed into their surface: the same curving L-shape, repeating over and over. Their body was striped with pastel shades of blue and orange. *Complementary colors,* Mawu thought and wondered if the color scheme had a physiological or decorative basis.

The three ex-operatives were waiting for Piekkat-dali-Nifar in Kheinu's main area, sitting in their shape-forming chairs. Dvora was fidgeting, and Hlaz-mlan made a slow grinding sound; only Anayāun seemed calm, but even her heart rate was elevated. She wasn't making her biosystems decrease it, so Mawu assumed she must be preparing for a confrontation.

Piekkat-dali-Nifar has a comforting voice, Mawu thought, despite not quite understanding where said voice was produced. It seemed to issue from the hub of the wheel. Dvora asked the auditor after the most cursory introductions, "Did Intelligence send you?"

Piekkat-dali-Nifar remained in place, but their blue and orange bands spun around on their surface. Mawu wasn't sure if they were wearing clothing; if they were, it probably covered their entire body. "No. Despite what I'd said earlier, I am here on entirely unofficial business. I owed someone a favor, and that someone decided to collect." They referred to themself with gender-unspecified terms, which somehow cheered up Mawu. "I was the only person in a position to be able to come unnoticed."

"Who will guard the guards themselves, hmm?" Dvora said. Mawu was almost certain this had to be one of those quotes from her sacred texts. Or maybe not?

Piekkat-dali-Nifar continued without missing a beat. "You must go to Eren. The System has summoned you. It is time. I only came to observe you and relay this information. You can jump there directly. The Barrier will allow you to pass through."

"I certainly hope so," Anayāun grumbled. Mawu remembered she'd mentioned seeing the Barrier being breached once? By force? Surely not by accident. The System of Eren was one of the most formidable groupminds in Alliance space.

"Will we be safe visiting Eren?" Hlaz-mlan asked. "Will *they* be safe from *us*?"

Mawu wished they'd ask the most pressing question: what would happen when Mushroom Rock's merging with their family finally ran its course?

The tiny courier was already outbound when Mawu felt the shifting, like giant panes sliding past each other. The process concluding—and Mushroom Rock finally sharing all their memories with their family?

Inside Kheinu's main area, the operatives were having a convoluted discussion. Why hadn't the System reached out directly? Should *they* reach out directly? Was the mysterious person who'd been cashing in a favor in fact the System itself? Otherwise, how could the System of Eren have favors owed to them in Internal Auditing? Why did the System need a physical observation? Why not contact Anayāun then, her being an Ereni citizen . . . ?

Sadness gripped Mawu for a moment. They'd been on the way to Ereni citizenship themself, but with all this disruption, who knew when that would happen. If it would ever happen. Even though they had the Ereni cognotype, even though they'd already prepared so much . . .

The courier ship hovered near Mushroom Rock's family. Observing, as they'd claimed. Mawu held their breath, but the fungal sentiences did not lash out. Mawu sent the video stream to the operatives.

"They wanted to see us in physicality," Dvora said. "I can't claim to understand the System's motives, but right now, we need every ally we can get."

Anayāun sighed—and Mawu wasn't sure if in frustration or in relief. "Time to go home."

Mawu wished deep within their bones that they could feel the same. But Eren wasn't their home yet.

Mushroom Rock's family let them all go. They calmly stated that they'd still remain connected to Anayāun, even through such a vast distance, and they were certain the ex-operatives would all be coming back. They did not raise the issue of Scattershot-4A again. They promised not to approach the smugglers again, and the ex-operatives were sure that the smugglers wouldn't try recontacting Mushroom Rock's family either. Their leader Minather—Peter's brother—agreed to the uneasy détente. That left the Alliance itself to be sorted out.

"Are you cold?" Peter spoke up, in range of Mawu's own ears.

No, why? Mawu responded through the ship.

"You've been shivering."

Mawu didn't know how to put it into words. They wanted to go back to Eren and its narrow streets and cramped buildings, a mining outpost turned city-planetoid; they'd come to know so many of the nooks and crannies already. But they were always, always afraid the System would judge them—and deem them unworthy. The Ereni never lied, and they were picky too. Mawu had lived through so much rejection on their planet of origin, they weren't sure they could manage another round of it in the Alliance.

Mawu had been to Eren enough times that they could manage the jump even without any elaborate aiming assistance. They were still apprehensive. Could they trust the messenger, or would they end up jumping face-first into the Barrier?

Mushroom Rock's family drew back to keep their distance, with an undulating motion that made Mawu question their own grasp on physics. It was as if the world itself had moved.

Time to focus on the jump.

At the moment Mawu'd initiated the cascade, the System of Eren reached out to them from where previously had only been silence, an absence, a void.

Like a hand grasping their arm and pulling, pulling—

Mawu was still woozy from the jump, but they could feel the System undergirding their thought processes, supporting their mind.

Mawu was worried and apprehensive and fearful and, yes, relieved. There was no pulse of disapproval, just the usual settling in, their mind gently locking into a larger pattern.

Anayāun noticed as the two of them were cycling through the small airlock. "Stop worrying about your immigration process," she said, looking straight ahead. "If we get through this alive, it will be fine. If we don't, it will be pointless to worry."

"I . . . don't know," Mawu muttered, getting used to their speech not looping through Kheinu. "Why is the System letting us in? Do you think the spores aren't a danger?"

"The System can potentially control everything Erenside down to a molecular level," Anayāun said. "It's just a question of priorities in energy expenditure."

Mawu didn't want to think of how much was involved in having them here, allowing them in. They stepped outside. The screening personnel were efficient, fast, entirely unlike the Alliance decon team they'd met earlier. The mental screening was uneventful, even though Mawu had been preparing for the worst, holding their breath remembering screenings from their birth planet. They ran away to the Alliance for a reason.

Most of the others were already waiting on the other side. Anayāun was taking the longest—unsurprising for a member of Ereni Security herself, Mawu thought.

Peter attached himself to Mawu like a puppy, eager and clueless in equal measure. "You have to explain about this," he said. "You're from here."

"I'm not from here," Mawu shifted on their feet uncomfortably. "I'm on my trial year after my asylum request was granted. I'm, uh, not a citizen, um . . ."

"Well, you'll be one soon." Peter seemed uncomfortably sure. "Please explain. Operative Anayāun, she is like, a police officer here, right? Delegated to Alliance Counterintelligence?"

"It doesn't work like that." Mawu was at a loss. Why were *they* expected to explain this?

"I don't get it. How is there crime if the System knows people's thoughts?"

"There is very little crime." Why was Anayāun taking so long? Mawu looked around anxiously. Dvora was chatting with Hlaz-mlan, both of them seeming entirely at ease. "And some of it gets, uh, stopped as it is being committed."

Peter's eyes widened. "What do you mean?"

"Try to hurt me?" Mawu blinked. "I mean, seriously."

Peter chuckled sharply and moved so fast that Mawu found their motions impossible to track. A blade flicking open, slashing—Mawu ducked—

The blade fell to the ground. Peter stared at his fingers, rubbed his wrist experimentally. Bent to pick up the butterfly knife. "I was wondering why they'd let me pass through with a knife on me," he said slowly with forced evenness.

The System pinged Mawu whether they had a need for assistance. Mawu shooed the query away.

Peter made slashing motions with the knife, unimpeded. "Hmm. It only stops me if I want to hurt you."

"Not *it*, *they*," Mawu said. "You shouldn't call a groupmind an *it*."

Peter flicked the knife closed and pocketed it. He furrowed his brow. "I'm honestly uncomfortable with—"

"Is there something wrong?" Anayāun came up to them.

Peter shook his head vehemently, the purple highlights in his straight brown hair glinting in the low light. "I shouldn't have trusted you people as far as I could throw you."

Was this some idiom from his planet translated to Alliance Common? Mawu wasn't sure.

He went on. "This is how you get by without policing, without coercion. No privacy. No free will."

Mawu blinked, unsure how to respond. "You mean you wish someone could stab you against your will?"

"Well, who decides? Who decides what's appropriate and—"

"Well, I decide! I decide what I want to be done to me—"

Anayāun cleared her throat. "I could in principle pry the two of you apart, stop you from yelling so loud my teeth hurt, but that would prove your point." She chuckled. "I have to let Mushroom Rock and their whole family talk to the System now. At length. The rest of you are free to go . . . though I have a task for you."

Both Mawu and Peter fell silent. Hlaz-mlan and Dvora came up to them.

Anayāun grinned. "Mushroom Rock's family wants to see life in the Alliance from up close. They can divide their attention—especially since Zsa is helping them. She's sufficiently independent, even incorporated into them as she is. Go, show them around."

Everyone stood silent, stunned into confusion.

"I hate to say this, but the last time we had some R&R, it did not exactly go as planned," Dvora finally said.

Anayāun grimaced. "For five seconds, we won't have to run for our lives. Use it for what it's worth. If the Alliance wanted to get us here, they'd have to bulldoze through the whole of Eren first."

"The advantages of totalitarianism," Peter snapped.

"The advantages of what now?!" Mawu was increasingly frustrated with him. First, his weirdly fetishizing comments about being a pilot, then this—

—*you listen to me for a moment?!*

Zsa? In their mind?

Finally. Listen. Mushroom Rock's family would like to be embodied.

Mawu closed their eyes to focus. It didn't help. Zsa went on but didn't make more sense to Mawu.

Now that I've been incorporated into the wider family and they in turn have gained some insight into someone with my cognotype and body template—

Mawu made some vague hand gesture to indicate to the others that they were occupied with a conversation. Peter groaned at them and rolled his eyes. Mawu ignored him and turned back their attention to Zsa. *Didn't we agree that connecting to Mushroom Rock would be dangerous to me?*

Yes, which is why I'm going to be embodied, and they'll only get things filtered through me.

Hold on, I haven't actually let you use my body yet either.

I've been trying to ask, but you just haven't been paying attention! What can I do?

It was hard to hold back the thoughts—so hard as to be ultimately unsuccessful. *Sorry, I was busy explaining to someone that not wanting to be assaulted is not totalitarianism—*

I have no idea where you're going with that, but I'd be happy to help!

Mawu sighed. Peter was annoying. Zsa was annoying in a different way. The two of them might argue that out while Mawu themself could . . . maybe sleep? Take a back seat in their own body for a while.

Mawu wandered off to sit on top of a crate. *Look, Zsa, I need to think this over.*

To her credit, she understood and withdrew.

Kheinu was amused. *You are practiced at sharing your mind with me. You should be all right if you wanted to give it a try.*

I kind of wanted you to discourage me. And you *don't want to walk around Erenside in my body.*

The amusement rolled over Mawu like waves. *I might be inclined to try,* Kheinu said.

You don't have the right body templates. You'd fall on your face. My face. Actually, that sounded like fun—teaching Kheinu how to be in a human body. Not just experience the environment through their senses but be *in* the body. Previously, the ship hadn't been interested, but Mawu knew through the network of pearls that in principle this was possible, though done relatively infrequently. It was uncomfortable if not practiced overmuch, and generally, both ship and pilot were too busy flying from place to place to have a great deal of time left over.

I'm worried that Zsa would do something nonsensical, Mawu finally hit upon what unsettled them the most. *With you, I'm not worried.*

You can co-front. Or draw up a list of things you'd rather she not do. Or . . . there are many solutions, Kheinu explained what both of them knew already. Still, it sometimes helped to see the options laid out one by one. *But if you don't want to do it, you can just say no.*

It might be fun though. And she could deal with Peter. What's his deal anyway? Zsa was giggly, blurty, scarily insightful, and had breathtaking situational awareness. Peter would underestimate her and fall flat on his face. Metaphorically speaking.

Mawu figured this was not the best reason to let someone in your body, but it was good as any. And if it would help Mushroom Rock have a favorable picture of life in the Alliance, so much the better. Maybe Mawu just wanted to feel some semblance of control while the vast groupminds were sorting out whatever needed to be sorted out between themselves. Mawu always felt small, but this time they somehow felt even smaller. Even more helpless.

They screwed their eyes up even tighter and thought of Zsa. *If the System allows this, I'm game.*

Mawu rubbed their face. The connection was somewhat asymmetrical; they would get Zsa's surface thoughts but nothing beyond that. Then again, that was probably for the better. Zsa was an Intelligence officer, and the less Mawu knew of those matters, the better, they decided.

Good decision, Zsa snorted.

After saying goodbye to Anayāun, they started to walk down a narrow loading ramp that never seemed to end: Dvora chatting with Hlaz-mlan right behind her, Peter tagging along after Mawu with a mixture of puppylike eagerness and great frustration.

"I've never been here before," he said. "They wouldn't have let me in. Not even as a tourist, I'm sure."

"Because of the war with your planet?" Mawu asked. They vaguely remembered him mentioning something like that, back on the ship—his planet declaring war on the Alliance and then surrendering unconditionally less than a day later? Mawu wasn't sure. They needed to find a calm, quiet spot where they could switch with Zsa. Zsa was savvy about politics.

"No, not really," Peter coughed. "Not because of that."

It's because he's a criminal, you know, Zsa said.

Space was always at a premium on Eren, but their room in a building near the docks was even smaller than Mawu'd expected. One room with four sleeping berths, almost like on a spaceship. Mawu told everyone that they'd need to deal with the *situation* with Zsa, and this was the magic word. The two operatives immediately nodded yes, and even Peter seemed cowed.

Mawu slunk into a berth and closed their eyes. They tried to think of how it'd worked with Kheinu the first time, but that had been very different, together with the bodily changes toward a jump pilot template. They sighed. They knew that sometimes the operatives formed a groupmind in various configurations, but Mawu themself hadn't been privy to that. No basis for comparison, they concluded. Maybe just relax and let things happen as they might. Focus on Zsa and draw back from body awareness slightly—

Zsa rushed forward, her mind the impression of a chattering brook. *Your limbs are very short. You are just very short altogether. I don't know, but for some reason I thought you'd be taller, even though I've met you before. I don't know. But this is cool, your body is nice. You're not very feminine though.*

Why am I supposed to be feminine? I'm intersex, and I haven't even decided about my gender yet. This is supposed to be a fun outing and not an exercise in misgendering. Mawu didn't want to think the second half *at* Zsa, but it came out that way regardless.

Sorry, I didn't mean it that way. It's just that I'm feminine, and I'm not really experienced with being in a different body. Like . . .

Welcome to the dysphoria club, I guess? Except I don't really have much dysphoria. I'm just trans because I don't like my birth assignment. But I don't like other options either. Mawu babbled. *We both talk a lot, I guess?*

Zsa felt tense in the body. Mawu tried to help her relax into it but wasn't sure how best to go about that. They were getting off on the wrong foot with this conversation.

Zsa tried to sit up. It worked on the second try, suspiciously fast. Mawu wondered, had she practiced this with other people before? Hadn't she just said she wasn't used to being in a different body? Did Intelligence clone people or something? Mawu drew up conspiracy scenarios. Maybe there were fifty of Zsa on various planets.

"I didn't even bang my head," Zsa said out loud. "But that's because you're so short."

Mawu winced.

I'm sorry. It's just weird. But I can talk to you mind-to-mind instead of out loud. It satisfies the urge. And don't worry, I know you're concerned, but I won't do anything you wouldn't want me to, all right? You can just kick me out anytime if I'm too annoying.

This was reassuring coming from Zsa at least.

"I want to eat before we go on an adventure," Zsa said, struggling to her newfound feet. Dvora helped her out of the berth.

Eating sounded good for Mawu. The connection needed plenty of energy to keep up anyway. They were dubious about the *adventure* part though.

Dvora took a long look at Zsa. "I don't know if *Mawu* would like to have an adventure."

"Just a small, moderate adventure," Zsa said. "Teeny tiny. We could see the sights. What are the sights?"

Um, there is the War of Independence Memorial, Mawu thought, *but that's more unsettling than exciting, I guess?* Eren wasn't much of a tourist destination.

What would you do? If you were back here on your own? Zsa asked.

Mawu felt put on the spot. *I don't know. Go to the pilots' lounge. I . . .* All their friends were off Eren at this point. *I'd message my friends, I guess, see if I could get word to them that I was all right. But Anayāun thought that was a bad idea, so I'm staying quiet for now.*

Mawu didn't want to explain about their friends, and mercifully, Zsa didn't push.

All right, so this is what we're going to do. Zsa was so loud in Mawu's head that the young pilot wished they could turn down the volume. *We'll go to the pilots' lounge. We'll grab a bite and hang out. Then Peter will try to steal some kind of crap to sell on the Periphery later. We'll get in a fight. The fight will go absolutely nowhere because this is some surreal panopticon of a country, as Peter would have it. Then we'll do drugs and chase each other screaming and crying through the five major tourist sites in the middle of the night while your ship will regret the day they chose you as their symbiotic partner. Deal?*

You're kidding. Mawu wished they had a cognotype that could deal better with sarcasm and irony.

Of course I'm kidding! Though not about Peter. Look. He's going to get into trouble.

Peter looked at the buildings as if trying to estimate their monetary value, and he also sized up every single passerby.

Look, kid. He's going to get into trouble, and we're going to let him. I enjoy myself, and Mushroom Rock and company get an extremely authentic demonstration of life in the Alliance while you . . .

While I basically cower in fear of what's going to go wrong next, Mawu finished the sentence. They were getting the hang of Zsa's thoughts, their rhythm.

Sounds like an extremely elaborate plan! Zsa giggled.

What could possibly go wrong, with the System having an eye on everything? Mawu tried to calm their tattered nerves. This was an adventure after all.

They did begin at the pilots' lounge. Mawu wasn't overly interested in conversation, and neither were most of the Ereni in general, but the dancing was always good, any time of the day. Pilot music was diverse in instrumentation and style but rather narrow on themes. Zsa felt a need to comment, like on anything else.

Go fast! Make magical things happen! Tear the world in half and scream, and

can I please have a tiny horse. I get it. It's highly relatable in fact. I love charmingly
weird subcultures like this.

Mawu thought that was annoyingly dismissive. Wasn't Alliance Intelligence
its own weird, exoticizable subculture? Mawu figured it probably was.

While Zsa was enjoying the music—if that was indeed the right word—Peter
pocketed at least three small decorations and did his hardest to provoke two
off-duty pilots to a fistfight by commenting loudly on the board game they
were playing in a corner. Mawu was dismayed that Zsa had been right. He
wasn't with the smugglers only because his brother dragged him into it; he was
with them because he was ultimately comfortable with trouble. Meanwhile, the
System did absolutely nothing.

"Through thunder and flames and fire and thunder and fire and lightning!"
a singer wailed and screeched. Newfound Perplexity wasn't one of Mawu's
favorite bands, despite the almost perfect name.

Finally, one of the pilots stood, tearing his eyes away from his game with
noticeable difficulty. He was tall, stocky, muscles filling out his dark-blue pilot's
robes. He wore a headscarf with a stylized pattern of flames—or tree leaves?
Mawu wasn't sure. He had a set of five matching, leaf-shaped earrings in each
ear. The patterns also continued on his skin in bright orange and yellow on
pink. The shapes bunched up as he grimaced. His face seemed just as muscular
as the rest of his body.

"I'll tell you what you need," the pilot started in a tone that would usually
suggest something like, "A smack on the head," as a follow-up.

Peter took a step back. The pilot glared at him.

"Through nights of starlight and acceleration and the force that grips your
solar plexus!" the song went on, less successful with each line. Mawu wished for
some Luminosity or maybe one of the newer local bands.

Zsa tensed and then relaxed her muscles—Mawu's muscles—preparing for
battle. Time perceptibly slowed. How did Zsa do that?

"I'll tell you what you need," the pilot repeated, giant chasms of microseconds
between each word.

Peter took a step forward.

Zsa grabbed a hold of Mawu's entire nervous system, or what felt like it,
and drew on their power, like squeezing juice out of an orange. Mawu/Zsa
shuddered.

"You need an arts project," the pilot said.

"What?" Peter almost squealed.

The pilot laughed, the tension breaking. "Look at you, all bursting with the need to do something, right now, and nothing to do. An arts project, I'm telling you."

Mawu felt Zsa's tinge of annoyance. More than a tinge.

"I'll challenge you if that'll help your competitive spirit," the man laughed. "One day-cycle to produce a fabulous work of art. The bunch of you, versus me. Then a round of public voting."

Zsa stepped forward, shoving Peter aside, brimming with power. "It's a deal."

"A deal all right. Now, go get all that grounded off"—the man paused only slightly to check their profile—"while you're a guest in the kid's head, or the two of you good folk will explode."

"You felt put on the spot, did you, Zsa?" Peter laughed with a sense of release palpable even to Mawu.

"Did *you*?" Zsa didn't even turn back to look at him as she trundled along the narrow street that passed for a main thoroughfare Erenside. "You might as well build all the knickknacks you swiped into our world-class masterpiece," she snapped.

"It's not theft if it's public property," Peter grunted at her.

"Evidently the System feels the same way," Zsa chuckled drily. "What masterpiece of larceny do you have in mind? Break into the Council Building and steal the crown jewels? See what happens then?"

Eren is a council republic, not a monarchy, Mawu protested. No one paid attention. *Um, this is a strange way of introducing someone to life in the Alliance.*

Mawu only hoped Zsa would ground off all the excess māwal at some point.

Zsa almost fried a scrawny tree in a tiny public park before Mawu could explain that there were specific places on Eren where one could let go of their excess and make sure it all went into the planetary networks. Then they all sat on one of the two benches facing the tree, discussing the supposed art project.

"I want it to be themed after the police state concept," Peter said. "Make the citizens think. The kid could also use some thinking."

I'm not a citizen yet.

"Mawu is saying they're not a citizen yet," Zsa dutifully relayed. *Also not a kid.* Zsa repeated that too: "Also not a kid."

"All the better to do some thinking right now," Peter nodded. "Second thoughts?"

Mawu was ready to tell them off: where else could they go? But there were plenty of places in the Alliance who would not hesitate for an instant to take a powerful māwalēni. If all else failed, they could go to Alliance Central, join Treaty Enforcement . . . no. Never.

Hey, it's not so bad, Zsa thought at them. Then with bitterness, *That was my ticket out.*

"So any ideas what would grab the hearts and the minds of the locals?" Peter grinned, oblivious.

"Maybe stop referring to them as 'the locals' first," Zsa grimaced, faster than Mawu could interject.

There was something about how Peter immediately positioned himself above everyone that grated on Mawu. But if nothing else, Zsa did at least take their side.

"Eyes! Eyes everywhere! The all-seeing eye!" Peter gestured broadly, almost dropping the can of vaguely alcoholic fermented drink he'd condescended to trying after a rant on how totalitarian states should always have artisanal liquor. The drink came out of a fabber.

Mawu had no idea what he was talking about. Again.

"The kid has no idea what you're talking about," Zsa said. "That won't work."

Mawu was so confused that they could even overlook the mention of *kid*. How did *Zsa* understand the reference? Did these two people come from the same planet? That would explain so much. Mawu was so busy cramming for Eren that their knowledge about the rest of the Alliance was rather nebulous. Was Peter and Zsa's home a planet with a strong Isolationist movement, like where they themself had come from? Mawu had no idea about, what was it, Earth?

"So what comes to your mind about surveillance?" Peter leaned forward. "Eh, Mawu?"

Um, awareness? I mean, it doesn't really work the same . . . Mawu did the mental equivalent of flailing. *I don't know how to explain.*

Allow me. Of course, Zsa was the expert. "This is not only a surveillance situation but also a *sousveillance* situation. Everyone observes everyone else. Panveillance?" She laughed. "Sure, you have the power differential between an individual and the state. But you also have a population where most everyone has some form of telepathic awareness."

Mawu thought this wasn't very representative of the Alliance. Mushroom Rock & Family would get a rather skewed notion of "life in the Alliance" by visiting Eren.

We think a lot about solidarity, they offered. *I guess.*

The whole team had assembled in their living quarters—with the exception of Anayāun, still busy with the negotiations.

"What have you gotten yourselves into? Well then, let's see." Hlaz-mlan read the plan, softly and slowly chirping to herself.

"*Panveillance: An Exploration of Solidarity.* Sounds good enough if somewhat academic. Mmm." She read on, going through the announcement that Zsa wrote. "So you're expecting everyone to offer you a 'found object,' which need not be physical, which you will then assemble into an . . . assemblage? This seems low-effort."

"We can't really ask people to do something complicated," Zsa pointed out. "It'd be unfair, and we only have a day."

"And presumably, you'd like to get some sleep at some point," Dovber—again Dovber—nodded.

"Sleep is optional," Peter grinned.

"Why would people give you these objects? As an expression of solidarity . . . I see." Hlaz-mlan made a little wave with her antennae. Mawu knew this meant that she felt dubious about something at best.

"Peter just wants free stuff," Zsa chuckled. "One way or another. And Mushroom Rock's family would be entertained by the variety, so I'm good."

"This will either bring you nothing or a whole mountain," Dovber said, smoothing down his beard. "It all depends on your marketing scheme."

"Good!" Zsa jumped up, almost banging her head into a low-hanging shelving unit. "I am *great* at psyops!"

Mawu was frustrated. Zsa was taking all of this so lightly. Of course, they reminded themself, Zsa had probably been engineered to take everything lightly. This was a terrifying thought. But maybe it was all right to take art lightly. It could not be as disruptive as an Intelligence operation, could it?

Zsa/Mawu walked across Council Square, trailing tiny, plastic sea life, floating in the air in their wake. The sea life was all printed from stylish, low-polygon models Peter found after spending all too much time browsing free-to-use templates in the fabber's directory. They looked vintage and charming. The gravity countermanding units were trickier to fit inside the small animals and plants, but Dovber proved handy. Colorful ribbons hung from the different little shapes bobbing in the air, tying some of the shapes together.

Passersby stopped to share, poked at the creatures—and received the carefully crafted message informing them about the project.

"I'd say this expresses our chosen values of cuteness, striking visuals, and blatant begging," Zsa said. "Now, we wait."

"There is surprisingly little, um, erotic content," Dovber said, browsing through the results. They were all sitting on a giant pipe in one of the many industrial areas.

"They don't trust us with that," Hlaz-mlan noted mildly.

In front of Dovber sat a giant, open crate, one of three fabricated to hold the pieces of the assemblage, whatever that might be.

"It's like a treasure chest," Peter grinned, all too eager for Mawu's tastes.

"There is a lengthy essay in the pile about tourists trying to beg their way through the Alliance," Dovber remarked. "It's rather scathing. And I'm still not sure how you want to explore *solidarity* with all this. Greed, maybe . . ."

"Don't use the glue gun," Peter yelled from the top of the scaffolding he'd erected. Dovber was fussing with the objects at ground level. "Everything needs to be detachable!"

To make sure passersby can investigate them? Mawu wondered.

No, to make sure he can take stuff with him to sell later, Zsa responded.

A small crowd was gathering. People came up to Dovber and handed him objects. There was something that looked like a tablecloth (Mawu realized they'd never seen a tablecloth actually being *used* on Eren), some sports equipment, something large and soft. A pillow?

Dovber chuckled. "It's like building a sukkah."

Mawu didn't get the reference, but Zsa did. "You also have that thing that you wave around? I always wondered what that was. There were those dudes standing on the corner around the synagogue, *Are you Jewish? Are you Jewish?* I'm not Jewish, so I never figured it out."

Dovber chuckled and sighed softly. "Lubavitchers. I'm surprised you didn't tell them you were Jewish."

"I know you make assumptions about my trustworthiness based on my line of work, but I'd rather you desisted from that." Zsa said maybe a trifle too grumpily.

At this exact moment, Hlaz-mlan slipped on the scaffolding, her many legs scissoring. Zsa acted so fast Mawu could not follow, even being as she was in their own body. Zsa steadied Hlaz-mlan with a fast mental push, shoved Dovber aside, and jumped right below Hlaz-mlan with arms outstretched.

Mawu's arms and legs were of a different length than what Zsa was used to, even though she'd acclimated to Mawu's body with alarming rapidity. Zsa/Mawu crashed into the scaffolding, falling down, and Mawu expected Hlaz-mlan to crush them from above any moment, but it did not happen.

Accidents were rare on Eren.

Hlaz-mlan softly floated down to the ground, the System catching her. Zsa was trying to stand, legs shaking.

The pilot, their challenger, came up to them. "I heard you were taking submissions for your project," he said, grinning. The effect wasn't all that different from his previous frown. He handed Dovber a large, greenish-yellowish cocoonlike shape with a loop hanging from it. Dovber thanked him, only slightly stunned, and hung it on the scaffolding. The man vanished as abruptly as he'd arrived, and other people with other gifts came to take his place.

"Do you think this is sabotage?" Peter yelled down.

"We sabotage ourselves quite effectively, thank you," Hlaz-mlan buzzed. "This arts business is not for me. I'll enjoy the results of your labor."

Labor it was, well into the night. Mawu had to convince Zsa, who had to convince Peter, that it was genuinely time to stop. He clambered down from the third giant, conical frame. "Is it a cornucopia or a Christmas tree? You tell me," he nodded his chin at Zsa.

"It's too askew to be either," Zsa said.

"Ooo, what's this? And this?" Peter was eager to sample the objects at ground level. "This says it's a drink," he poked at an opaque, iridescently glowing flask. "I'd say it's time for a drink."

"It can hardly be a poison. No one would risk that in this police state, mmm?" Zsa said out loud, then thought at Mawu. *Watch.*

Peter drank.

Whatever it was, it took effect slowly. Peter licked his lips. "Tastes like bananas. Or maybe beef. Let's take a look at a few more of these."

He popped open something that looked like an oversize raspberry.

A giant, sparkling flower jumped out and began to bounce.

Peter tried to catch it, but the flower started multiplying. Each time Peter tried to make a lunge at it, it split into two, emitting a puff of what looked like confetti. At first, Mawu thought they'd cover him entirely, but then the flowers arranged themselves into a ball-like composition and made a run for a side alley, expanding in size with each bounce. Peter gave chase. Zsa gave chase. Mawu watched, helpless and only somewhat horrified.

"Can you stop," Zsa yelled at him. "Stop chasing it! It can't keep on duplicating forever!" She swore.

Limiting factors! Mawu yelled.

"Have you heard of limiting factors?! What kind of occultist are you?!" Zsa shouted after Peter. "It will run out of whatever fuels it, and it will be ALL DONE!"

"I must stop the invasion!" Peter screamed.

The three of them, in two bodies, sprinted along the street, Peter chasing a giant ball of sparkling, dancing, and . . . *singing* flowers, and Zsa chasing Peter. Was this an effect of the drink, or was he just unable to let go of anything potentially expensive in his possession?

Close your eyes, Mawu thought at Zsa in desperation.

What?

Close your eyes, or it will be a lot harder!

To Zsa's credit, she did. Without slowing down.

Then, a discontinuity, and space flipped around—

Mawu jumped in front of the flowers. The giant ball steamrolled them with softness, pushed them off their feet and came to a halt. Zsa reoriented faster than Mawu did, snapped an arm out to the side, and tripped the fast-approaching Peter.

They lay in a gasping, wheezing pile amid myriad iridescent flowers.

Peter muttered something entirely incoherent. Mawu scrambled to their feet, Zsa's hold on their mind momentarily loosening. Mawu mentally grabbed her and shoved her back at the front of their mind. The two of them stared at the High Council Building.

Peter blinked too. "We weren't supposed to be this close to here. This is strange."

"Hey, the kid can teleport," Zsa shrugged. "Spacetime is weird."

Weren't we supposed to chase each other screaming and crying across the five major tourist sites while being high or something? Mawu asked.

Believe me, I didn't plan for this, Zsa said.

The flowers attached themselves to their clothing. They made half-hearted attempts to pry them off, and then, they trundled back to Dovber, Hlaz-mlan, and the fabulous work of art.

Can you please keep the flowers? Mawu asked Zsa. *I think they're awesome.*

Sure, I can be a walking Christmas tree for you, kid.

Whatever that was, Mawu figured that it had to be bad.

"It is time to open the exhibit for public viewing," Dovber said to the audience that seemed to be increasing by the minute, despite the early morning hours.

Mawu was still anxious about the pilot-artist Wowanā's cocoon. They'd looked him up while Zsa slept, and he was apparently famous. Surely, famous-on-Eren kind of famous, which wasn't famous-in-the-Alliance kind of famous or even famous-on-Central kind of famous, but it had to count for something.

He wouldn't try to prank them, would he? Mawu reminded themself that while misdirection was sort of an Ereni virtue, people scoffed at yiniyaisun, which could be best translated to Alliance Common as . . . mean-spiritedness? Surely, the multiplying flowers, the strange drink, the herd of wasps, and the object that combined a variety of smells until they were all too *smelly* . . . were all meant in a kind spirit too. People had unusual interests.

Their newfound artist-rival was standing to the side, his mind well-warded—not that Mawu was inclined to poke. He had something on a floater pallet that looked like a small sculpture covered with . . . a tablecloth, for all that was worth. He was dressed in a much more flamboyant overcoat than the pilot's robes he wore the day before and a silken garment under that. The fiery pattern remained the same.

He nodded affably to Dovber to go first. Anayāun had taken a break from the negotiations and was now standing next to Zsa/Mawu, curious but reserved. Mawu had no doubts that Mushroom Rock and their family were also following the proceedings, now from multiple vantage points.

Dovber was giving the audience a hard sell of *Panveillance: An Exploration of Solidarity* with Peter illustrating his points. Mawu felt that a bunch of people probably only donated to the cause of art because they felt sorry for the embarrassing foreigners. But if it worked? Mawu was uneasy about the whole matter. Still, some people were already getting in line to take a closer look. Out of curiosity—or pity perhaps? How could someone compete with a professional artist who understood all the fine details of social context? How could someone come in from outside and think they could—do what?

When it was Wowanā's turn, he snapped his fingers, and the cocoon opened with gleaming light. Crystalline tendrils snaked out of it, embracing the scaffolding, running up and down and twining around the objects, holding them gently in place.

The result looked like some kind of ideal type of their original art, infinitely more glorious than they could have ever achieved. The effect took Mawu's breath away.

The crowd cheered, finger-waved, applauded, jumped up and down. Zsa clapped vigorously.

Anayāun chuckled. "I had no idea you had it in you," she said.

"Um, this was all the Ereni dude," Zsa said.

"Sure, but . . . you can see that"—Anayāun waved at the installation—"this was all inside your work. It had the potential. He just actualized it."

Mawu thought back on art class in school, back in the day before they had to go to the Navy academy—before they ran away to the Alliance. At one time, they were struggling mightily with watercolors. The two heads of cabbage and one pepper that they were trying to paint just didn't come out right. The painting was dull, lopsided, lifeless. Their art teacher stepped next to them and added just a few well-chosen strokes. Effortlessly. It was clear to Mawu that those had been the exact strokes that had been needed—even though they themself could not have placed them there. But they were learning.

Even now.

Wowanā quieted the crowd and made a sweeping bow, his many earrings clicking against each other unexpectedly loudly in the newfound silence. "Dear fellow sentients, my small contribution to the exploration of solidarity."

Another round of cheers.

"He beat us at our own game," Peter whisper-hissed.

"Well, he expressed solidarity with us struggling artists," Zsa said. "It's only fair. I'll take it in good spirits."

The voting went overwhelmingly in Wowanā's favor.

He walked up to them and spread his arms.

"I could not have done it without you," he said, "and that is as strictly interpretable as it gets."

But what is under the tablecloth? Mawu asked and Zsa repeated.

"This?" He smiled. "A misdirection." He unveiled the object with one smooth motion. "I jest. I made you a gift—a prize if you will. Something to take home."

It was around this point that Peter realized that the objects wouldn't be coming off the gigantic crystalline structure. He moaned.

The gift was highly abstract, multicolored, three-dimensional, and to Mawu's eyes, it clearly depicted Mushroom Rock even as it looked nothing alike.

"It's titled *Something You Hold Dear*," Wowanā explained.

We do? We do, Mawu realized.

There was some kind of yank, something pulling and snapping. Mawu's connection to Zsa wavered and vanished. Mawu reached out to Kheinu, but the ship seemed to be unaffected and still well within reach.

Anayāun held up a hand. "We have a problem here. Our friends very much like what they see. They like it so much, they want to eat it."

Dovber gasped. "What do you mean?"

"An expression of solidarity." Anayāun waved at the sculpture in exasperation. "This *expression* ate everything, consumed and incorporated the other art. Mushroom Rock's family have decided that by analogy, they could also eat everything. 'It won't diminish the existence of anything, it will only add to it,' they said."

"Zsa might have something to say about that," Mawu spoke up.

"The entire Alliance might have something to say about that," Anayāun groaned. "Mushroom Rock can't just go on and consume everything."

Wowanā said, "I don't understand, but I'm listening. I get the impression I set something larger in motion."

The System is opposed to being eaten, the System said, words resonating clearly in everyone's minds. An overwhelming, unquestionable presence.

The System, they've already eaten everything, Mawu thought. *They don't want a rival? Maybe Peter was right after all.*

Zsa didn't respond.

What am I getting myself into? Mawu hugged themself. *Ereni citizenship . . .*

Then a realization. *This is like Scattershot-4A. Mutually assured destruction? If not that, a balance of power.*

Mawu wasn't sure who would win in a direct confrontation. The System of Eren was known throughout the Alliance and generally mentioned with a respect mixed with dread. Awe? Whereas Mushroom Rock's family was an unknown with unknown potential.

Why did so many of these vast beings function on the premise of incorporation? Dovber's planet, the System of Eren . . . Mushroom Rock's family? *That is one way to become vast,* Mawu thought.

"The System hasn't consumed *everything,*" Mawu said out loud. "Neither has Dovber's planet. Maybe they can teach this restraint to Mushroom Rock's family. And then, um, not everything in the Alliance gets eaten? Most things in the Alliance don't get eaten?"

Anayāun crossed her arms. "I agree. Haven't we just negotiated conditions and processes of linking and information sharing for a whole day? Could we not throw that away just because someone got greedy all of a sudden?" A faint shudder ran through her, Mawu noticed. "There are plenty of large groupminds in Alliance space, existing in a balance. Surely more can be added, details can be worked out." She frowned. "It's all *I've* been doing anyway."

"What will the Alliance *say* though?" Hlaz-mlan said. "Eren can't negotiate all this behind their back."

"The Alliance was ready to commit mass murder," Anayāun replied.

For the benefit of all sentience, as they say, Zsa snarked, and Mawu was so relieved at her reappearance that their knees sagged.

"Eren will certainly pursue this through available official channels," Anayāun said. "Once the System finally agrees on all the details with Mushroom Rock's family, they can propose the solution to the Alliance."

Dovber sighed. "We might not like the answer . . ." He turned to Wowanā, who gently nudged the floating pallet toward him. "As for now, I am keeping the art."

CHAPTER EIGHT: A FORM OF COUNTERSELECTION

ONE NIGHT'S SLEEP." ANAYĀUN HAD MADE SURE TO REQUEST THIS during the negotiations, and she got her wish. In the morning, she felt incomprehensibly relieved. The rest of the team was off causing chaos on Eren, and she'd had absolutely no desire to participate. Before sleeping, she had been at the point where everything grated on her nerves, as if her fingers and toes were each bent backward, one by one.

Her limbs ached. She was worried this was a consequence of having merged with Mushroom Rock, but at least, the pain wasn't getting any worse. She'd see a doctor once this was over.

Now that they were all back on Eren, she could almost start believing it would one day be over. Unfortunately, the negotiations offered less of that hope.

Anayāun got herself presentable with only moderate difficulty and dragged herself back to the meeting hall. The High Council meeting hall. She'd never before presented her case before the Ereni leadership. She was already familiar with the councilors and the other attendees, like the head of Ereni Security, Commander Morosewi. But the entire situation was disconcerting.

She sat across from a young, stocky, brown-skinned woman who spoke for the System and wore the traditional blue robes. *We are both here on behalf of a larger being,* Anayāun thought, and that gave her a tiny bit of solace. The woman seemed as tired as her and shuddered occasionally.

The System could speak to all attendees directly, but their attendance via proxy was a longtime custom. Their proxy rose to speak.

"To circle back to yesterday's discussion, we are glad to offer both sanctuary and supervision to the being known as Mushroom Rock and their family." She put an odd emphasis on *supervision*, and Anayāun wasn't sure she liked that. It played into preconceptions about the way Eren was organized.

One look at the three Alliance representatives and she realized that the System was performing for them. They all nodded in a grim but brisk manner, almost entirely in unison, navy-blue cloaks rustling. Their leader was a broad-shouldered, light-skinned man with hair a glossy shade of teal, tied back in a ponytail. He rose to speak.

"We appreciate your offer, but we cannot see this situation as anything other than a serious breach of Alliance security." Anayāun was certain he'd uttered this exact sentence before.

The Alliance representatives all seemed resentful that she and her fellow operatives had survived. They wouldn't state that outright, but the impression was clear, even across cognotypes.

A bureaucratic error, counted in lives. Anayāun wanted to stand up and yell, *You folks tried to get us murdered just so that you wouldn't have to deal with a so-called* situation!

Something in her had broken. She'd never quite believed in the goodness of the Alliance and would quote the motto usually with an ironic snort: "For the benefit of all sentience." Indeed. But she hadn't minded being delegated to Alliance Counterintelligence, appreciating the daily, procedural aspects of the job.

For all her difficulties, her cognotype clashing with other people's in the Alliance, their glaring unfamiliarity with Ereni culture, their dismissal of it as peripheral and irrelevant . . . despite all that, she'd thought she was keeping people safe. At least, before she'd been rapidly reclassified as a risk herself: a risk that needed to be eliminated, though the Alliance reps would never say that out loud.

She still hadn't met an actual First Contact team. She was beginning to feel skeptical that they existed.

The woman speaking for the System sat back so abruptly after making an argument that her chair crackled to readjust. She was a System operator, and she looked like she'd rather be working. Anayāun knew someone like that who'd been kept from their work by other tasks, and she sympathized. There was nothing quite like being part of the planetary groupmind, they'd always say. A distance from it brought pain.

Anayāun herself eased back into the awareness of Mushroom Rock. Unfortunately, Mushroom Rock could have been best described as grumpy.

Grumpy, hungry, and oddly enough, sad.

They assume we'd only take and take. Just because we're hungry. The thoughts resonated in her mind.

Anayāun wasn't sure how to react.

We'd like to give, Mushroom Rock said. *The System understands, but they're not mentioning it.*

The Alliance is worried about Eren as is, Anayāun responded. *Too much of a concentration of power. With your people added into the mix . . .* she leaned back in her own chair.

Eren is supposed to be a small, peripheral state, she thought to herself, but Mushroom Rock still understood.

Anayāun didn't want to go back to working with the Alliance. For her, it was an option, as she'd only been temporarily delegated to Alliance Counterintelligence from Ereni Security. Commander Morosewi on Eren would be glad to get her back—if she wanted to return at all. But what about the others? Dvora owed her existence as a rapid response shapeshifter to the Alliance. Hlazmlan's whole life was uprooted just when she'd been about to retire. Zsa could not live independently of Mushroom Rock any longer, but with her, the situation was easier, and she didn't look like she wanted to do that anyway. Peter's desires were a mystery.

All of them were tossed and turned by these events—even Mawu, who'd only been hired to ferry the operatives. And for what?

Alliance Treaty Enforcement. She'd never before considered how chilling it sounded.

"I need to go for a walk," Anayāun said after a few more rounds of endless offers and counteroffers, once someone had finally suggested a pause. She needed to do something, something physical. She wished she could go for a few practice runs on a floater racetrack.

Where was Alliance Internal Affairs at a time like this? Why couldn't Eren lodge a formal complaint?

She wondered if there was a way to force a decision. Something that would unbalance the status quo, yet at the same time, something that didn't involve letting Mushroom Rock eat whole planets.

The System operator also got to her feet. "Mind if I accompany you?"

"I'd be glad," Anayāun said and meant it.

They were walking along one of the wider boulevards, though Anayāun supposed it wouldn't count as a boulevard on a more spacious planet. Maybe a street. Definitely not an alleyway? She struggled to focus. What did this person say her name was?

"Mōnisirun," the System operator said. "But names feel odd sometimes. It feels like they produce . . . distance. This name is all right for me, but the concept of names, I struggle with that sometimes."

Anayāun nodded. "That makes sense."

"I've been an operator for a long time," she said. "I'll have to begin preparing to retire. But this is the point where I don't feel like I can live entirely independently of the groupmind. Technically, one is never fully independent of it, but it would certainly be much more of a distance." She sighed. "Too much."

"I . . ." Anayāun wasn't sure what to say. That she could relate? She couldn't, not really. But on Eren, it was acceptable to share how one felt in response to someone sharing how they felt, so she went ahead with that. "My situation is rather the opposite. I'm linked to Mushroom Rock—and now to their entire family too—but I'm still getting used to it, and it's not really comfortable. Neither for the mind nor for the body. If there is such a firm separation between the mind and the body." She stared determinedly at the planters affixed to the wall on her left, as a way to hold on to at least something familiar.

"Yes, it's different," Mōnisirun said. "The System isn't so hungry, for instance. Which is probably for the best. Eren and these fungal newcomers, if we teamed up, we could take over the entire Alliance." Her voice remained level.

Anayāun gritted her teeth.

The System operator laughed. Noticing her emotion? "It's a good thing we are not interested in expansion," she said. "Maybe consider, you've been thinking of eating and hunger as *taking*. But can they also be thought of as *giving*?"

"Giving. What do you mean? This kind of endless consumption and expansion?" Anayāun grimaced, made more uncomfortable than she'd have liked by the fact that Mushroom Rock had also just raised the issue of giving. *Are we reconceptualizing* taking *as* giving *now?* She sighed before going on. "Limitless consumption led entire societies to ruin. And that's ignoring the societies that permanently balance on the edge of collapse. Believe me, I've seen a few in my line of work. Even if there's a lot of room in space, they don't want to be *there*. they want to be where the action is—"

She never got to finish her thought. Mawu sped past her on a transportation pallet entirely unsuited for floater racing. "I can't stop this thing!" they screamed.

"Hold on." Anayāun quickly sent out an override command. "I'm slowing it."

Mawu reacted as if they'd expected a sudden stop, so the slower deceleration confused them. They overcompensated and fell off, hitting the ground rolling. But in the span of another breath, they were already up on their feet. "That was problem number one, er, but I also have problem number two," Mawu said. "The person from Internal Auditing?"

Anayāun thought for a moment. "Counterintelligence Oversight Section? Piekkat-dali-Nifar?"

"Yes, they are here and one of the Alliance negotiators wanted to shoot them!"

This made no sense to her. "You can't just shoot someone on Eren. It won't happen."

"Well, he *tried*! And then Peter—"

Anayāun glared at the System operator—though pointlessly because she wasn't actively operating anything. Mōnisirun nodded at her. "Go."

Anayāun unclipped her combat staves from her belt, joined them, and flattened them into a floater pallet. Then she jumped on and flew back to the High Council building. The boulevard seemed even narrower than before, and she rose just above the passersby to avoid them, almost back to . . .

You're rushing into a standoff, the System informed her.

Is that a problem? She snapped back.

We are just providing information.

Anayāun shook her head. This wouldn't be a physical confrontation, but it *would* be a diplomatic one. Even though she was close to a point where, for all her enormous restraint, she really wanted to just whack someone with a shortstaff.

Not today.

The wheel-shaped sentient was standing across from the chief Alliance negotiator, both frozen in place. Held by the System? Anayāun checked, and it was indeed so. A relief. Peter was standing farther back, shaking, but not held still by anything beyond his own common sense. Also a relief.

The negotiator was pointing at Piekkat-dali-Nifar, who had also grown an odd protrusion. Pointing back at him?

"I am with Counterintelligence Oversight," Piekkat-dali-Nifar raised their voice, as melodiously as ever, and changed colors rapidly from teal to purple to a marbled orange, as if rotating in place. "I'm arresting this man, and I would appreciate the cooperation of Ereni Security!"

"*I* am with Counterintelligence Oversight," the negotiator screamed. "Verify my credentials! I'm arresting this person, and I would—"

Anayāun was confused. They were arresting *each other*? With the same verbiage? Both of them were asking for *her* cooperation?

"I bet you'd appreciate their cooperation, asshole!" Peter shook in place. "I'd appreciate an explanation why you were carrying this!"

"You swiped something off him?" Anayāun was trying to get a handle on the situation. Where was Hlaz-mlan?

"Well, if I couldn't beat him up, this was the least I could do!" Peter grinned at her.

Anayāun's thoughts rushed ahead, faster than any words could serve. Peter got something dangerous from the negotiator, but what? The System hadn't taken the negotiator's mystery object upon border control, or even later? Was it a weapon after all? Mawu had mentioned *shooting*, which would imply a firearm . . . yet the negotiator got to keep the item. Why?

Anayāun already knew the answer, but she suspected the Alliance man had never realized. He was being provoked into a confrontation, and he'd taken the bait. He wanted to take a weapon onto Eren and into the negotiations? The System let him, just to see what would happen once he thought he could get away with it. The Alliance could've sent more skilled officials, Anayāun wondered. *I'm beginning to see a pattern here.* A pattern of incompetence, to be honest?

She could think about this later. She had to resolve the situation. "Deny, attack, reverse victim and offender?" she called out loudly. It almost sounded like a command, though it wasn't.

Piekkat-dali-Nifar made a sound that could be best described as someone trundling through chest-high tallgrass. A sound of amusement, Anayāun guessed. Reacting as they were supposed to react.

The chief negotiator blinked, taken by surprise, not recognizing the term at all. That decided it.

Anayāun took a step forward, crossed her arms. "You know, I had to sit through the basic Alliance counterintelligence training when I was delegated to the Alliance—and let me tell you, it was not very exciting or novel—but at least it provided me with something important I hadn't realized up till now," Anayāun said slowly, savoring the moment even as her toes felt like they wanted to curl up. Mushroom Rock and their relatives, pushed into the background of her awareness, relished the moment, startlingly so. She went on, ignoring them. "I found out much . . . about the training people receive in the Alliance. I would expect someone from Internal Auditing, overseeing Counterintelligence no less, to be conversant in communication patterns related to abuse." She condensed her floater into a longstaff with a gesture and then split it into her usual two shorter staves, twirled them around her fingers for emphasis before clipping them to her belt. "And not just those patterns but also the terminology used to describe them."

The chief negotiator trembled, ever so slightly.

"Your supposed colleague here immediately recognized the words," Anayāun said. "The name of a specific strategy. Anyone can *employ* this strategy without any special training. They just need to counterattack verbally every time they're accused of something, trying to pin the blame on the other person. But what needs to be taught is the awareness that this is a specific strategy with a *name*. You might work for the Alliance but definitely not in a counterintelligence capacity. You didn't recognize the name." She took her time to take a leisurely breath.

"Now, the question is not, *why did you overreach so badly with your bluff?*" She shook her head. "The question is, why did the Alliance send you and not someone more skilled at bluffing? Furthermore, why did the Alliance send you, with who-knows-what training, and not actual diplomats—even as this is turning into a full-scale diplomatic incident? Because one thing is clear: you're not a diplomat."

She began to pace in a cloverleaf pattern around the three, keeping her eyes on the Alliance man. She preferred not to keep eye contact but knew it made for better intimidation when she did.

People of different cognotypes in the Alliance always told her to stop monologuing at people. That it was annoying, exasperating, and a variety of similar adjectives, all pejoratives. She could never get it across to them that this was how her cognotype worked, which would have been a monologue in itself.

Now, she was on Eren, and she would monologue as much as she wanted. She still had important things to say. Besides, the two quasi-combatants had been frozen in place.

She could feel her grin slowly spread on her face, almost as if of its own accord. She went on.

"Maybe a bluff like this worked other times. It probably did. Especially when your words were backed with a threat. You don't need to exert any effort when the balance of power is on your side. You don't need to be excellent. Things will go your way regardless. Familiar?" She looked the man square in the face. He flinched. "A form of counterselection, if you will. Alliance bureaucracy, a place for the non-excellent ones."

A crowd was gathering, and the System was doing nothing to keep them away. The off-duty System operator she'd just talked to was among the onlookers with Mawu, but Anayāun still didn't see Hlaz-mlan or Dvora. There'd be time to find them later. She went on.

"That explains so much about our recent experiences. The incompetence we only truly noticed once things began to go abruptly wrong. The incompetence we experienced over and over and over." She wouldn't get into the details, not in front of strangers, but many in the crowd were nodding. She felt encouraged.

"When responsibility is distributed in a group, what happens to accountability? Your answer is that no one is accountable. There's always someone else who should've done something else. But our approach, the Ereni approach, is that everyone is accountable." She waved toward the crowd, enjoying the sympathetic resonance. "I'm sure there are *some* people who think that way in the Alliance too. Think that way, and act on it." She nodded toward Piekkat-dali-Nifar in turn, though she had her doubts about the sentient's motives, whether they were really employed by Internal Auditing, and how much dirt the System had on them to nudge them into action. But it worked as a rhetorical flourish.

Piekkat-dali-Nifar made a satisfied sound like a balloon deflating and reinflating. It wasn't accompanied by any visible change in their body shape.

Anayāun stopped pacing. "So what happens with you now?" She wasn't sure about the man's name, but it was irrelevant: first, his identity might only be a cover, and second, the way he'd acted was systemic, bigger than him. She could've looked up his name, but it would not have helped at all. "The question is—"

The man interrupted her, grinning. "The question is, if you're so much better, why have you walked into the trap?"

Anayāun's muscles stiffened. What?

Then, a sinking feeling deep in her guts, from Mushroom Rock and their family. Something bad was happening out there—

A diversion. All this man needed to do, all the entire Alliance delegation needed to do, was to keep them busy—and a good way to achieve that was to create chaos, as Dvora also liked to do. A failed shootout, accusations randomly flung about, and there it was: their goal reached.

That didn't make any of what she'd said incorrect though.

The chief negotiator chuckled. "Everything you'd said applies to your ragtag team of operatives as well. Aren't *you* incompetent?"

Anayāun ignored him and spun around to face the System's representative while at the same time trying to direct at least part of her attention inward, to Mushroom Rock. The words hurt, and they also felt inaccurate in a way she couldn't quite place, but she'd deal with that later.

"*Alliance warships are jumping to the location of Mushroom Rock's family,*" the System said, the words resonating both in Anayāun's mind and coming from Mōnisirun's mouth.

An attack? It had to be. And coordinated on two very different locations. "Can you do something?" Anayāun was close to shouting.

"*We need to keep most of our resources in localspace,*" the System responded. "*Or we risk a successful attack on Eren.*"

Not much to do about that. Where was her boss—where was Commander Morosewi? Screaming at the Alliance higher-ups, no doubt. The actual diplomats. Or at Counterintelligence? Treaty Enforcement? Who else could help? Anayāun had originally wanted to involve as few people and organizations in this mess as possible, but the stakes had changed.

She suddenly wished she *had* given the Scattershot-4A to Mushroom Rock's family. Could the Alliance warships destroy them before they'd get eaten in self-defense? How much damage could these sentients take?

"This is genocide," she hissed at the gloating Alliance man.

"This is *risk management.*" He paused, almost as if not believing his own words. "They were the first to attack."

Anayāun yelled at him. "They were trying to communicate!" Had they been? There were those lingering questions about the saboteur . . . still, that didn't justify destroying an entire species, even if it was formed of just one groupmind. "Would you kill them over that?"

"It would be entirely within the realm of—"

"Can you just shut him up?" Anayāun asked the System.

"An argument could be made that his continued communication represents a security risk."

The man's mouth closed with an audible clap. Anayāun exhaled.

Dovber and Hlaz-mlan came running. "Have you heard—" Dovber took one look at the scene. "I guess you've heard."

Mawu broke in—emboldened by their sudden appearance? "Look, I know you don't like it when I say this, but I could jump you there and—"

"And what, fight dozens of warships by ourselves?" Anayāun felt that came out sharper than she'd intended.

We have agents on thirteen of the Alliance vessels present and open communication lines, the System messaged her in private. *We can commandeer those vessels if the need arises.*

That still leaves how many more? Anayāun responded.

Twenty-four.

A decent percentage—Anayāun was glad for a moment that taking over warships or installing agents on them wasn't one of her job responsibilities. But not enough. Who else did they have on their side?

"Our Planetmind—" "The net of pearls—" Dovber and Mawu said simultaneously. They stared at each other and said, "They can help," again simultaneously, blinking at each other in confusion.

Slightly excessive synchrony between team members aside, these are both viable ideas, Anayāun thought. "Go for it."

The Alliance aside, they've been building alliances of their own.

"I can get you to your ship," the System stated.

Anayāun nodded. "That'd help too."

It was like being tossed—or shoved? Abrupt and more than slightly painful. Anayāun doubled over. Dovber and Hlaz-mlan were whimpering on Kheinu's floor alongside Peter, who the System must have decided belonged with them, but Mawu was already up and scrambling into the connection berth. Mawu was used to this, Anayāun thought, resenting the inevitable second gut-punch when Mawu jumped the ship to Mushroom Rock's family.

Anayāun didn't notice the moment Mawu had called on the net of pearls—could it have happened *during* the jump, somehow?—but all around them, ships like Kheinu were popping into existence, jumping to localspace. How did this work? Did they get the locations from Mawu? Anayāun remembered that Kheinu and Mawu had, if not outright disconnected from the net of pearls for the earlier mission, still disassociated somewhat. When did that change? She had to remind herself that Mawu was not, strictly speaking, answering to her.

She knew little about the net of pearls, but she imagined a fishing net, one corner of it yanked and the rest following suit. Not as automatically as that because the ships kept on arriving, gradually rather than all at the same instant, and clearly not all the ships came because she remembered there were thousands in the net. The numbers were still formidable. And not just formidable but outright threatening. Beings that looked like angry pufferfish were filling the space between Mushroom Rock's family and the warships.

Dovber also tuned into the outside view. "They look like vintage naval mines."

That had to have been more *ancient* rather than *vintage*, but Anayāun was glad Dovber was feeling well enough to look. She'd need him to call on the Planetmind of his home.

He shook his head. His beard was sticking out in all directions, some geometrically unlikely. "Mawu, can you help me reach . . . ?" He seemed uncomfortable for some reason—but then it seemed to Anayāun that the connection was formed to the Planetmind. Dovber fell silent, and Anayāun didn't want to intrude, not the least due to being linked to Mushroom Rock's family. Best not to drop that kind of awareness on anybody unwarned.

At least, whoever was commanding the Alliance warships wasn't comfortable ramming several dozen sentient ships with various allegiances, all coming in from various corners of Alliance space and beyond. But Anayāun wasn't sure how long that hesitation would last.

Yes! I can! Mawu yelled suddenly over the comms.

Dovber made a face that was just a slight improvement over when he'd turned into a sea monster.

Anayāun's stomach sank. "What *is* it?" she demanded.

Hlaz-mlan came up to her. "Something to be performed loudly and while moving fast, I assume," she said in her best crochety voice. Anayāun was never sure if it was an act.

"I will do it. Let me unlink," Mawu said.

"Don't," Anayāun said, being acutely aware that Mawu was not in her chain of command.

"It will be fun," Peter croaked, still sitting on the floor, "as long as *I* won't have to jump again."

"Feel free to throw up, the flooring will absorb it!" Mawu gleefully marched into the main area.

"I will *not* throw up," Peter said.

"Quiet," Anayāun raised her voice. She considered for a moment whether to appeal to Zsa, who was probably still sharing a body with Mawu. Then again, Zsa was also a representative of the loud and messy school.

To their credit, everyone fell silent.

"I want to hear this plan." Anayāun winced. "Correction, I don't *want* to hear this plan at all. Alas, I *need* to hear this plan."

"The ships aren't warded very thoroughly," Mawu said.

This was going exactly where she'd supposed it was going. Anayāun remembered very well that Mawu had once destroyed an orbital weapons platform. In comparison with that, some hastily mustered Alliance warships had to present a trivial obstacle. But over two dozen of them?

Though if Dovber's Planetmind were also to help, that would be much more doable.

"I would jump to the ships and break things and jump back," Mawu said, the words blending together. "It would be all right!"

How big was the Planetmind of Bayit Ledorot anyway? Dovber had recently gone back to visit, and that'd seemed to help, but at this point, Anayāun was hesitant to rely on the content of any conversation she herself hadn't experienced . . . and Dovber hadn't given her the details. The planet only had a tiny human town with people from Dovber's religious group, but surely the Planetmind was larger than that. She remembered that the entire planet of Bayit Ledorot was supposed to be made of the same material, and wasn't it all technically a substrate for the Planetmind?

This could be workable.

"Ignore the ships with agents of Eren on them. I am sure they can find a way to take control of the situation," Anayāun said.

"Wait, there are?" Mawu blinked rapidly. "How many?"

So much for anything even resembling operations security anymore. Anayāun wished she was anywhere else, doing anything else. She responded, "Roughly one third, and the System will give you an overlay if they trust you with it." She was at the point where she was happy to offload at least a tiny bit of responsibility. "The Jump Pilots' Union will hate me for this, you know."

Mawu gestured in the direction of the standoff outside. "The Jump Pilots' Union is right here!"

That made sense. Anayāun supposed it'd set a terrible precedent if the Alliance were allowed to kill pilot and ship alike with impunity, even if they claimed it had been an accident. It wasn't just about Kheinu's conspecifics showing up for them via the net of pearls, an instinctive kind of solidarity. It was just as much a political demonstration and a carefully considered show of force.

But she wondered why it had to be Mawu doing anything.

Anayāun shook her head. "Are you sure you don't just want to be the one to save the day?"

"No, it's a team effort!" Mawu was scandalized. "I couldn't do it without the Planetmind! I'm good at this, like *very* good, but not twenty-four jumps good! Twenty-five? I mean I need to come back too." They looked like they were about to start counting on their fingers. "Twenty-four? And the ships will block the ships. That didn't come out right. I mean, okay, you get it."

Wouldn't Mushroom Rock's family be doing anything? Anayāun supposed it would be best for them not to be doing *anything* if at all possible. She did her best to convey that over their link. *This is not an attack on the Alliance. We are of the Alliance, and we are showing our disagreement.* She had her doubts about belonging to the Alliance, but she tried not to think about them.

"Let's hope they don't bill you for the damage afterward," Peter said, his voice as hoarse as if he'd thrown up after all.

"I still need to bill someone for my house," Hlaz-mlan added, almost offhandedly. At the same time, she messaged Anayāun: *I will hold you personally responsible for the kid's life. If we had a better solution—*

You don't have a lot of time, the System reached out to all of them, and Anayāun knew that if the System decided to make the effort it had to be important. *We have sent word to sabotage or take over the vessels. Those remaining are yours to handle. We have deemed other routes exhausted, and we estimate the Alliance will give an order to fire once they have decided how to manage the Jump Pilots' Union.*

Anayāun had no doubts what *manage* meant in this context. But it wasn't the Alliance who held all the power.

"Go do it," she said. "Focus on the drives. The higher the energy concentration, the clearer the signature."

Mawu nodded. "I've asked Zsa to withdraw. We can start."

Peter got to his feet. "Let me send you off with a boost," he said. "I'm an occultist after all."

"As long as it doesn't involve spit," Hlaz-mlan waved her antennae at him and turned to Mawu. "Just so you're aware, this is exactly the situation I warned you about, and more. Act accordingly."

Mawu nodded, serious for once. Then Peter waved his arms around—which was more effective than it should have been, Anayāun noted with bemusement—and Mawu vanished.

"So now we wait," Dovber said.

Anayāun couldn't just wait. She reached out carefully to Mawu.

Want to watch? Mawu thought at her. How did they have time and effort to spare to pay attention to Anayāun?

Suspecting it unwise, she still wanted to watch.

The first ship, the first engine room—Anayāun didn't notice the moment of passing through the wards. How? She was about to yell at Mawu to be careful, to disable the engines without blowing them up. The goal was to get through this all with no loss of life. Not that she should yell at someone who wasn't in her chain of command and besides was doing her a favor—

But Mawu had a surprisingly graceful touch—or how much of it was the Planetmind? It felt to Anayāun as if some panels slid askew, not entirely in 3-space, she couldn't quite follow the motion. It looked like the air itself was glittering, tiny particles scattering away as Mawu moved—

Something wasn't right, Anayāun thought. She was forgetting something. But she had no time to contemplate it as Mawu rushed forward—

Then the second ship—a similar motion, same momentum—and the third ship—faster and faster—it was too much in a way she hadn't expected and—she could tell through their connection—in a way Mawu hadn't expected either—

Somewhere, elsewhere, Anayāun felt her body tilt, her arms reaching out to break her fall, the forward movement bending into a roll as her own body's systems decided it was time for the safest possible emergency shutdown. Then all awareness ceased—

Hlaz-mlan was looking at her, gently moving her antennae. How much time had passed? Where was she? Anayāun struggled to orient herself but gave up.

She didn't want to know. She suspected that out there, in the world, was a massive *situation* she'd need to fix when all she felt able to do was to lie in one spot, unmoving, breathing only because it was required to sustain her life.

Surely, Mawu had made a mess. For some reason, she had no doubt Mawu had survived. Survived only to create an even larger jumble than at the outset. Surely Mushroom Rock, surely Dovber, surely all those sentient ships out there, surely the Alliance—surely, something was broken, possibly without any chance of repair—

You don't need to fix anything, Mushroom Rock said with their whole family, the thought resonating with such gentleness that it stunned Anayāun's mind into silence.

She sat up so abruptly that her breath caught, and something inside her chest seized—her diaphragm? A hiccup morphed into a cough.

"No rush," Hlaz-mlan said. "It has been taken care of."

Yes, but how? Anayāun wanted to say, but she struggled to produce speech sounds, let alone words.

"Ssh," Hlaz-mlan rustled. "Let me act out my grandmotherly fantasies."

Anayāun still had trouble telling whenever Hlaz-mlan was being ironic, but she decided that once, just once in her life, she would let someone take care of her. She leaned back onto the soft surface—a bed?—and slept, seemingly endlessly. Just slept.

She dreamt of glitter.

Anayāun woke with the words of the chief negotiator ringing in her ears.

Aren't you *incompetent?*

Her mind was stuck on the sentence, producing variations with differing emphasis.

Aren't you *incompetent?*

Aren't you incompetent?

Aren't *you incompetent?*

She was afraid of facing reality. What had happened while she was out? She was still alive, and that had to count for something.

She opened her eyes, rubbed her face. She was alone in one of Kheinu's small sleeping berths. *Incompetent.* No. Besides, there would be time to contemplate this once she'd assessed the situation.

Maybe, not everything was a *situation* in need of *assessment,* she reminded herself, but this—this certainly was. She'd have to report back to Commander Morosewi of Ereni Security in any case. The Commander loved to micromanage those delegated to the Alliance.

Anayāun sat up. She was fully dressed, and her black dress uniform helpfully unwrinkled itself as she got out of the berth, the silver highlights readjusting. She picked up her combat staves, which someone had deposited next to her pillow, and clipped them to her sides.

Now it was time to wander around and get information out of people who were all ignoring her, she assumed. She stretched out, yawned in displeasure. *Incompetent.*

Hlaz-mlan chirped so loudly from the neighboring berth that Anayāun reflexively spun around, reaching for her staves.

"I assumed you'd like to be briefed," Hlaz-mlan said with a warm buzzing undertone.

Someone *knew* her, after all. Anayāun felt sudden gratitude.

"That woman of Intelligence . . . possibly formerly . . . she made you a report."

"Made *me* a report?" Why would Zsa do that? "Is everyone reporting to me now?" Anayāun said with a trifle more annoyance than she'd meant. Was this becoming a habit?

Hlaz-mlan buzzed an octave higher. "You know, you can let yourself relax for once."

Anayāun laughed. "You see through me, old comrade. I admit I'm grateful." She accepted the file transfer. "I'll just sit back in my berth and take a look then. Just . . . one thing first. Tell me, did everyone survive?"

"Everyone and then some," Hlaz-mlan replied.

Anayāun wasn't sure if that was meant to be as ominous as it'd sounded.

"This is my executive summary to you because I know I like to babble, I mean, that's on purpose," Zsa said in the introductory video, twirling a lock of red hair around her fingers. Anayāun wasn't a fan of executive summaries, but she'd give it a try this once. She did appreciate that Zsa had taken the trouble. "In a tiny nutshell, no one died." Anayāun wondered why everyone felt a pressing need to tell her just that. "In a bigger nutshell, this is a mess. The kid teleported around to knock off the warships' drive cores, which all threw in the towel—that was all really good and politically expedient I'd say—BUT THEN THE SHIPS GREW MUSHROOMS, and now everyone is screaming at everyone else! Okay, I'll stop yelling. Check out the table of contents."

Anayāun wasn't sure about the "towel" but guessed it had to be a figure of speech unfamiliar to her. As for the mushrooms . . . what mushrooms on the ships?

Suddenly, it all clicked into place. They grew on the ships, like in Hlaz-mlan's house.

In the desperate rush to stop the Alliance warships, they'd forgotten that on Eren the System had actively been making sure the spores they were carrying couldn't spread. But the spores were still there. Even if they'd been removed for the duration of their visit—had they been?—they went back to their own ship afterward only to get some new spores to spread to the warships. They'd relaxed too much during the visit. Why didn't the System warn them? Anayāun was wondering if the System wanted to achieve exactly this, whatever *this* was.

She pulled up some of the video streams that looked like data feeds from the various vessels' bridge cameras. The familiar scenes from inside Hlaz-mlan's house played out at high speed as she scrolled forward: the increasingly complicated structures, the flowering, the ships being consumed. She hadn't imagined the glittering particles in the air after all, had she? She thought the spores weren't visible to the naked eye, but once one's perception is extended beyond its usual confines, all sorts of other information might be gleaned . . .

Aren't you inc—

No. She stopped herself. She'd watch.

Would it have made a difference if any of them had anticipated this scenario? She reminded herself that she had been bemoaning that she hadn't given that box of Shattershot-4A to Mushroom Rock's family. One weapon of mass destruction replaced by another. Or was it? Mass construction? Hlaz-mlan's house, entirely consumed. A replica of the smuggler outpost, built from scratch. Anayāun shook her head, but her thoughts kept on pushing forward.

A fabricator the size of a planetoid.

The size of a *planet* for all she knew. She couldn't even begin to estimate the full extent of Mushroom Rock's family out in deep space.

Was this how Bayit Ledorot, Dovber's planet, had been created eons ago, even if the exact process had been different? Everything made of the same substance—a garden world where everything bled silver if cut, flora and fauna meticulously recreated—

After it had been consumed.

Anayāun hoped, for Mushroom Rock's sake, that the entire crew of the warships hadn't been *processed*. She ran through the data. There were timelines, visualizations. A red dot blinking around the display, flickering through the tokens marking the vessels: Mawu. Anayāun was glad her mind gave in and resisted being strung along for the ride. She watched the animation of crew movements, tiny little dots of escape capsules spraying from the warships. Had the whole process happened faster than with Hlaz-mlan's house? She checked, and yes, definitely. The material was getting accustomed to interacting with what it found—an unsettling thought. Also, she didn't see any attempts to produce mobile forms like the walkers. There was no need to produce a communication partner.

How did the current situation look? She found the right document.

The ejected lifepods of crew members were gathered up by one of the warships the Ereni had taken over. Had the crew taken no spores with them, or had the System ensured by some unknown means that they would remain dormant? Anayāun wasn't certain.

The warships Mawu had visited had slowly coalesced into another Mushroom Rock. The remainder of the vessels taken over by the Ereni waited, inert.

The sentient ships held the line—the lattice, rather.

The politicians, bureaucrats, and diplomats were all screaming. Still.

Anayāun wasn't sure how long she'd slept, and she felt hesitant to check, but that had to be a long time to spend screaming.

Anayāun got back to her feet. Genocide had been averted, and even the Alliance diplomats finally appeared on the scene alongside a very confused First Contact team—so they did exist after all. Mawu would get to learn about linguistics. Anayāun grinned.

She gingerly reached out to Mushroom Rock, felt only reassurance, though of an oddly tense kind. She didn't understand why. Even if they hadn't expected to survive the confrontation, things should surely have stabilized somewhat by now? As Zsa had told her, on her planet, they had a saying: the dog that barks doesn't bite. Screaming is certainly preferable to shooting.

She finally dared to look at her personal messages. There were several from Commander Morosewi, but he'd respected her rest and didn't put in an override. She was startled not to hear anything from Counterintelligence Dispatch or the team's direct supervisor. Surely, at this point, they might want to talk to her? Even Fake-Counterintelligence-Guy with the teal hair had deigned to talk to her. At least she wouldn't need to put in her resignation. She could just ask Commander Morosewi to cancel her status of being delegated to the Alliance. Dovber and Hlaz-mlan would probably need to resign though.

She walked back to the ship's main area, feeling suspended in air, everything all too silent. She was supposed to be the one to convey the words of Mushroom Rock's family, so she'd need to reenter the fray. She was already bracing herself.

Dvora looked up at her from one of the chairs, now in her woman shape and with her identifier saying Dvora. She appeared similarly exhausted. "Glad to see you," she smiled. "From what I hear, the Alliance higher-ups are expecting a statement, but take your time to recover."

"They are just running in circles," Hlaz-mlan added. "They're not sure what to do. They're just waiting to react to us."

"Take it easy?" Mawu piped up, lounging in a chair rather than being connected to the ship. "It's Mushroom Rock who needs to make the statement. You just have to speak, right?"

Anayāun sighed. "I was hoping I could convince them of a reasonable course of action first." Fear suddenly shot through her. "I can record the statement, is that correct? Or would I have to speak live?"

Dvora chuckled. "I made sure to argue for you. The Alliance will accept a recording."

Anayāun was slightly apprehensive what form this argument had taken, but it was time to trust the people who'd proven over and over that they were on her side.

Anayāun closed the sleeping berth, the only place where she thought she'd have some privacy on the not very spacious ship. She lay down and locked down her voluntary muscle control, so she wouldn't make rash motions and bang her limbs into one bulkhead or another. She expected she'd get angry.

She turned her attention inward. *Before you start dictating your statement, we have to talk,* she thought at Mushroom Rock and, by extension, their entire family.

The vast being radiated acceptance—of this one request at least.

Anayāun mentally sighed. She was already wishing for her voluntary muscles. *You need to tell me how much control you have over your spores. Dvora left a box of your substance at the smuggler outpost, and it didn't take over the entire station. But just now—*

It is something we need to relearn each time we are built anew, Mushroom Rock said.

But it can be learned. You are capable of quite delicate control right now. Not like earlier. Anayāun couldn't help it, and she thought of one spore, just one spore carried on a ship, passing through a jump point, spreading, spreading—

The jump points do not seem to like us, Mushroom Rock interrupted her thought.

The jump points aren't sentient. Anayāun tried to be firm about this, if only for the reason that she had no desire to deal with two potentially Alliance-destroying emergencies at the same time. She redirected her argument: *In any case, you could spread, by latching on to individual people or ships who can jump without the points' infrastructure. You have just done so.*

Mushroom Rock hesitated, just an instant. *That is essentially correct.*

The Alliance will continue to see you as a massive threat. There is no way around it. At least *she* saw no way around it.

Allow us to phrase our statement.

There was little to respond to that.

I'm not going to lie for you! Anayāun put considerable power into the thought. She felt a chill run up her spine, motionless as she lay in her berth. *I'm not going to lie about what happened to the box—the box of Scattershot-4A. I'm not going to say you have it!*

You would not be lying, only conveying our statement. Mushroom Rock seemed determined.

Yes, but you're lying. About a weapon of mass destruction! And I'm aware of that!

She chided herself. Of course—why would an enormous, unknown sentience necessarily tell the truth? Just when she'd grown to accept that people were on her side, something like this had to happen.

We are on the same side, Mushroom Rock said, slightly hurt.

Anayāun considered releasing the hold on her muscles just so that she could punch a bulkhead, but she thought surely Kheinu wouldn't like that. She resisted the impulse.

One way exists to make our statement true.

Don't even dream of it. Anayāun fumed. *And why are you playing up your alienness? You don't speak like that.*

Yet for all her anger, she understood Mushroom Rock's tactic.

Only one problem remained. *Hold on,* she said, *I need to contact Commander Morosewi.*

Anayāun opened a simple, text-based channel, but even through that, she had the impression the commander of Ereni Security was not in the least bit surprised. He had to have already asked his forecasters to examine the trendlines. Or for all she knew, asked them to manipulate the probabilities just right to get his desired outcomes. Make his own future.

"Yes, we can certainly dispose of it in a safe manner," he said.

Anayāun wasn't sure he would. Commander Morosewi clearly understood that because he added after a pause, "With the power backing the System, we don't *need* additional weapons of mass destruction."

"I just don't want to be the one left holding this box." Anayāun vibrated with tension. "Surely, you know."

"We'll do what we can."

She knew that'd have to be enough.

It is hard. Some of us ate the box, but we could not reincorporate them. Mushroom Rock came across as . . . mournful? *Technically, we* have *it in some senses of the word, but we do not have access to those fragments of us, and . . .*

Anayāun cut them off. *And you won't. You should be satisfied with your lie.*

Sentence by sentence, finalizing the statement took time.

"We are the being. We are Mushroom Rock and their family. We are."

This is excessive. Honestly.

We prefer to obscure the extent of our communication capabilities independent of you.

"You are the Alliance. You have threatened us and attacked us. We understand our actions to establish contact have caused damage."

Stop it. Those were not actions to establish contact. We established contact quite easily. Then we ended up on the run. All together!

We have no wish to remind them of their malfeasance.

Fair enough.

"We do not seek to create damage. We do not."

I think you should cut the repetition.

We do not.

If that's what you want . . .

"We wish to live in a peaceful manner. We wish to be safe from the Alliance."

And achieve this by lying.

By any means necessary.

How will that work out for you in the long term?

"We possess one of the weapons the Alliance intended to damage us with—known as Scattershot-4A."

If you use this kind of syntax, you need to keep it consistent. Also, I already spoke for you during the negotiations and sounded much more polished.

They will assume you interpreted our words. You did not utter our words directly.

That's true. Still . . .

"We employ this weapon against a threat. We also employ our spores against a threat."

You can try to spin it as starting over from the beginning now that the situation has changed so drastically.

You will be able to say that. We are also protecting you. You will be able to claim that we stopped listening to you, that we broke off negotiations.

. . . I appreciate that, but I do not lie.

We trust you will manage, one way or another. Also, we have stopped negotiating.

"You leave us alone. We leave you alone."

But Mushroom Rock, you'll be alone out here without anything to eat.

We consumed several Alliance warships. We still need to process them. That will take time.

"We respond to peaceful contact. Not from the Alliance. Not from organizations. From individuals."

That's a nice touch. Do you think people will come and seek you out?

We remember the System operator who had trouble separating from the System. There will be not only people who come to meet us but also people who will want to stay.

Eventually, I suppose.

That would be sufficient for us . . . it might happen sooner than you expect.

"Please, respect our wishes."

Look, Mushroom Rock, I'm thinking . . . remember what the System said? About how eating can also be a form of giving, not just of taking?

We considered it and arrived at the conclusion that both an expectation to give and an expectation to take are externally imposed on us. We do not wish to define ourself in terms of those concepts.

Hence leaving?

Hence keeping our distance.

Anayāun released the lock on her muscles and got out of the sleeping berth with some difficulty. Her body was still protesting all that had happened to her in the very recent past. How much of it was due to the changes after she'd connected to Mushroom Rock, and how much was due to being chased across space by the largest political entity near and far?

When this is all over, would you prefer to remain linked to us?

She realized with a startle that not only wasn't she sure of the answer, but she hadn't even contemplated the question. She had been struggling to believe the situation would one day "be over"—and that it could end in a manner that did not involve her death.

When this is all over, I'll reassess, she told Mushroom Rock. *After getting some more sleep and rest for a change.*

We will respect your decision, the being responded, their immense extent showing to her mind just for an instant and receding again.

Mushroom Rock seemed—as impossible as that would appear—sad.

Dovber was pulling at the fringes of his garment and rocking back and forth in his shapeforming chair in an unexpectedly Ereni way. Anayāun was wondering if he was changing shapes because he was nervous. "I can't believe the Alliance stood down after reading this," he said.

Anayāun chuckled. "This, and the alternate risk assessment presented by the System. The Alliance assessment had assumed that if they tried to destroy Mushroom Rock, they would succeed on the first attempt. We didn't make that assumption."

Hlaz-mlan walked up to them, gingerly, like someone attempting to minimize pain. "Trying to destroy Mushroom Rock, failing, and arousing their ire is certainly a bigger danger to the Alliance than just leaving them alone."

Mawu stretched, accidentally elbowing Peter. "You're just more open to . . . to consider your own failure, I suppose. But like, not considering your own failure is also a failure?"

The memory resurfaced, *Aren't* you *incompetent?*

Anayāun sat down in one of the empty chairs. *Incompetent because . . . ? Because we didn't expect that the organization we served would turn around and attempt to murder us—casually, almost as if by algorithm?* Her hands closed into fists.

For many others, an Alliance position was a given, something they would have as part of their career mapped out from birth. They could safely fail and keep on failing.

That wasn't the same situation as hers or her team's. She was Ereni, delegated to the Alliance and having to deal with people of a cognotype drastically different from hers. Dovber ran away from his home planet because he couldn't come out. Mawu was an asylum seeker from a planet embroiled in civil war. Hlaz-mlan . . . even Hlaz-mlan didn't fit the pattern of the classic Alliance man, who had an I-type body and most definitely wasn't an insectoid. Who was most frequently a *man.*

Failing while having all the world's resources at your disposal wasn't the same as failing when you had been set up to fail. She wished she could tell the chief negotiator, but she'd been warned before ever leaving Eren—warned that she would often only understand how to respond to someone long after the pertinent situation had already passed. *Staircase wit* was the term, and it was common in interactions between sentients of different cognotypes.

This was all right. This was expected.

Not to mention, they did not fail—in the end.

She could return home, after all.

She closed her eyes and leaned back, tears streaming down her face—tears of relief.

ENVOI

It was feeling more and more cramped inside the ship, but they were all still waiting for Mushroom Rock to finish retrieving their errant material from localspace. The danger had passed, but not having anything to do was grating on everyone's nerves.

"I've decided." Peter's voice was only slightly trembling. "I'm staying with Mushroom Rock." Anayāun noticed he was already looking in the direction of the airlock.

"Because you have a crush on Zsa?" Mawu blurted out.

"Mawu! Even if he does, that's not polite to say." Anayāun turned away to not see Peter's reaction, but what she sensed of his mind already showed her that even if Mawu had not exactly hit the mark, they'd hit a nerve. Best to redirect both of them. "Focus on the fact that you're going to become an Ereni citizen, and act accordingly."

"Responsibilities, responsibilities," Hlaz-mlan buzzed on a low tone. "Hopefully, the Ereni will take better care of you."

"I'd still like to work as a pilot, and Kheinu agrees, but . . . yeah, I'll be cautious about which jobs to take." Mawu bit their lip.

"So young man, you've made up your mind?" Hlaz-mlan poked at Peter, who twitched in response.

"Yes. I have . . . no future in Alliance space. Or a desire to stay anyway." He swallowed. Anayāun hoped Mawu would not ask something inquisitive yet again. She trusted Mushroom Rock to keep Peter out of trouble, at least. Stealing quickly becomes meaningless if everything is made up of the same substance. Even though it must have occurred to Peter . . .

"Well, *I'm* retiring," Hlaz-mlan said with such expansive delight in her voice that Anayāun sat up straight. "Need to start working on a new family home, in any case . . . and I have had enough. More than enough."

"How would you even retire? They still have all of us operatives on file as deceased, I'm sure," Dvora chuckled. "Or if not, then certainly not employed by Counterintelligence anymore."

"We'll get reinstated," Anayāun said. "Commander Morosewi told me the Alliance bureaucrats were working on it. I've already told him I wouldn't want to go back. I'm not entirely sure about going back to Ereni Security either. I'd rather do something else. Maybe involving floater racing."

"Why is it that *you* hear from *your* boss, but neither of us hear from *our* boss?" Dvora looked like she was about to spring up and start pacing. "We haven't even heard from Dispatch. In any case, I'm resigning. I probably need a good lawyer because my body might fall under some anti-proliferation treaty."

"I'm sure the System can help out with that." Anayāun had no qualms volunteering the System at this point. She felt like the entire universe owed her a favor.

It is time, Mushroom Rock said, and Anayāun echoed their words.

The entire chamber began to glow, even the walls themselves, and something protoplasmic began to coalesce at its center, floating in the air about waist height to Anayāun. She remembered about her lungs and tried to forcibly exhale, but there was no reason, for the air streaming out of her nostrils and her mouth was glittering with the mysterious substance already.

Anayāun startled. *Wait, we haven't discussed—wait, are you going to reverse the changes in my body?*

She still wasn't sure what she wanted.

I'm removing my mobilizable material from you, but the structural changes remain, Mushroom Rock said, their presence as clear as ever in her mind. *Those we have yet to discuss.*

She wanted to remain in touch. She wanted to preserve their lines of communication. She realized by how much she'd startled when she'd assumed it was all going away. But she wasn't sure if her body was dealing with the changes all that well. She'd need to go back to Eren, get expert opinion, consider the benefits and tradeoffs . . .

It is certainly all right to wait, Mushroom Rock said, oddly approvingly. *To wait and consider.*

Anayāun closed her eyes. *I'm not going to pass spores on further, am I?*

Not after we are done here.

That was probably for the best. But the more she thought about it, the more she felt she wouldn't ask Mushroom Rock to break off their link. She could deal with some side effects, some inconvenience. She genuinely liked Mushroom Rock, even if she disapproved of some of their decisions. And who knows, those might have been, if not the best decisions, certainly good enough. Besides, these changes weren't entirely reversible.

She stopped herself, and for just a fleeting instant, considered something as privately as she could, thoughts locked away tightly. If Mushroom Rock was influencing her mind to make her more amenable to them, she would be able to find out about that back on Eren too. Certainly, the Ereni were experts on mental influence.

She opened her eyes and stood. The glow was gradually subsiding.

If you would be as kind as to cycle the material out of your airlock, Mushroom Rock said and Anayāun repeated. *Then you can go on your way.*

They did not come across as sad, but to Anayāun, it seemed as if they had put a lot of effort into a pretense of neutrality. Had they been aware of her hidden thought after all? Or was this about what she'd said about floater racing? She meant that she did not want to return to Security, delegated to the Alliance or not, but she hadn't quite considered how Mushroom Rock related to all this.

"I'll take the extra material with me. When I go," Peter said, already on his way to the suit locker.

It was time to say goodbye.

Dvora cleared her throat. "Remember I said the Planetmind wanted to meet us once this was over?"

Anayāun had to wrack her mind. Everything had seemed implausibly distant, stretched out over time, even as the original events had happened in rapid succession. Stress, she reminded herself. Trauma.

"We might as well head there once we drop off Peter," Anayāun said. "We need some rest."

She regretted it the moment the words were out of her mouth. How would they handle Dvora's family? What would be a fun outing for Anayāun, an intriguing new planet, might as well prove to be a nightmare for Dvora. But Dvora proposed this after all . . .

Anayāun's thoughts must have been plain on her face because Dvora nodded at her. "It's going to be all right. And if not, I have backup." She laughed.

"I am *not* going to fight your family," Mawu yelled back. "Folks, why are you laughing so much, this wasn't that funny?"

Some kind of tension released—something not within any one of them but in the group as a whole—that Anayāun hadn't even noticed. How many more times would she feel an all-new relief before she could entirely unburden herself of the events of this assignment?

She suspected it would take years.

The landing on Bayit Ledorot was smooth, but all the while, Anayāun was already considering every possible issue she could have missed, as carefully hidden from Mushroom Rock as possible. She was a security professional after all. Who had warded the saboteur they'd first come across, and how had Mushroom Rock recruited them? Dvora had mentioned they had been of some unfamiliar body template. Maybe Mushroom Rock had indeed had more influence over sentients than they'd revealed to her. Why did the saboteur need to release the spores? Was that a contact attempt as well? Was it connected to Mushroom Rock having to learn about spreading? Even more frighteningly, about the jump points and ascribing intentionality to them . . . no. She wouldn't think about this any further.

Or rather, she would, once back safely on Eren.

At least she didn't need to worry about spores here. Dvora had told her that Bayit Ledorot had a means of getting rid of them that she'd already tried on her previous quick visit, and it seemed to have worked. Even if Mushroom Rock hadn't been entirely truthful or just missed retrieving some of their spores accidentally, the leftover spores would be eaten by this other planetmind. It struck her as an odd kind of rivalry.

Once she resolved to do all this, she managed to redirect herself. Everyone else was already disembarking, and she had gotten up too, body almost entirely on autopilot.

"I'm so excited," Mawu came up to her. "I got a favorable decision on my citizenship . . . thing. Application. And also! I'm excited to meet the Planetmind and Chani who speaks for them, and Dvora said that Chani specifically wanted to talk to me, and . . . ! That's just awesome." Mawu went on and on. Anayāun grinned at them, something else unclenching in her, something that had constantly worried about the young pilot.

"I know you will accuse me of having a one-track mind," Hlaz-mlan chirped, "but I must say. If this planet is also made of some kind of mutable substance, maybe I should build my house here after all. It would take much less effort. Or at least a vacation home . . . if the Planetmind proves amenable to the idea. Truth be told, I've been worried about my great-grandchildren living in such an insular region, back on our planet . . ."

Dvora laughed again. "This is the first time ever *my* town isn't called insular! You might want to rethink this! Do you like kosher food?" She chuckled and sighed, her face suddenly overcast. "It comes with a serving of binary gender norms, at least on this planet." Anayāun expected her to change to her man shape, but it didn't happen.

Past the airlock, the sun shone in a spectrum pleasing to Anayāun, the grass was green and looked just slightly damp, and someone who had to be Chani was walking up to them all, sunlight gleaming on her curls. She was wearing a blouse and long skirt in different shades of muted blue, the hem wet from the grass.

A glance passed between Chani and Dvora that Anayāun could feel was heavy with not just intent but information. The Planetmind had a plan.

It will take many years, Dvora messaged Anayāun, *but it will turn out all right, this complication with my family . . . provided the System can get me a good lawyer to handle my resignation from Counterintelligence, first of all.*

"I can tell what you're thinking," Hlaz-mlan said. "You're thinking of making some changes in how the Alliance does its business altogether. Some radical changes. Oh, that's not what you're thinking? That's a pity because that's where *my* thoughts went . . ."

"Quitting helps us, personally. But if we join our forces afterward, that could help everyone in the Alliance."

"You'd go up against the entire Alliance?" Anayāun was only slightly incredulous. To her own shock, she found herself tempted. Her motivation was always to protect people. "How do you propose we do that?" *We,* she said, almost despite herself.

"Count me in," Dvora said, suddenly serious. "Just count me in."

Mawu giggled. "Well, let me and Kheinu know if you're in need of a ride." She poked Hlaz-mlan, and her legs twitched. "You said I should be on my guard about recruitment attempts."

"I . . . meant it the other way round," Hlaz-mlan tilted her head in response.

"Maybe we should get some food first," Chani offered, tilting her head to the side, the breeze tangling her hair. "I'm turning into a Jewish grandmother."

"Some grandmotherly coordination wouldn't be amiss," Hlaz-mlan buzzed. "Snacks and plotting our next steps."

Anayāun nodded. "As long as I get to have my well-deserved sleep."

AFTERWORD

T HANK YOU FOR READING MY BOOK! I WANTED TO REMARK ON A FEW things now that you're done. *Song of Spores* was originally serialized on the Patreon of Broken Eye Books from November 2017 to July 2022. I lightly revised the text for the book publication in 2025 but did not make drastic changes. This also means that if something in it strikes you as very timely, it was probably not intended as such. Then again, King Solomon said that there's nothing new under the sun, so if something seems very timely now, it was probably present in the world much earlier, just maybe in a less visible way. Shifts and asymmetries of power are enacted again and again.

Over the years, I've seen much discussion about how there are no good cops, for if there ever are good cops, they end up quitting. I also wanted to write a procedural, not necessarily a police procedural per se but some kind of investigation, involving some kind of organization, not a private detective. I chose counterintelligence in the end because, in part, they always have rivalries with the police (and with intelligence), but they often aren't all that different. So how does it work if you have a procedural, but they quit? My answer is that the investigation goes off the rails, but the way it goes off the rails is very much inspired by the way I've seen large, repressive organizations function. I've never been a police officer, nor a counterintelligence or intelligence one, but as a scholar of Communist-era Hungary—and specifically a scholar of censorship—I think I do have some insight into this. Still, at the same time, this is also a space adventure with many lighthearted moments, and also just general chaos, because of course no plan survives contact . . . not only with the enemy but also with one's own allies.

At the same time, KGB officers in the Soviet Union were fond of saying, "Once a Chekist, always a Chekist." Can one really quit, or does one still preserve the mindset needed for one's former job? After all, if one decides to quit only after one's organization turns on oneself, that's also in some ways less of a moral decision than quitting upon seeing others mistreated. Though here, the organization turns both on the protagonists and on the unknown sentience on its periphery simultaneously, once they become associated with each other in a way they can only be in speculative fiction (or . . . ?). I'm saving these questions for the time, if I ever write a sequel, but they are always worth considering.

Take care,
Bogi.

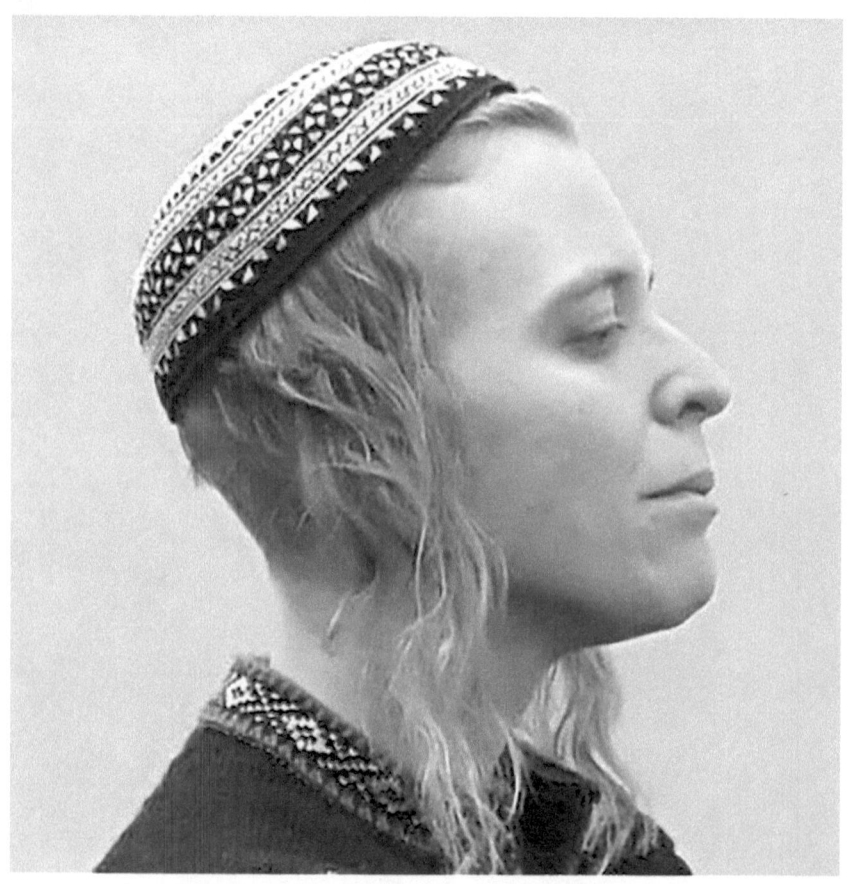

§

Bogi Takács is a Hungarian Jewish agender trans person (e/em/eir/
emself or they pronouns) and an immigrant to the US. Bogi lives
in Lawrence, Kansas, with eir family and a congregation of books.
Bogi writes, edits, and reviews speculative fiction and poetry. E is a
winner of the Lambda Literary award for editing *Transcendent 2: The
Year's Best Transgender Speculative Fiction*, the Hugo award for Best
Fan Writer, and a finalist for the Ignyte award, the Locus award, and
the Hexa award for advocates of Hungarian SFF. Bogi talks about
books at www.bogireadstheworld.com, and you can also find em as
@bogiperson on various social media websites.

BROKEN EYE BOOKS

Sign up for our newsletter at
www.brokeneyebooks.com

Welcome to Broken Eye Books! Our goal is to bring you the weird and funky that you just can't get anywhere else. We want to create books that blend genres and break expectations. We want stories with fascinating characters and forward-thinking ideas. We want to keep exploring and celebrating the joy of storytelling.

If you want to help us and all the authors and artists that are part of our projects, please leave a review for this book! Every single review will help this title get noticed by someone who might not have seen it otherwise.

And stay tuned because we've got more coming . . .

OUR BOOKS

The Hole Behind Midnight, by Clinton J. Boomer
Crooked, by Richard Pett
Scourge of the Realm, by Erik Scott de Bie
Izanami's Choice, by Adam Heine
Pretty Marys All in a Row, by Gwendolyn Kiste
The Great Faerie Strike, by Spencer Ellsworth
Catfish Lullaby, by A.C. Wise
Busted Synapses, by Erica L. Satifka
Boneset & Feathers, by Gwendolyn Kiste
Alphabet of Lightning, by Edward Morris
The Obsecration, by Matthew M. Bartlett
Better Living Through Alchemy, by Evan J. Peterson
The Mosquito Fleet, by Andrew Penn Romine
Trail of Shadows, by Mike Allen
Song of Spores, by Bogi Takács

COLLECTIONS

Royden Poole's Field Guide to the 25th Hour, by Clinton J. Boomer
Team Murderhobo: Assemble, by Clinton J. Boomer
Who Lost, I Found: Stories, by Eden Royce
Power to Yield and Other Stories, by Bogi Takács
Team Murderhobo: Flaming Love Icosahedron, by Clinton J. Boomer

ANTHOLOGIES

(edited by Scott Gable & C. Dombrowski)
By Faerie Light: Tales of the Fair Folk
Ghost in the Cogs: Steam-Powered Ghost Stories
Tomorrow's Cthulhu: Stories at the Dawn of Posthumanity
Ride the Star Wind: Cthulhu, Space Opera, and the Cosmic Weird
Welcome to Miskatonic University: Fantastically Weird Tales of Campus Life
It Came from Miskatonic University: Weirdly Fantastical Tales of Campus Life
Nowhereville: Weird Is Other People
Cooties Shot Required: There Are Things You Must Know
Whether Change: The Revolution Will Be Weird

Stay weird.
Read books.
Repeat.

brokeneyebooks.com
facebook.com/brokeneyebooks
instagram.com/brokeneyebooks
bsky.app/profile/slgable.bsky.social

www.ingramcontent.com/pod-product-compliance
Lightning Source LLC
Chambersburg PA
CBHW020240030726
47497CB00009B/3178